# WOLF BROTHER'S LEGACY:

# *Resurrection*

## DIANA CASTILLEJA

Purple Sword Publications, LLC
www.purplesword.com

**WOLF BROTHER'S LEGACY: RESURRECTION**
Copyright © 2011 DIANA CASTILLEJA
ISBN: 978-1-61292-004-7
ISBN 10: 1612920047
Cover Art Designed by Anastasia Rabiyah
Photographs Copyright Dreamstime.com.
Edited by Stephanie Taylor and Traci Markou

Published by Purple Sword Publications, LLC
Tucson, Arizona, USA
www.PurpleSword.com

# Wolf Brother's Legacy:

# Resurrection

# Chapter One

The hand rendered diagram image haunted Angie's every waking moment, taking two solid days of searching the Natural Museum archives where she worked as an archivist and researcher, but she finally placed it. The Anga Talisman. The sacred artifact could be anywhere, but the stored photos and dated drawings with the deduced hypothesizes were from the dig in Oregon. The *big* find. The Jahehn ceremonial home. Their largest camp to date. There were others, several in fact, but the canyon site had been a phenomenal treasure trove of their ancient world.

Lost in the crags of the northern Rockies, the encampment was in deep Oregon, a near-impossible to access canyon, filled with shadowed and mysterious caves and crannies, the kind that could make a mountain goat faint with joy. She remembered every single mile she'd hiked while on that dig, along with the grumbles of her dozen volunteer students and staff. There had been so much information there. She knew they'd only scratched the surface of all the secrets left behind during that trip. Many of those finds were on display at the museum on loan through Inglewood's generosity.

Dragging herself listlessly down the grocery store aisle on tired legs staring at, but not seeing, the packages of food in the freezers, she was lost in her thoughts and memories of that excavation. She had to be missing something in the photos. There was proof all through their history that they'd held an honored place for the talisman, an object of reverence and power in their community. Everything collected and dated seemed to say the last place they'd held their ceremonies was in the canyon. It *had* to be there. It would be equivalent to finding the Holy Grail for these people, if it still existed.

A teasing thought floated through her mind. A tale regarding the talisman's history. She refused to take this one particular theory to heart, or allow herself to fall victim to its tantalizing thread of hope. *There is no proof,* she reminded herself. It was a fanciful idea to begin with, yet it was so hard to dismiss it completely with medical science, modern and ever expanding, failing her. Ever since the talisman and the impractical possibility reappeared in her search in another file, it had been impossible to banish. A single, slim chance of hope.

*The talisman could heal.*

The Jahehn had believed it, had written tales and legends in their own language over the centuries. She shook her head, her logical brain wanting to deny it, but *what if it could*? That was her little voice refusing to let her simply brush it aside. What did she have to lose if she wanted to believe in a shaman's tale when more than a dozen doctors were leaving her with nothing?

Something about those historical photos... The talisman itself had been on the fringes of her mind for months, and seeing the images of the long-ago artifact had merged everything into one concrete desire. Angie knew better than to believe in the intangibles, but it was those same intangibles gripping her relentlessly and not letting go. A mystery to solve. A puzzle to unlock. It wasn't the healing power drawing her. She could admit that much. But...

She sighed, knowing she wasn't going to convince herself it could or couldn't, one way or the other, only that she needed to risk one last effort to find it. For herself. To stay moving.

Freezer doors stood in front of her vision, her thoughts running like a tempestuous dust storm over her latest finds and questions. Not hungry for anything in the freezer, she tugged open a door. Angie was reaching blindly when a voice she hadn't heard in months jerked her to her surroundings.

"Angie?"

Cold glass slipped out of suddenly stiff fingers. She turned to face him, and the woman with her ex.

"Neil. Hello." Her voice was as cool as the air teasing from the freezer to whisk over her frame. All she wanted was to step around them and continue with her unexciting evening when he stopped her.

"Angie, are you feeling all right?"

Her eyelids sank, and her stomach heated in revolt at the concern—the fake concern—she heard. Months later, his lying voice still sounded the same to her. "I'm fine, Neil."

"Aren't you going to introduce us?" the woman at his side asked with curious interest. One hand was looped through his arm possessively. The sun-drenched watercolors on her sundress danced playfully with her movements. Along with Angie's fatigue, it was enough to give her a headache.

"I'm sorry, honey. This is Angie, a very old friend of mine," he commented to the tall, tan blonde. "I've told you about her. Angie, this is my wife, Ilene." His remorseless gaze collided with Angie's, flashing in warning to not correct him, mocking her feelings and everything they had once shared together.

Her gut twisted with renewed pain from the knife he'd left there when he'd asked for the divorce. *Well, that didn't take long*, was her next angry thought. Bile-flavored humiliation rose to coat her throat. She managed a nod, unable to speak.

"Oh, it's nice to meet you!" Ilene delivered a beaming smile. "Neil mentioned you two had dated in college, then stayed friends after. Friends are so hard to keep anymore."

Angie shot Neil a disbelieving, furious glare at the obnoxious lie. He shook his head with a snap then flashed Ilene a huge, too-bright smile when she tipped quizzically to glance at him.

Angie ground her teeth. She choked a strained, "Nice to meet you," through a painfully tight jaw.

Angie wasn't typically a violent person, but even she had a limit. By the way Neil was avoiding her stares, she knew her wishes for his sudden death dazzled like flames in her eyes.

"I guess we're almost family, then," Ilene continued, oblivious to the undercurrent raging between Neil and Angie. She passed an adoring gaze over him, then cheerily said, "I have to tell you. We're pregnant! I've been telling everyone. We're so happy."

"What?" The floor tilted beneath Angie, and she staggered a step. The mammoth-sized wave of shock, anger, and disbelief made her waver on her feet.

Ilene giggled, glowing, holding him closer, as though she feared he might get away. "I know! Isn't this wonderful? Neil has wanted a baby forever, and now that we're married, it all came together. I'm five months tomorrow."

Incredulity rocked her until the lights overhead swam dizzily. The emotional roller coaster sent her stomach into another threatening somersault.

*A baby.* He was going to have a baby, and it wasn't with her. Her gaze sank and stuck to the barely-there bulge at Ilene's middle. Angie blinked to push hot tears far, far away.

"I'm... I'm happy for you." The radiating happiness on Ilene's expression didn't appear at all forced. Angie did a double take. "Wait. I'm sorry. Did you say five months?" Ilene nodded in pregnant, ignorant bliss.

Volcanic anger and humiliation soared again. By her behavior, Angie was positive Ilene had no idea Neil had been married to her when she became pregnant! She took another escaping step in the opposite direction, wanting to run as far and as fast as she could.

Ilene curled tighter into his side, beaming at him with absolute adoration. "It was so sweet too, the way he proposed. On the cruise to the Caribbean."

Angie stopped fleeing and swallowed, hiding the bitterness, her gaze landing on Neil like piercing daggers. Was she the only one who felt Ilene was bragging here or what? Angie had no intention of trying to take him from his new wife. She could have—and keep—the two-timing bastard. The ass didn't even have the nerve to look guilty. *Now* she was learning the full, sordid story when he'd given almost no reasons behind their divorce.

"A cruise? How...wonderful. When did he ever find the time? He's always been busy on some account or with a client since I've known him." His eyes flashed at the underhanded score. So what if Angie knew more about him than his new wife might appreciate? Neil finally lowered his stare, finding the floor to be much more interesting than the seething anger boiling behind her own glares. He had no excuse for the reality hitting her with a full-frontal impact.

Eager to regale their trip, Ilene replied, "Oh, that was in March. It was beautiful." She thrust out her left hand. "Isn't this gorgeous?"

Tears that could have fallen dried to steam. She refused to allow the few in her eyes to fall, blinking rapidly to keep them off her lashes.

*March. A ten-day business trip.* She remembered it. It wasn't long after that trip when Neil had asked for the divorce. And now she was meeting the reason why.

"I'm sorry." Angie fought to not choke on the words. "I need to go home."

Neil finally deigned to meet her glacial stares. There was something she didn't want to acknowledge waiting for her when she did. Whether it was an ounce of remorse, guilt, or some part of the man she had once loved, it was enough to make her pause. Though she hated herself, she hated him more for even thinking he had the right at this point to plead his case.

He told Ilene, "Honey, go on to the bakery. I'll be right there."

She leaned over, reaching up for his cheek and gave him a quick kiss, saying, "Don't take too long. You know I'm eating for two. I'll go overboard."

He laughed. It sounded forced to Angie as he nodded in answer.

"You're a real ass," she hissed when Ilene was out of sight.

"Angie. Wait."

"For what?" Fury laced her words. She was physically shaking with her outrage. It was a good thing they were the only two people in the freezer aisle. No one deserved this much humiliation, much less having witnesses to it. "How long were you sleeping with her? How long was I trying to get pregnant for you, when you had plan B waiting in the wings? You're a class-act fuck, you know that?"

He rubbed a hand across his forehead, his expression torn and apologetic. She doubted either was real. "I deserve that."

"No. What you deserve I can't put into words. You lied to me, lied to her! You were cheating on me for months!" Emotions too strong to curb spilled into her voice and made it crack. She spun on a foot and raced for the front of the store, oblivious to everything around her. At the last second, she tossed the forgotten frozen square clutched in her hand into a cart. Her appetite was completely shot.

THE NEXT MORNING, after yet another night of almost no sleep, she slipped into the museum sneaking downstairs bypassing her office. The basement storage door closed with a definite do-not-disturb clang as she stumbled to her work area to numbly spread out her research. The only comfort she had left.

She submerged herself in her notes and drawings to not have to think. She didn't want to think about anything or anyone. Linkin Park was cranked, bouncing off the basement walls. At least the soundproofing kept her angsty music from being heard beyond the doors. The noise couldn't stop her mind from tormenting her, though.

Angie blinked, focusing on the pages in front of her for what had to be the hundredth time in an hour.

*Five months pregnant.* Bastard. He'd even bought Ilene a larger ring. Angie muttered a curse. She'd listed hers online the day the divorce was final.

Tears clogged her throat, making it burn. She remembered all the months they'd tried to conceive a baby, all the money she'd spent on tests, feeling like a failure when she'd faced negative results, over and over.

She swiped a hand across blurring eyes. Ilene would never know that sense of expectancy already carrying a child, to crash into a debilitating wall of hopelessness. Angie had avoided fertility testing, praying. It was one test she couldn't subject herself to when she was already suffering in ways that no doctor could explain. With a defeated sob, she acknowledged what she hadn't wanted to accept. She was incapable, barren, and Neil and Ilene's baby only sealed her judgment.

She'd tried to talk to Neil, but it hadn't been an issue for him. Now she realized why. It was the one thing she'd wanted to believe. That the doctors would find a cure for her and tell her she wasn't barren along with it, but she'd feared learning the truth more. Running into them destroyed her last illusion. Any test would be anticlimactic now, a stake through fragile dreams. Ilene had been more than capable of delivering the killing shot.

Angie refused to dwell on the times she had been depressed and worried, sleeping with her husband while he was screwing another woman. If she did, she'd only throw up.

Later that afternoon, with a look at the clock, she started cleaning up her desk. Bumping into Neil last night and reliving everything she'd already dealt with, including the whys and the woman behind it... It was more than she could take. It was no wonder she was exhausted today. She'd managed nil's worth of sleep the night before.

With all the scattered research pages in their respective files in the vault, she sighed in weary relief. How long had it been since she'd left this early, anyway? Her gaze swept toward the basement doors and she thought of Mark, her co-worker and assistant, and a renowned etymologist in his own right. Shaking her head to break away from the memory of his eyes that glittered when he laughed, she focused on cleaning her desk.

He'd caught her one time too many working late into the night and had berated her for not taking better care of herself. Pursing her lips, she heard his admonishing voice between her ears, telling her to get a move on and get out. Friends like him were too hard to find to strangle out of frustration. She refused to tell him to his face he was right. No man's ego needed that much stroking. A rare, uninhibited laugh bubbled up, but her musing was cut short. The abruptness was as frightening as it was painful. Her eyes widened as the familiar sensations bombarded her, threatening to split her down the middle.

There was no known reprieve from the coming moments, and she had no idea how to avoid the blistering pain. She lifted the weight of her hair from her neck, though experience had taught her it was an exercise in futility. She searched her surroundings frantically, grateful if for nothing else than to find herself alone as pain soared. Towering racks and shelves warped in her vision as she propelled herself past them. The surge roared through her. A hand slapped cold chrome the instant heat exploded upward and outward from her spine.

Sound disappeared, eclipsed by the ragged rush of her heartbeat against her ears. All she heard was her own desperate breathing rasping through tortured lungs. Pain-filled screams burst upward as if a dam had burst, flooding her throat. She ground her jaw tight to keep them jailed behind her lips. Tears forced their way from behind clamped eyelids. She tipped her head back, fighting the tears and pain.

Fighting didn't help, and wouldn't stop the agony from growing worse.

A fireball rocketed down her spine mere seconds later, a red-hot rod of flame that slipped under her skin and between her aching bones. It was anguish from her hair to her nails. The intense agony of twisting muscles was the worst she had experienced yet. Sensations of ripping and tearing barraged her body as the spasm overtook her completely. There was no sense of time as the contortion rolled over her, only the never-ending deluge of torture.

Unable to stay standing against the pounding waves of heat and pain, she lost her balance. With a guttural whimper, her legs vanished from beneath her, throwing her into her chair by sheer luck.

Her entire body clamored to fall apart at the seams. Racking twists and jabs swelled and collided across her frame. She sprawled forward, the intensity of the spasm making her gag and wheeze, gulping air to breathe as her throat constricted. The coldness of the metal research table shocked her overheated skin as if she were being crushed under an ice block. It was impossible to blink. She knew moving wasn't even an option.

Cramps and pain tromped over her without regard as the spasm receded. Her fingers ached, her back burned, and she wasn't sure, but she thought she just might throw up. She inhaled cooler air in measured draughts and fought the urge. With her eyes finally able to close, she could almost make herself believe she had it under control.

Moments melted together as shapes and colors swirled when she did open her eyes. Nothing sounded right; nothing smelled right. Not one part of her physical being was granted immunity from the spasms. Tears pooled on her lashes to dribble down her cheeks. Their damp trails cooled as they dried on overheated skin.

"Ang? Hey Angie, you down here?"

*Christ, Mark!* He couldn't find her like this! She whimpered when she tried to move and only managed to cause fresh tears. Not a single hair on her body was willing or able to move yet. She closed her eyes to the world before her and breathed. At least that she could do, even a little easier now that the pulsating shocks and wrenches to her frame had calmed.

She heard his steps before he rounded the last row of stacked shelves, but it was unavoidable. Unless lightning struck indoors, he was going to find her.

"Hey, Angie, I was going to head out— Hell!" he exploded. "What happened?" She heard him sprint the last few paces to skid to a stop at the edge of the table. His broad shape was blurred by the welling tears.

"Angie?" The sound of her name cracked with worry as he brushed her hair clear to examine her face. "Angie, talk to me!" She shivered uncontrollably when he grazed sensitive skin with cautious fingers. They were like ice against her. He ripped away as though he'd been shocked. "Shit! You're burning up. You need to go to the hospital." He reached across her body, yanking the phone toward him. She had to stop him. There wasn't a point in wasting the doctor's time.

She forced the strength to roll her head, feeling chilled smoothness beneath her cheek. Each heave of air was louder than a vacuum sucking air. "No. I'll...be all right. Need a minute." She opened her eyes but snapped them closed again when her world tilted to an odd angle. She refused to be sick. *Breathe. You can breathe through this.*

"Angela?" His voice was strangled, alarm and concern woven through every syllable. She didn't hear him moving, probably frozen solid watching her for any twitch. She was sure she didn't have long before he'd make the call regardless.

It was a struggle to sit up with every muscle screaming in pain. By his frown, she wasn't hiding it either. "No. This isn't the first time." She swallowed her stomach into place and leaned into the support of her chair, closing her eyes once more to halt the room's spinning. Sheer will blocked the remnants of pain, shoving it out of range. "I'll be okay in a few minutes."

"What happened?" The sound of the phone settling into the cradle told her she'd hit a reprieve.

With effort, she was able to fling her arms across her middle. They were limp and heavy as lead.

"I have no idea. Neither do the doctors. They say I'm fine, but..." She shook her head from side to side, knowing it wasn't exactly controlled. There was no way to know if any other part of her was functioning yet, not without making it obvious she really *wasn't* fine. She refused to allow any more of the dissipating pain to show.

Mark hovered over her like a mother hen, watching her from beside her desk, ready to leap forward at any second to help her. Any sign that she was still in pain was sure to have him calling an ambulance for her with record speed. Angie didn't even need her eyes open to know where he was or what he was thinking. Some things were just a given, especially with a friend like him.

"Angie, tell me. Talk to me."

She wiped her eyes dry, feeling the lingering heat on her skin. It seemed to be taking longer to fade this time. "You really want to know, Mark?" She couldn't look toward him. He was about to laugh his ass off at her. "I think I'm dying."

*Brutal silence.* Seconds slipped by them both.

At least it wasn't the laughter she'd feared. She attempted to push out of the chair, demanding her body to obey. She stumbled, catching herself on the smooth chrome edge of her research table, her legs cramped and sore. She raised her hand when he lunged for her from around the desk. He froze, not taking his worry-filled eyes from her.

Her legs trembled in blatant warning, and she gritted her teeth refusing to crumble. It was too much too soon after the worst of it. She never pushed herself to move like this so quickly after a seizure. Most of the time, she curled up and didn't move for hours. No such luck today.

"Don't, Mark. I don't know what it is." Her shoulders slumped in defeat. "I just want to go." She felt whipped inside and out.

"But Angie," he pleaded. "You almost blacked out. I saw you." He pushed past her hand to tilt her face up and search her. "Your color is almost normal, but you need to see a doctor."

She snapped her chin out of his fingers. "What makes you think I haven't? I've been seeing doctors for four months." She raked a hand down the length of her hair, sweeping it up and over her shoulder then braced herself on flat palms on the desktop. The icy blast of cooler air on her neck dropped a shiver the size of Kansas down her spine.

"The doctors say I'm fine, but at least twice a month, I have severe spasms. I ache and burn from my hair to my nails. Even my teeth hurt. I've been MRI'd to death. I've given blood until I can't give any more. Nothing shows up. Not a damn thing. By their records, I'm fit and healthy." A drawn gulp of air, and all her pain burst free, unfettered and no longer denied. "There isn't one God damned reason why I couldn't conceive either," she blurted with a choked sob, all the buried emotional disappointment layered on the physical, everything she'd been stuffing inside for so long pouring out in an onslaught of words. "But I never did. Barren is still barren."

She fought for control. The sudden release made her answers short, agonized outbursts of frustration. Closing her eyelids tight, leaning on her palms, she refused to let the tears she felt run free.

"Second opinions?" he asked with subdued concern. Mark's tender hands curled over her shoulders, holding her steady.

Angie licked her lips and shook her head. "Try fifth and sixth. I even went to see a neurologist in San Francisco to find out if it was between my ears. Everything that's there is supposed to be."

Mark stroked her neck with the roughened pad of his thumb. Gentle silence settled between them, and she was desperate to soak it up. His next words were very subdued. "This is what's been wrong, isn't it? Why you've been so withdrawn and working like a slave, long hours and staying late. This has nothing to do with your divorce."

She shuddered, relieved, finally, that someone else knew about her suffering, that she wasn't imagining it, yet she still felt utterly lost.

"Yes," she managed. "It has nothing to do with him at all." Fearing she was running out of time, if that spasm were any marker, her shoulders collapsed beneath his fingers. The trembling in her legs grew until her entire body was racked with them. Angie was on the verge of breaking, and she knew it.

MARK FELT THE tremors beneath his steadying hands. He should've expected to find her in the basement. He'd hoped she wouldn't be there, especially after she'd promised him she would slow down and take a break, get some rest. Discovering her huffing like a freight train and burning up terrified him. When he'd thought she was hiding, depressed over her divorce, something far more insidious had been going on with Angie. And he was just now finding out about it.

She started to talk again. He had to strain to hear her, each word dragged out of her.

"In the beginning, it felt like a hot fever. The spasms didn't last as long as they do now. Like walking in front of a radiator and not stopping. They were irregular, easy to ignore. Now..." she said, not meeting his gaze, her arms wrapped defensively around her body avoiding him. "Now, it feels like I am the radiator, like my skin is peeling it's so hot, and my bones ache." She swallowed a hiccup that sounded too much like a sob.

He brought her into his body, tucking her under his chin. Her entire body shook. "Christ, Angie. Why didn't you say something?"

"Because I don't want it to be real! I don't want to die." She whimpered brokenly into his chest.

Mark hugged her closer. "Angie, you know you aren't dying. There has to be a reason for this. A mental malfunction with synapses, or a nervous system problem."

She stiffened, then shoved herself clear of his embrace. "You think I don't know there *should* be a reason? I've been suffering like this for a year. A whole year!"

"You've been seeing the doctors for that long, and nothing's been found?" Mark couldn't believe with medical science advances, nothing had been diagnosed for what he'd walked in on today. There was a little flame of guilt in his gut that he should have suspected something more than her divorce had been going on with her. He'd known her for years, and he'd never suspected.

Angie rubbed her temples, then let her hands drop. "No, just the last four months." She tossed an arm in agitation, punctuating her next words. "But nothing, absolutely nothing, is showing up. This hurts, Mark. Whatever it is, it hurts. I don't know how much longer I can take the spasms. They *burn*. I don't go numb, stiff, or even black out. God! I wish I could. I'm about to go crazy with this."

She dug her fingers deep into her hair, pulling it in anxious frustration to drop them, mirroring the slack defeat in her shoulders. Warm skin, much warmer than it should have been, slid beneath his palms when he curved them over her once more.

"There has to be an answer somewhere, Angie," he tried, wanting to calm her, wanting her to be okay and not sure how to go about it. "Maybe a different doctor—" A derisive curl of her lip stopped him cold.

"I've seen them all." Tears were building in her eyes, making them large in the overhead lighting. Tears he hated because he didn't know how to stop them. "Every last one in LA, San Francisco, and San Diego. I've been everywhere, to every doctor they've suggested." Her head sagged forward to his chest with a noticeable thump, her voice breaking on every word. "I even went to therapy because I thought maybe Neil did have something to do with this." She drew a shuddering breath, rolling her shoulders in acceptance under his palms. "This started long before he and I began to have problems."

He drew her into his body in the silent void of the basement, surrounded by the blank faces of boxes and shadowed shelves holding bits of historical information. Most of it her successes, achievements he'd shared with her or watched her gather. The only scent on the air was her skin, and a soft peachy sweetness he discovered in her hair, tingling his senses, making him want to taste her. He closed his eyes holding her in his arms, shamelessly enjoying it, if only for a brief stolen moment in time. It didn't last. Reality had to be faced.

# CHAPTER TWO

"DAMN, ANGIE," he whispered a few minutes later.

His eyes closed in pure bliss. He then swallowed a hungry groan when she wrapped her arms neatly around his waist. Maybe she needed him, or just this moment.

Mark didn't know, didn't really care why, because he knew he needed her. Badly. He had for so long, warning himself to step away from the dangerous edge of the taunting cliff over and over, everyday, knowing once he plunged off into the unknown, he'd never be able to return to what they shared right now. And he feared the consequences almost as much as he wanted to take that last forbidden step.

There was a little-girl-lost quality in her voice he'd never heard before when she broke the companionable silence moments later.

"I ran into Neil at the store last night."

He hadn't expected that. She rarely talked about Neil now that they were divorced. Steeling himself to be the friend she needed, he relaxed. If she wanted to talk, then it was that much more she let out of her system. She'd been bottling up quite a lot lately, and he'd been without a clue.

"What happened?" he coaxed, nuzzling his chin against her in comfort, in support, in contact.

She drew a deep breath, and he felt the way her body molded into his. Comfort was slowly turning into its own kind of torture. He usually didn't touch her so much, but tonight he couldn't seem to help himself, too worried to keep his usual level of restraint in place around her.

"I got to meet his new wife."

He bit off the expletive on his tongue before it gained momentum. "Already? The jerk just couldn't wait, could he?"

"Apparently not. She's lovely, sweet," she muttered into his shirt, "tall, big boobs, blonde, darker than me..." She rattled off all the pertinent facts like a shopping list. Then bitterness made her voice harsh. "She's five months pregnant."

His arms tightened when she dug her forehead into him, despair weighing heavily on the air. He touched her with his cheek with the last bit of news. His heart broke a little knowing how deeply that alone cut her.

Angie had wanted a baby for several years, and added on top of the fear that she was dying, it was just one more devastating blow to her world. His arms tightened without thought, bringing her closer.

Mark counted the months absently, then snarled silently in anger, adding a few more curse words. "Shit! What the hell? You haven't been divorced five months! It was final less than three months ago." He knew when to the day. A rage he didn't know he possessed leaped to life.

"I know," she replied, devoid of emotion, sounding wrung out.

"That ass was cheating on you?" Her husband had ignored her, what was happening to her, then put her aside like yesterday's newspaper? Mark wasn't a violent man. He avoided irrational anger, but if Neil had been around... He curved himself around her to protect her more because he knew what he would have done if he wasn't holding her. Envisioning the punching long bag at the gym, he counted it off in his mind instead. Calming but not nearly as satisfying.

She rocked against him, her forehead pressed to his sternum. "I don't want to talk about it, Mark."

"But Angie—"

"No. It isn't worth the effort, and he isn't worth the oxygen. It's over."

After a few strained, quiet moments between them, Mark told her, "You know, I do have some friends at the gym. Big, big friends." His grin was wide, begging for retribution. Lucky for him, she couldn't see it. If the other man had been anywhere nearby, Mark would be the first in line.

"Thanks, but you should probably hold on to that favor."

"Just say the word."

"I'll save it for when I really need it," she told him.

A subtle shift of her body flattened her breasts into his chest again. The innocent movement made his breath catch. Hard. He arm-wrestled the urge to answer the physical pull she had on him. This was not the right time for any of the fantasies running rampant through his head.

"Thanks for listening, though. I hadn't realized how much that had been bothering me." She sighed, snug within his arms, at ease. Probably the most relaxed he'd seen her in weeks. "You're a good friend, Mark." She sniffed, burrowing deeper into his embrace. A friend seeking comfort and nothing more.

He cringed at her words. He was through with being the shoulder. He'd been there for her during the divorce, through every stabbing rejection she'd suffered because Neil had, with the sensitivity of a bull elephant, asked for the divorce one night over dinner, as calm as if he were discussing the weather. Except you don't expect to get a lawyer's letterhead packet passed with the dinner rolls. She'd spilled her guts not long after that happening when he'd found her devastated and hiding, like today. Like a wound needing drained, she'd let it all out. His estimation of Neil dropped by glacial numbers that day.

Mark heard her pain, heard the arguments she'd given to deaf husband ears. She had entrusted Mark with almost every private thought she'd had in the strong friendship they'd shared over the years. Except, he couldn't just be her friend any longer. Not if he wanted to stay sane, or ever take a hot shower again. The last few months had been a growing hell of frustration and restraint, fighting himself every step of the way. It was time to make the last fight or walk away.

Her breath whispered through his shirt, tingling the skin beneath those pouty lips where she rested. The way she affected him was impossible to ignore, even though he tried. The edge of that cliff loomed before him. Fear or not, he'd never been the kind to walk away from what he wanted. And right now he knew *exactly* what he wanted.

It was time if he was going to make his stand with Angie. If it meant finding out what was wrong with her, stopping it, or finding a cure, then that was where he would start.

Smooth skin slid over his palms as he searched her face, following the curve of her eyebrows to slight cheekbones, gliding to delicious, inviting lips.

"There has to be something, some way to find out what's wrong," he said, nearly choking on the final implication. "You can't die." Just saying the words created a knot that seared and twisted his heart.

After what he had seen moments ago, her skin so red and hot to the touch, her body no more than a rag doll flung across her desk, left no doubt this was serious. The memory would haunt him forever.

He wasn't going to lose her when he finally had a chance to embrace everything about her. Starting now, he was going to take care of the precious woman in his hands. The way he'd craved, the way he'd yearned to for years.

Standing together with their gazes locked, his arguments waned and his intentions grew fuzzy. Angie had incredible dark and vibrant eyes, like spring leaves. Falling into them, he couldn't quite remember what he'd been about to say. But he did know what he wanted to do at that moment.

Mark leaped off the cliff's edge and didn't even realize it.

Her lips beckoned to him. Mark knew right before he touched them it was ludicrous, but the charge didn't stop him. He caressed supple, pink lips. Heat ignited between them, spearing him straight to his groin. Everything he'd imagined and so much more was in her kiss. Lust, desire, longing. Sweetness and sin. She molded their bodies together, her mouth fitting his perfectly, and his world shifted. It happened so easily, so naturally, there was nothing else in that moment but Angie.

Mark cursed Neil once more for hurting her, for making her believe she was less of a woman because she didn't become pregnant, or intimating she was somehow physically lacking. Mark didn't want to think of all the times he'd secretly pictured her pert, rounded breasts, desiring her, craving to touch and caress, feeling guilty because they worked together. He was only male, but it had always felt wrong. Not even that admonishing truth stopped him. There wasn't one thing that felt wrong about this now.

Blood rushed through his body as desire grabbed hold and shook him, the long-withheld desires breaking free of his iron control.

Everything about those desires bombarded him at once with her in his arms. The imagined way she would taste on his tongue. The silken smoothness of her skin. Gliding his mouth across the top of her breast, swirling around her full shape until he met her peak. Discovering the weight of her in his hand. Too many nights he'd fallen asleep aching for this woman and all the ways he wanted to please her, love her, adore her. And the man she'd been married to hadn't even known she'd been ill. Instead, Neil had been a selfish bastard, tossing away the greatest gift Mark had ever known in another human being.

Now that Mark knew the truth about her illness, he wasn't letting her out of his sight until something was done, and done right, to help her.

Angie was perfect to Mark. Beautiful. He tried to show her how perfect she was nestled flushed against his chest, his fingers loose but holding her face to his, directing her movements. Sips and nibbles escalated to a thrusting passion. He wanted to taste every nuance of her. A roaring, uninhibited need overtook his body, enflaming him, begging for fulfillment. The last tendril of common sense vanished when she pressed into him chest to chest, thigh to thigh, and what was in between became impossible to hide. She was better than perfect. Angie was heaven.

In those few seconds, he fell for her in a way he'd never dreamed, never envisioned. He'd carried feelings for years, but until that moment, he'd never *known* how much or how deep they went. With her lips pillowing his, her touch hotter than a livewire along every nerve, Mark's life changed forever.

Angie gasped scant heartbeats into the sweet plunder of her mouth, breaking herself out of his arms. "Mark!" She lifted her shaking hand upward to cover quivering lips. "You— You can't do that."

Fearful, he froze. Had he gone too far? Been too forceful? Expected too much? He plowed a hand through his hair, bringing himself back to where they stood. He found himself standing in the basement once more, as much metaphorically as literally. His entire body felt ready to explode, and it had only been a kiss. He groaned a low sound, wary of meeting her eyes, anticipating the accusations and anger he'd find.

"I'm sorry, Angie."

What he found when he met her gaze was not what he expected, and for a brief heartbeat, her hesitant expression gave Mark hope. He'd taken her by surprise. *She wasn't the only one caught off guard*, he thought ruefully, *but she liked it*. She'd enjoyed his kiss. It was in the new sparkle in her eyes that matched the soft pink on her cheeks. He hadn't lost his chance. Relief pounded as deep as lust. There was no doubt now that he'd tasted her, he was going to find a way to have more.

She swallowed, the rising beat of her pulse ticking at the curve of her throat. "Just...don't do that."

Mark lifted a hand, and she ducked out from underneath. She bit her lip, her eyes wide and uncertain now.

"Angie, don't," he pleaded. "I'd never hurt you."

"I know," she stammered but leaning away just the same. She slid one more step, then whirled and raced for the doors to the outer hallway of the lower floor.

"Shit." It slipped out between clenched teeth. She may have enjoyed it—he knew he had—but he'd still screwed up. A purposeful breath filled his lungs, forcing a rational calm he didn't want to deal with.

Mark needed her in his arms, her soft body lined up with his enjoying the newness they'd found between them. Instead, he waited and when she didn't return, he had no choice but to follow, but the hallway was empty. He'd give her a few minutes and then apologize profusely.

He shouldn't have done it, shouldn't have let it happen. He'd fought the temptation for years, though it had been easier to deny when she'd been married, but remove the single obstruction, and he was a typical, unthinking, caveman male.

See.

Want.

Take.

Mark chastised himself over and over for the lack of finesse and poor judgment of timing. It was callous of him to take advantage of the moment. The last thing Angie needed was for him to be following her around like a hound dog with his tongue hanging out. Although he'd been feeling exactly like that for a long time, she hadn't known it until today. He tapped his head in punishment against the metal security door in his hands, then let it slip closed behind him, leaving the utilitarian hallway empty to scuffle to his office. Not a peep filled the lower floor. He left his door open to listen for her. He had to apologize.

An hour passed and he didn't hear a single sound. Finally, unable to sit on his own thumbs, feeling the guilt burrow into him, he trudged to the basement and was surprised to find her desk cleaned and her chair in its place. She never left on time, much less early. His stomach fell like a stone hanging at his feet. She'd run. He'd have to apologize in the morning.

But Angie didn't come in.

For two days Mark waited patiently, taking extra time, skipping workouts at the gym to try to catch her, but he seemed to miss her every day. He couldn't help himself, and he began to worry. He called her at home, but no one answered. The final straw came at the end of the week when Mr. Singleton, the museum curator, informed him she'd requested vacation time and asked Mark to fill the gap if he was needed. The news came as a shock, and it created a raw fear, infiltrating his conscience. Taking off unexpectedly was out of character for Angie.

He rushed to her office and then to the basement, searching every file and cranny for information on why she was gone.

The more he searched, the more his stomach plummeted. It held worry for her, and self aimed anger. Real fear kicked him in the gut not long after he started digging through her research desk. After an hour of hunting for any clue to what was going on, he found the one thing that had the power to make him break out in a cold sweat.

The crisp, linen pages shook in his hand. He didn't want to believe what he held. He sank into her chair and read. *Her will.* Completely executed, clipped to a power of attorney. There was also a letter to her mother, a final goodbye. Reading her words for her mother made his heart race painfully. It was a copy, which meant the original was probably with her attorney, along with the original will. He swallowed, slackening in disbelief, tasting cotton balls on his tongue.

Slowing to try to think reasonably, he spotted the drawing of the Anga talisman on the corner of her desk, pinned like a reminder beneath her favorite statue. A mountain lion perched atop a high rock, peering over its kingdom. The animal had a very noble bearing. It was the silent, regal appeal of the pose that she'd always appreciated.

He pulled the page out from beneath its weight and stared at it. Memories about that exact same symbol and what it stood for, what she knew about it, returned to him. At the same time, a sense of disbelief swept over him.

"She wouldn't," he muttered, but with a sick feeling swiftly rising, he knew she would. It would be the very thing she would do to push herself above the unknown factors of her illness and what it was doing to her. With her tenacious ability to focus on one thing, it would help her put the worst of her fears behind her, to search for something as elusive as a missing artifact.

After years of working together, he understood that about her without a doubt. It was *exactly* the kind of thing she would do. He leaped from his spot and yanked out cabinet drawers. Huge gaping holes mocked him. Dozens of her personal files were gone.

His feet dragged him to her desk. Two seconds more and he had another answer he didn't like. The file of maps was gone. He stood straight, eyeing the vault with trepidation. He feared what he would find, or worse, not find at all.

Physically chilled and numb, his head sank to the cold vault door moments later, finding only the empty case that had held the in-depth information on the talisman. The language interpretations and the legends he'd helped her decipher. Legends and stories that weren't possibly true, except at that moment, truth held little leeway considering why she'd gone hunting for it in the first place. Distraction. An unhealthy attempt to push her head into the sand.

There was no doubt she'd gone to search for the talisman, a witch doctor's ploy of magic, nonsense and insanity. He'd had no idea until he saw the entirety of what she'd taken, how desperate she was to not have to deal with her illness. To not have to think at all.

There was no way a mysterious, long-lost artifact of an extinct culture could do anything more than keep her from getting the help she needed. He wasn't even sure he could get her that help, but he had to try. There simply was no other option.

# Chapter Three

THE BUSTLE OF the diner during lunchtime in Inglewood didn't disturb Angie's thoughts as she examined and reordered the notes, photos and drawings before her on the table. Somewhere out there was the talisman. She couldn't prove it, but she wanted to believe it. She bit her lip between her teeth. Nervous energy made her bite it lightly. Was it possible? She'd reread every word she had on the tribe and on the talisman itself over the week. Somewhere in the collection of symbols was the hint that it could heal. She knew, *knew*, it had to be a myth, but...what if it wasn't? What *if* it could heal?

So many legends and myths had been proven false because of common human ignorance, people misinterpreting or misunderstanding some natural action and reaction in their lives. Humans were weird and sometimes gullible creatures. Was she falling into the same trap? Was she allowing herself to believe in a mirage from millennia before for nothing?

She knew it wasn't logical. It would be phenomenal but remained astronomically unlikely. Rather impossible really. Just finding it, though... She sipped at her water, her chin resting on a fist as she studied the maps and cave entrances to the areas where she wanted to start searching first.

If it could heal, it was the farthest reason from the truth of why she wanted to find it. She was firm on that. She already knew where her last moments would most probably be exhausted, and if she could spend those moments doing what she loved, communing with these people, what else did she have to lose?

Silently, the word mocked her: nothing. Doctors across the state gave her nothing to hope for, nothing to work with, and nothing to help her believe that medical science was going to come through when she desperately needed it to. It wasn't rational to lay her hopes on something that probably didn't even exist any longer. A relic long since lost in the dust of time. There was as much of a chance that right at this moment, it was sitting in some shoebox in a nature hiker's closet as there was of it being somewhere out in the deepest parts of the canyon. Even if it did exist, it was the hunt and only the hunt that she wanted.

She sat straight in her booth, letting her gaze wander until she was staring blankly out the window. She would be happy, ecstatic to have one last achievement, one last connection with these people who weren't even a people any longer. Was there any real harm in hoping for that, asking for it after devoting her entire life to this enigmatic and cryptic culture?

The whoosh of the restaurant door opening swung her attention to the front of the diner and to the man who stood there. She almost felt the heat as his gaze burned into her, through her.

In a leisurely fashion, his gaze swept her form in the booth, first up, then down, then rising to meet her eyes. His attention confused her. She squared her shoulders, wondering what it was he was seeing with so much interest. She'd tied her hair behind her, so that wasn't what had drawn his attention.

But there was something in his gaze nonetheless, some spark. He approached her with a slow, easy, swaggering walk. He tipped his chin in greeting.

"Ms. Merrick? I'm Loren Falcon. Erick said you needed a guide."

She swallowed, stunned speechless by his brazen appraisal now that he stood only a foot away. Those same eyes were such an intense golden hue, they danced in the darker caramel of his skin.

Then what he said registered. Right, the guide she'd asked about. Remembering her manners, she arched a hand and offered the opposite bench.

"Please," she managed, reaching for her water to clear the lump she suddenly found in her throat. Her composure returned in segments. "Yes, I spoke with Erick at the hotel front desk." Loren nodded in agreement. "Thank you for coming."

He shrugged in indifference. They were interrupted for just a moment by the waitress, and Angie pounced on the chance to find her heart and shove it back down into her chest where it belonged. She couldn't explain her unusual reactions to this man's arrival. He set her off balance, but there seemed to be almost a sense that she knew him somehow. Angie was positive someone who looked like him would be hard to forget. Especially with those penetrating eyes. She wondered if it was merely her imagination, or if he really could see anything through them. She certainly felt as though he could every time he looked her way, as if he were staring right through her.

Loren Falcon was the perfect example of Native American Indian blood. He was lean, tall, and gorgeous, with thick black hair that swept over his skull with little concern until it danced over his shoulders where the edge swayed. He had the kind of presence that could make a charging bull think twice—cool and commanding.

Suddenly, Angie wished Mark were there with her, someone familiar, someone she could trust. She knew what she was doing in Inglewood and exactly what she was going to ask of the stranger across from her. With a regretful twist of her fingers in her lap, she realized she'd been hasty coming to the town nearly hidden in the mountain passes. In hindsight, telling no one probably hadn't been the best laid plan.

She watched as he sipped his coffee, then placed it on the table in apparent satisfaction. "What did you need a guide for, Ms. Merrick?" he asked with a casual roll of his shoulder.

Was he uncomfortable? She had to wonder at the glances he kept passing her way. Like he wasn't able to relax talking to her, or with her. Did he feel the same? Sense something about her? Was it even possible? Did he know her? She prayed not.

An arched eyebrow prompted her when she didn't answer right away. Time to put it out on the table. Wrestling out of her thoughts, she pulled out several photos of caves from her stack of pages. "I want to get into the canyon." She pointed to the face openings. "To go here."

He nodded absently. "Beaches are more fun," he said with a lazy disdain in his voice.

"This isn't for vacation. I'm looking for something."

He drank, slow and unhurried as if bored with her, then asked, "For what? There isn't much but dirt out there."

"The Anga Talisman, a relic of the Jahehn tribe that lived in this canyon over three thousand years ago."

The rise of his cup halted, then lowered. He gave her his full attention. Her heart stuttered painfully when he locked her down with his piercing gaze. "The talisman is a myth. There's very little left out there that would be interesting. Rocks, dirt." Distrust rumbled between them now.

She tipped her chin, hearing the challenge in his voice. "I'm aware of that. It wasn't found during the original encampment excavation, but I feel it still exists."

"Treasure hunter." It was a low-slung accusation. Angie winced inside, keeping it from showing on her face, refusing to become defensive over his attitude. She was the one invading his home, though it still stung. All she wanted to do was look. Angie knew what her odds were of actually finding the needle in the haystack.

Swallowing her pride because she knew she needed him to guide her to those caves, she told him, "I swear I'm not." She leaned in, casting furtive glances around to see who was near enough to hear her, then lowered her voice. "I'm here on my own time. If there is a chance that it still exists, all I'm asking for is the chance to look for it."

He met her stare, his jaw growing tight as his voice lowered to an unwelcoming growl. "Ever since your museum's excavation," he all but snarled, scorn falling on the table and shattering like glass against her nerves, "more and more people have come here trying to find pieces of anything that they can call Indian and sell for money." He straightened on the bench, eyeing her with suspicion. "What makes your search different? To me, to this town, they are one and the same." He pushed his coffee away, his stare cold and inhospitable.

Her hands began to tremble when she dropped them to her lap. Firming her resolve, she dared to meet his eyes once more, determined to give no indication that she was sharing anything less than the truth. Because she wasn't.

"Honestly, Mr. Falcon, it's personal."

He grunted. She was losing ground.

"You're going to have to do better than that."

"I'm dying," she whispered, taking the ultimate plunge. She found the tabletop, unable to keep his gaze with her own. "I'm dying and I need this, this one last connection. The Jahehn are my entire life and have been since I was in school and became enamored with the Cheyenne peoples. Only I found a thin record of another culture, another people, older, and discovered they weren't Cheyenne. They weren't even recent, but extinct. They fascinated me. They have been my life's work." Her voice dropped as memories through the years bombarded her. "In the hard times, they were more of a family to me than my own. I understood them when no one understood me. There have been others who came and went along the study, but it has been and always will be my project."

"Hard times?" The shift in his voice was noticeable. The scorn was gone, replaced with an element she couldn't decipher.

Angie debated. She'd already come this far and spilled her guts. *What's the whole truth at this rate?*

"My divorce, for one. My best friend calls me obsessed. He's probably right," she allowed, thinking about Mark. "But I also know I'm running out of time to do anything. My life is over. It's either try this or huddle in the corner and wait for my illness to finish the job."

Taking a deep breath, she went on, the final push. "All I'm asking for is the chance to look, to spend the last few days or weeks of my life doing something I love, to not have a reason to die. Whether I find it or not isn't relevant." If it was found, that would make it completely relevant, but she wasn't about to tell him her thoughts on the matter. He'd stalk out, leaving her no options whatsoever.

Loren started tapping out a rhythm on the table edge with a finger, his coffee cup ignored. "I see."

Both swung up when a person stopped at the table, and it wasn't the waitress.

"Loren," the newcomer said with a nod, a disapproving air contained in his greeting. The man at the table's edge gave hardly a glance to Loren, apparently more interested in Angie, and not because she encouraged it.

"River." There was even less welcome in Loren's greeting at the interruption.

The man standing shifted on a foot and smiled, but it felt shallow to Angie as he extended his hand. "You must be the archeologist Erick has been speaking of." *Small-town grapevines,* she thought.

She allowed a quick handshake, unable to avoid it when he offered. She did not want to touch this man at all. The instant their hands clasped, though, she was filled with an immediate sense of déjà vu again, as if she could know this man. It made her skin crawl, not at all the way Loren had affected her. It was the polar opposite.

Her hand dropped beneath the table, unobtrusively wiping the feeling against her jeans leg. She nodded in answer, giving him her first name.

"It's a pleasure to meet you. I hope you enjoy your stay in our town. Forgive the interruption. We rarely get visitors as lovely as yourself." He gave her another insincere smile, then turned to Loren. Any pretense of friendliness fell like a stone. "Don't be late, Falcon." Without giving him a chance to respond, River spun on a heel and left them.

"Am I keeping you from something?" Angie asked him after several tense minutes. She managed to drink more of her water, erasing the odd and awkward sensations she was encountering in the presence of the two men. It was something almost instinctual in feeling, purely reactionary, and totally unexpected and unknown.

Loren shook his head. "I have to meet with the council this afternoon. He's just like that."

Her grin lightened in understanding. "An ass, you mean?"

For the first time, his expression relaxed, and he chuckled. "Yeah. Exactly."

She gave him a sage nod, her expression knowing. "I've known one or two myself. I work in a mostly male-dominated field. Let me tell ya," she said, her laughter slipping out behind the grin, more relaxed than she had been since the minute Loren entered the diner.

He reached for his coffee, seeming to be more at ease, with humor in his eyes warming them for the first time. "When did you want to leave?"

Relief filled her from the inside out. She must have convinced him. She'd take the victory.

"I'm open from tomorrow. I want to search the town archives and meet with the historical matrons, but I can do that later if it works better."

He drank the rest of his coffee, then stood. "I'll be in touch. I'll leave you a message at the hotel this afternoon."

She reached for a napkin. "You can stop by if it'd be easier." She wrote down her room number. "I appreciate you doing this. I am prepared to pay you."

"Money doesn't have anything to do with it," he said absently, looking away from her.

Loren stuffed the napkin in his pocket, then paused. Something sat between them, that peculiar feeling again. When he turned to her, his gaze was watchful. He was studying her. There was no other way to describe the glint of confusion in his expression, like he was trying to figure which puzzle she had come from. Several seconds passed them by, and he remained silent until he made some decision. She dismissed the gnawing impressions that he was judging her, that he was trying to find something more, something hidden. As if reluctant, he finally nodded and left her, striding out the doors into the noonday sunlight. She watched him leave with a quizzical scrunch to her brow.

He had been about to say something. She was sure of it, but what? She mused for several minutes with the sounds of the diner and patrons barely infiltrating, then gathered her pages from the table and filed them in her document holder. Rather than dealing with the unmanned register, she left money under her water glass for the time. She'd never ordered anything but the water. Food was still too much of a hit-and-miss effort for her. She left out the same front doors to the sunshine outside.

The fading summer aromas coming off the mountains were rich on the swirling breezes wafting through town. There was still the tang of hot asphalt, fumes from cars and heated buildings, but to her it smelled far sweeter than the air she was used to in LA. There were other things to be found in the air. Pine trees and tilled soil from somewhere beyond the town. There were the sweet scents of potted flowers in huge urn-sized planters on the sidewalk, painted and obviously cared for during the seasons. Several stores even had decorated fronts with Indian graphics or whimsical window designs. They appeared to be individual to the stores. The entire street made a unique picture.

Angie imagined the little town lost in the mountains during the winter. Snow drifts towering over the mountains, miles and miles of beautiful, pristine white to dazzle the eye. She sighed with a touch of regret. Living in LA, she'd never seen it.

She wondered what it would be like to live in such a small town as she strolled to the hotel. Traffic reached them from the interstate outside of town, and quite a few people were around, but it was calmer, less frenetic than she was used to. It had to be very different, laid back, but harsh at times, unlike in the city where if something wasn't to someone's liking, they just moved, changed, or replaced that part of their life that wasn't a good fit. Angie imagined it would take some adapting to live at this pace. It was definitely an appealing idea to her, to get away from the nonstop chaos of the city.

She crossed the street, her mind not exactly with where her feet were going, and her foot snagged on the uneven roadside change to the shoulder. The near fall jarred a few slips of paper out of one of the folders in her grip. They flipped and fluttered like fall leaves to the ground. Grumbling under her breath, she knelt and found them, grasping for them before the breeze snatched them and carried them away.

A puff of dirt erupted barely inches from her fingers. She yelped as she yanked her hand away, staring at the now indented spot. The dust rose and swirled, but her mind seemed to be watching it in slow motion.

Time warped. Her breathing hitched with her lungs dragging in surprise. She heard little beyond the receding echo of the single shot that seemed to come from so far away. Seconds passed before it all registered. The impact, the thud of it hitting the ground, the sound echoing in waves off the mountain higher up caused her heart to thump hard against her chest as the rest of her remained frozen in shock.

The tableau sank in—that first shot was someone shooting at her. She snapped out of it in a rush, clutching scattered papers between trembling fingers. Strong arms plucked her from the ground with a snarled curse. A second shot echoed a heartbeat after she'd been stolen from the ground. The spray of dirt was right where she had been kneeling.

A kill shot.

# CHAPTER FOUR

"CHRIST, ANGIE! Someone shoots, you run!"

"Mark!" She squeaked his name, shaking, scared, and with her head spinning with the realization that he was the one carrying her. "Where did you come from? What are you doing?" She gasped as his arms tightened into a viselike band around her body, practically squeezing the air from her lungs. Dizzy, she managed to put what happened into order and shivered viciously in his hold.

"Someone shot at me." Her voice cracked, the words making it all too real.

He barked a crude laugh, not slowing until he stood outside her room door. His breathing rasped, harsh and rough right over her ear from the sprint he'd run to get them both safely to her room.

"Key." She didn't argue, handing it over after digging it out of a pocket, clutching the held files closer to her chest. As tight as he was clutching her, however, she was perfectly safe from falling to the ground.

He slammed the door shut with a heel, then plopped her down on the standard harder-than-bricks double bed, folders and all. He tipped the corner of the blue and teal curtain to search outside through the slit. He twisted and pinned the excess door locks, glancing once over his shoulder to find them. After several tense seconds of staring out the lifted curtain, he dropped it and turned to face her.

"What the hell?" he exploded. "What did you do?" Veins pulsed in his neck as he fought for control and his breath. It had to be over half a mile from the diner to the hotel, and he'd sprinted.

"Me?" She leaped from the bed, pages falling and folders flipping to spill their contents as she disentangled herself. "What the hell did I do? Someone shot at *me!*" She jabbed a finger at herself for emphasis. "I didn't exactly have a target on me."

Fine lines radiated from his eyes, anger deepening their rich color until they all but snapped with electric energy. He cursed, pressing the heels of his hands to his temples and sucking air. "Damn it, Angie," he finally muttered, his hands falling. He took two steps and captured her shoulders beneath his palms. Surges of adrenaline raced up and down her body, making her tremble. She felt his answering response through his hands.

Before she could comprehend his intentions, he crushed her into his chest and found her lips. Powerful and commanding, he devoured Angie to her last sane thought. His hold was masterful yet remained gentle. He'd shocked her so intensely, she couldn't possibly get to the point of even thinking of pushing him away.

It took several minutes, but the rush of the moment and the heat of his kiss calmed. With tender care, he formed her to his frame and she answered in kind, her hands rising on their own to meet over his head. Whips of lightning ignited along her nerves with every touch, each caress. His palms warmed her spine in sweeping motions as he pressed her closer into his embrace. She quivered with reawakened life, a passion she'd thought she'd lost. Nerves tingled with raw desire.

Mark's frame was rock solid and shuddering beneath her. He tilted his head, and she moved with him. He teased her lips with his tongue, and her breath escaped in a low moan of desire. She answered him, dueling with him, savoring the bolt of heat that rose.

Mark's first kiss had been a shock so many days ago, but she hadn't forgotten it. It had been one of the most tender kisses she'd ever experienced. Unlike now. Passion and desire licked at them both, her body growing achy and hot with every sip of his lips and swipe of his fingers.

His palm glided, spreading learning fingers across her back, and heat flared over her skin. He tipped her head, causing a windfall of shivers when he nipped at the skin of her shoulder, moving upward, creating a new wave of sensations to pool deep within her.

She wanted to drown in the feeling. It had been so long since she'd been held, kissed, felt so wanted. "Mark," she sighed, the sound filled with need and desire.

Angie blinked and stiffened. *Mark?* Confusion eclipsed the passion, cooling her. What was going on? Why was he kissing her? What was he doing there? What was going on here? "Wait."

He lifted to stare into her eyes, though he didn't drop his hands. Instead, he tightened his hold on her. His molasses brown eyes opened, and the desire warming them shot through her. His chest rocked as he drew a breath.

Had she ever noticed his eyes could hold so many shades? From molasses to teddy-bear brown. Or that they burned with want when he looked at her? It took effort to loosen her fingers from his thick hair, leaving her surprised at how effortlessly she'd fallen under the spell of his kiss. She followed their path as her fingers trailed down his neck, watching his reaction to the single stroke.

Hunger lit his eyes while tension left a wake behind as she grazed his pulse, dancing over the shape of his body until her palms paused on his shoulders. Want filled her, feeling him so acutely, skin to skin. He felt amazing—warm, solid, male. His pulse pounded deliciously beneath her exploration.

She took her time learning the shape of him, taking in the expanse of his body, the width of his shoulders beneath his pullover shirt where the top buttons had been left open in a tantalizing tease. Her fingers stretched across his body, and she discovered the hard hammer of his heart.

A smooth, cotton scent rose from the fabric warmed from her touch and from his skin. A heated maleness and she wanted to get drunk on it. With each new caress, he shuddered, but he never told her to stop, didn't let her go. She was awed by every rumble her explorations created, but Mark didn't move. He didn't say anything at all, simply let her learn what stood before her, what had been waiting for her for a long time.

"How long?" Her voice was breathless with a desire she'd accepted she wouldn't find again. It stunned her, though, to find it because of Mark, the last person she would have expected to reawaken her fantasies.

He tilted his chin, a question in his gaze.

Angie swallowed to clear her throat and her brain. "How long have you felt like this?"

He molded his lips to hers in a seductive surrender of pleasure, then pulled away. "Since the Christmas party two years ago. I saw you in that black dress, and I almost kissed you the way I wanted to, under the mistletoe, in front of everybody and not giving a damn who would see it. Everything I thought I'd been imagining until then became clear. You were stunning." A shudder rocked his chest, and his arms tightened a fraction.

Angie remembered that Christmas party. She'd spent a lovely evening with Neil, her friends and several work associates from the museum society, dancing the night away. She even remembered the dress. A strapless, slit-to-the-knee traffic stopper. It was still in her closet. "Two years," she murmured, unable to believe it. "I had no idea. None."

A curl took over his mouth, creating a devil's grin. "I have you now, and that's all I care about."

Chills hit her at his words, erasing the newfound wonder of his kiss with a swift strike.

"Mark, you don't understand." She wanted to scream as her hands fell away from him. Strong arms encircled her waist with a loose loop, anchoring her to him. Instead of giving her freedom, he pressed her into his shoulder.

"What I do understand is that I need to be here." Suppressed tension resurfaced. "I found your will, Angie." He nuzzled the top of her head. "You aren't dying. There has to be something, some way to help you."

Defeat left her unmoved. He continued to hold her close in a way Neil never would have, offering unconditional support. "I've told you everything already, Mark. There's nothing to work with, nothing to treat." And he'd seen her at her worst. He might have let a lot slide when he'd found her after her seizure, but if he'd arrived to say goodbye five seconds sooner, she would have been in an ambulance, courtesy of Mark.

He shook his head against her, arguing. "What I saw was something." There was a new strength in his voice. She'd never heard it there before. Possessive, protective, the sweetest sound she'd heard in a long time. "We can find out what is happening. You didn't have to run away. I'm sorry I did that to you, that kiss. It was more than you needed, and it wasn't the right time for it."

She extricated herself from his arms, unable to think clearly with his hold so warm and natural around her. It shocked her how much she wanted that embrace, to feel the wall of his chest cradling her, and the tender sweep of his hands soothing her. Her world had tilted.

This was *Mark*. She slid him a glance. He looked the same, the same short hairstyle, the brown eyes, the easy smile, but he was different. He was watching her differently, not suppressing. There was a burning desire and pleasure to be with her evident in his deepening gaze. This new image of Mark after working side by side for so long was going to take some adjustment time.

"I didn't run." When his eyebrow lifted, she conceded, "Okay, yes it was more than I was expecting from you, and it shocked me, but it's not why I'm here."

A frown cut into his features. "Are there more doctors here?"

She shook her head. He angled a glance at the bed and the strewn files there.

"Somehow I didn't think so." He leaned a hip against the door, crossing his arms, following her every step with an unrepentant stare. "So tell me why you have all this information on the Jahehn, and then we're going to find out who would shoot at you."

She paced a few steps, wrapping her arms around her body, feeling his worry follow her the entire time. "Honestly, it hit me when I ran into Neil. I felt desolate. I've wanted a family ever since I was young. I want to be a mother. I want a real family for my children, and when I met Ilene, it almost killed me." She drew a breath, shuddering beneath the impact of what she was finally telling him. What she had no choice but to accept. "I know Mom had me, but not knowing what would happen with Daniel's job, they agreed to wait for more children." She paused, thinking back to those young years. "She was hurt, burned badly by the guy who was my father, so I can't blame her for wanting to be cautious when so many other things were up in the air around her. I adore my dad, and he loves Mom and me. They didn't know when they married she had cysts that would rupture her ovaries. I was so young when they met, they felt they had time. So I was the only child."

He nodded. Now he was seeing the whole picture. "I've heard so many negative test results, this was just the icing on the cake. I didn't want to be barren, had prayed, but..." She swallowed down the growing lump of heartache. "After seeing her, I had to accept it was me all along. Now it's too late to worry about testing. I'm here, I'm divorced, and I'm running out of time." The weight was there, but she refused to let the tears fall, tired of crying over what was happening. "I came here to bury the pain, because I can tell you, this goes way beyond disappointing."

She turned away from him, staring at anything but him. "None of it matters. The last spasm hit before I left town." Another quake rocked her, emphasizing the absolute knowledge that there was nothing left. "It was even worse than the one you walked in on." She didn't want to dwell on the pain of that last seizure. It had taken her almost an hour to just be able to move again. Thanking every deity she'd ever known of that she'd been at home when it had happened. She'd been able to stumble to her own bed and convulse in moderate safety.

He pushed off the door and was holding her again in an instant. "We'll find out something, Angie, although coming here wasn't what I would have expected you to do. We can get you back to town tomorrow."

She shook her head, rocking against him. "No. I'm here. I'm going into the canyon tomorrow."

"Damn it, Angie! You can't do this. I won't let you give up!"

Anger gave her strength to shove him away from her. "I'm not giving up! Giving up would be not caring that the doctors can't help me. Giving up would be not bothering to get out of bed in the morning. I am *not* giving up," she told him decisively, her steel conviction giving her the strength to meet his incredulous gaze without flinching. "I have one last dream, one last hunt driving me. So long as I have something to live for, I'm going to fight this."

Mark twisted to look at the bed, eyeing the pages there. Dawning realization whipped his head back and forth. "You can't possibly think—Christ!" he shouted, the one word echoing for a moment in the room. He stomped to the bed and riffled through the pages, picking out the drawn image for the talisman. "This? You really think this is going to keep you alive because you're looking for it? It's lost, Angie. It probably doesn't even exist anymore. Focusing on this is not going to make what's wrong disappear."

She lifted her chin, meeting his challenge. "It's either try to find it, or find a grave right this minute. Either way, in minutes or days, I'm going to die."

"You're morbid." He tossed the paper down to the bed with a disgusted jerk of his hand. "You really are obsessed over this, aren't you? There is something wrong with you, and I want to help you, but this..." He tossed a scathing look at the bed. "This is not going to help you. It's a legend, a lost myth. You even said you didn't think it had survived when we did the excavation and deciphered the drawings and writings."

She drew a breath, making her stand, knowing he would either stay or he would leave. She was prepared for either. "Are you going to help me or are you going to leave me here? Because I know I'm not going to make it back to LA."

He cursed under his breath, sinking down to the bed capturing his head in his hands. Silence stretched between them, punctuating the battle of wills. His voice was pained when he finally asked, "You're certain you have no other options? Everything has been done?"

Angie knew he didn't want to believe. *She* didn't want to believe. She didn't want to die.

"As much as medical science has cooked up as of three days ago, yes."

Gruff mutters were heard from Mark until he stood and stalked up to her. Concerned eyes reflected like hard quartz, lines of worry returning around them. "I should just throw you over my shoulder. This is insane. I repeat—insane." He cupped her chin, not letting her look away. "I will do whatever I have to, Angie. If this is what's going to happen, then..." He sighed with obvious misgivings. "Then I

48

will do what it takes to make you happy for as long as you have."

Relief made her sag where she stood. "Thank you, Mark."

"But," he stated with emphasis, a grim determination marking his features, "don't think I'm going to just sit on the sidelines and watch you die either. I will think of a way to help you somehow. Something has to be there." He pressed a finger to her lips when they popped open in rebuttal. She was perfectly aware of what was and wasn't there. "No. Right now you're going to turn around, and we're going to report that shooting. Someone was determined to hurt you not an hour ago. I just happened to see you before you saw the car. Those shots had to be heard by others in town. You thinking you're dying is bad enough. Another person intent on killing you is only going to piss me off."

"It could have been a misfire." She gave him a halfhearted smile, knowing how unlikely it was. The thought that someone would shoot at her, wanted her dead, made her stomach climb upward.

"In the middle of town just after lunch, with half the town at the diner?" His tone spoke volumes. "I spotted you walking this way after I found your car here and decided I'd drive around when I didn't find you." He shook his head with more force. "No, sorry. Not believing it."

"You're right." A harsh chill skittered along her spine. "But who? I don't know a single person here."

He opened his arms and she sank into them willingly, surprised at how comfortable she felt there, how well she fit against him. She nuzzled in closer, relishing the rub of his shirt against her cheek. There was no hesitation this time when she wrapped her arms around his waist. Something new and hungry invaded her.

Outside of the known walls of the museum, without any reservations between them, she considered Mark as the man in her arms rather than her work assistant, and was shocked at the immediate flare of recognition for him as a male. A *gorgeous* one, not that she'd come right out and tell him. Some men needed the constant confirmation for their egos, but Mark had never come across that way. She felt the blush on her cheeks, glad for the moment that he couldn't see it the way he held her, or have a notion to her thoughts.

He was the good-looking, guy-next-door type. Your best friend but not the kind she would have been attracted to, except she *was* attracted to him. He had tender brown eyes that warmed when he looked at her, with thick, dark blond hair the color of winter sand and a smile that could melt ice at fifty yards. All-American in a lot of ways. And he'd been her friend for years. In hindsight, she probably always had been attracted to him on some level, but the timing had been wrong.

She didn't have that problem now. It was like a switch turned on, allowing her to see him as the person before her, really seeing him for the first time as the man who held her rather than a work friend. Maybe it was because he had been her friend for so long, she found it easy to revel in his touch, in the way it ignited her like dry kindling. It wasn't like he had touched her often, if at all, until the last few weeks. She wouldn't have been able to accept more than his support even if she had felt more for him then. Without the distraction of work in her way, it was very noticeable what being touched by him felt like. And she wanted more of it.

Time. If she only had more time.

Frustration made her blink hard, denying the building tears. All she'd done this week was cry. This was the worst thing she could think of happening—to have a second chance at something special but knowing she would probably die before they could find out where it would end.

Warm lips trailed down her cheek as if he sensed her torment, seeking her mouth, and she curled into him, refusing the despondent thoughts the chance to fester. She had this moment, and right then, this time was all that mattered. She didn't want to think about what the next few days would bring, especially now that they'd both admitted to...well, whatever this seemed to be. An attraction?

Angie really didn't want to hurt him, and right then she didn't know how she couldn't. It would be wrong to let this continue, but she couldn't dredge up the strength or any real yearning to pull herself away when he kept dropping those hot-lipped kisses on her skin.

He shifted, burying his face into her throat, nipping and biting gently. "You're beautiful, Angie. It feels so good to hold you, to tell you."

A whip of awareness seared her from the inside out at the sexy growl of his voice. She sank into the sensual fog he was creating around them. It had been so long since she'd been held or touched with any kind of desire. Mark made sparks flare on her eyelids, brighter, longer, and hotter.

She melted against him when he leaned back to the wall and brought her into his body, his legs spread to hold them both. He angled her into the V of his legs, and his chest staggered with the contact. The friction made her dizzy with need. Her breathing hitched as his mouth grew hungrier. Warm fingers caressed her spine, her sides, sliding and learning as he glided his lips over the nerves in her neck, spiraling her into newfound passion. His breath tickled the side of her mouth, and she turned to him, almost greedily. He groaned once, long and low.

The kiss he gave her was demanding, commanding, and dragged up more moans of passion from within her. She clenched and burned, aching with renewed desire up and down her body.

The heat of his lips warmed her, sent shocks through her until her blood pulsed with a new tempo against her ears. Her breasts ached as the desire built, wave after wave washing over her. A low mewl slipped free when he caressed her lips with his tongue. Mark's taste was heady, rich. Male. Shivers of need piled onto each other until she knew he could feel them also.

A knock at the door made Mark snap up, which was good. Not that he pulled away, but that he stopped. This was too much to take in all at once. *He* was too much, and he made her want too much.

"Expecting someone?" he asked, setting her behind him to look through the door peephole. "It's a guy. Dark hair, and he looks pissed."

Angie's brow knitted. *Pissed?* Now what did she do? "Black T-shirt?"

Mark's mouth tightened, not at all pleased that she seemed to not only know who it was, but that she knew what he was wearing.

"It must be Loren, the guide I wanted to hire for tomorrow. He's okay. You can let him in."

He shook his head, giving no room for argument. "No offense, but I'm not letting anyone in."

Her mouth popped open, an indignant retort on her tongue, but something in his eyes made her hesitate. Relenting, she nodded. With a second peek outside, he cracked the door to open only as wide as the chain allowed.

# CHAPTER FIVE

LOREN WAITED IMPATIENTLY outside Angie's motel door, surprised to find a walking steroid blocking his view when the door finally opened. Loren's frustration flared when the guy before him seemed uncooperative to move out of the way, leaving the barest of slivers to converse through. Actually, both of them frowned, and that seemed to be the start of it. Loren thought she'd come alone. She'd been alone at the diner and hadn't mentioned anyone else to go into the canyon with her. This was not going to help her case with the council, arriving with a *notse*.

"I've been asked to escort you to meet with the council," he said in way of greeting, trying to find her around the ass in the doorway.

"Why?" She took a step forward but was again blocked. She put a hand on the man's hip and shoved. "Knock it off, Mark. I told you, he's okay."

Mark looked over his shoulder long enough to warn with a snarl, "No one is okay, Angie. Someone shot at you." Then he faced Loren again with a flat expression, no welcome intended.

Loren blinked. "Shot at you?" He'd been in the council house talking to his dad when he'd heard the muted noise. He hadn't been paying a whole lot of attention, and if he were honest with himself, too disgusted with the orders his dad had been making on behalf of the council about this woman. He was still furious at the dictates. "It wasn't someone on the mountain? They do hunt up there."

Mark's lip lifted into a sneer. "If it was someone hunting on the mountain, their aim was nearly deadly, and in the wrong direction. It was closer than that," he stated. "They were shooting at her."

Loren saw Angie pale, and she swallowed a gulp of air. He heard her clearly.

Mark spun, his hands on her shoulders instantly. "Hell, I'm sorry, Ang." He tucked her into his body, tilting her up to see him. "This isn't something you can pretend didn't happen."

She shuddered visibly, then nodded. "I know. I just don't understand why someone would," she whispered. A moment passed. "I'm okay." Mark let her go with a light caress to her chin.

Angie stepped into Loren's view, but Mark continued to keep himself between her and the doorway. Loren realized it wasn't just to keep him from seeing her; her friend was hiding her behind his larger body, keeping the whole world from finding her through the doorway. Grudging respect rose for the *notse*. He wasn't dumb after all.

Mark's voice cut the silence with authority. "We were on our way to report the missed shots. The council, or whatever, can wait."

Loren stopped the frown before it appeared. They wouldn't like it, but Mark had a point. "I'll take you there," Loren offered, knowing the other man wouldn't be swayed. Loren didn't want to take them anywhere, least of all the other male, but the council had all but ordered him to watch her, and he had little choice in the matter. Which meant he had to watch her friend, as well.

Ten minutes later, he sat across the Sheriff's office as Steven took the report from both Angie and Mark. Loren watched them unobtrusively from under his lashes, rolling a pencil between his fingers in outward boredom.

He was definitely not bored, and not relaxed either. His gaze repeatedly grazed over her as she described the day she'd had, his gut fighting to turn into a jungle of knots. Who was Angie Merrick? Just what was she doing there? Why was she really looking for the talisman after so long?

Loren knew she'd been there once already with the museum and all that had entailed, though he'd still been in the service at the time. He'd found out the finer details from his father and the internet reports she'd written. She also had quite the elaborate background studying the Indians that had once lived in the area, from as far back as her college days. That was also making Loren adamant in watching her, but not for the alarmed reasons his father had given.

There was the one question that he refused to ignore, even if his father and the council wanted to obliterate it from anyone's thoughts. As a guardian, he needed to know just as much as the council seemed deliberately inclined to ignore it.

How could she be half-breed Jahehn? Did she know? How could she not know? Those knots in his gut were winding faster than spring weeds as his thoughts raced. At the moment, he and the council were not seeing eye to eye on Angie's arrival in Inglewood. He hadn't made up his mind yet, but he felt it deep down that they were wrong about her.

The tribe was very strict on their mating and breeding to keep their continued secrecy, yet there she sat. Blonde, beautiful, and without a question, one of them. He'd known the second he'd walked into the diner that afternoon, as had most of the living male population. Hell! He'd *felt* her, and that was disturbing in a recognition kind of way he didn't fully understand. Loren had never seen this woman in his life, yet he *knew* she was one of them, somehow knew her in ways that shouldn't exist. Her signals were stronger than any in memory. It also meant she was dangerously close to merging.

It was his duty to help her meet the wolf brother, what tribal males and a few of the women suffer through during the merging. The tribal secret that every member of the Jahehn carried whether they were called by the brother or not.

The council was arguing the obviousness of the facts because she wasn't one of them, of the inner circle. Angie was unique in many ways, and none of them made him comfortable enough to trust her, being one of the tribe or not. The guard dog with her wasn't helping her situation, Loren's decisions, or her position any either.

Mark's voice rose with disgust when he reiterated that someone had shot at her. He couldn't begrudge Mark his anger in that regard. Steven was one cold son of a bitch when he wanted to be, and considering the circumstances, Mark was getting his fair share of Steven's treatment. Mark had refused the seat Steven had offered in front of the desk. His behavior and stance were very telling. The occasional touch to Angie, the protective aggressiveness, and the tone edged in fury. Loren frowned, realizing the man had claimed her.

The scowls Steven gave whenever Mark touched her proved Loren right. He wasn't any happier that she was there with this other male. Steven recognized her as one of them as well, and her friend wasn't welcome around her. Their instincts were to protect their own to the last, even if she wasn't from there. He was *notse*, an outsider and not one of the people. It was only another confusing matter to try to balance.

It wasn't unusual for people to marry outside of the tribe. They were brought in and if worthy, shared the tribal knowledge to pass on, but not everyone needed it. This, her, all of it was an explosive situation. She was an unknown, an outsider returning, and on the edge of her final merging. And every male in town knew it, whether they were hitched, mated, or asleep. They protected the women who had the calling to merge. It was rarer for the women than the men, but not any less dangerous. That vibration of awareness also drew couples together, kept the wolf brother's pact alive.

Except her parentage was unknown. And someone had tried to kill her.

He flexed his fingers, his thoughts exploding with new questions as fast as he tried to find answers.

The shooter could have been anyone in town today, anyone who knew of her arrival the day before. Too many people. But why?

Was it because she was an outsider? Unmated? Looking for the talisman? Loren had too many questions to possibly choose only one.

His focus leapt up to them again when she mentioned the talisman.

Steven slowed in taking their report, stopping altogether to sit straight. "You really think it's still out there?" He gave both of them a blank expression, letting none of his own thoughts show. Loren knew him well enough to know what those thoughts would be, regardless. Much like his own, except Loren had a much more personal stake in the talisman.

She shrugged feminine curved shoulders. "If it is or isn't, all I want is the chance to look."

Loren caught the scowl as it first appeared on Mark's face, then on Steven's. He doubted they had the same reason for their irritation, though. Steven's first duty was to protect the tribe on their own terms, the same as Loren's, then to protect the people as law enforcement from the rest of the world. Right at that moment, no one was happy she was there.

Loren understood the conviction behind her reasoning to search for the missing object. She wanted a distraction from her current problems. Except, he knew Angie wasn't dying. She hadn't been raised with the training, without the knowledge of what was happening or why. Loren doubted she knew anything at all about the Jahehn heritage. Those within the tribal community were raised with the knowledge. He guessed, since her birth wasn't recorded in the communal base, she'd been raised without it. Watching her sitting on the edge of her chair, Loren hid the wince, knowing exactly what she would be facing in the near future. The exact same thing almost every member of their tribal blood faced.

The merging wasn't guaranteed. Just because the wolf brother called to a person didn't mean it was as simple as changing clothes. He'd witnessed his own brother's death from the transformation and toll that overcomes a body during the merging. It was a death he'd been held powerless to try to stop.

Forcefully, he loosened his jaw, pushing Dance's screams out of his head. He wasn't the only one still living with that nightmare, but no one could dare argue that he felt it the deepest. His place *was* to help his people, but the tribal law forbade it during the merging with the spirit brother.

He glanced again at the woman who was currently getting so much attention throughout the council, and she didn't even know it. Would she survive? Could she? He was bound not to interfere—the council were fearful enough about her intentions that they'd already bound him to silence, and breaking it had severe consequences.

*But if she had no idea...* Loren couldn't finish the sentence. He knew exactly what could happen. The memories were an experience he didn't want to ever repeat again. He flipped the pencil to the desk he sat next to, the sharp movement causing three sets of eyes to whip toward his direction.

"Is she almost done, Steven? The council is waiting." Which Steven was perfectly aware of, as a guardian himself.

Steven signed his name to the bottom of the report. "She can go. I'm not sure what we can do about an errant bullet," he informed them with a loose shrug.

Mark hissed through his teeth. "There was absolutely nothing errant about it. One could be misfired, not two."

Angie put a hand on Mark's arm in an effort to restrain him, and Steven frowned at the contact. Loren pushed himself out of his chair, wanting to put space between her and the *notse,* too. It was reactionary, but knowing that didn't stop the rush to protect her from the unknown male at her side, even if she didn't need that protection.

"Don't, Mark," she said with quiet warning. She slowly swiveled to glance over her shoulder at Loren, not flinching, almost challenging. She turned to Steven purposefully, giving Mark a little push away from both men, placing herself between them all. Loren took a second to think and realized what was wrong. She must have sensed their agitation. Reading it as hostility but for the wrong reason, thinking it was against Mark for being confrontational. Rather than simply because he was there and too close to one of their own.

*All right*, he conceded. Steven probably was ticked with Mark, but his inclusion in this situation wasn't the real reason, and Loren knew it. He bit his tongue. Damn but this was getting worse and worse. She *shouldn't* have felt any of their reactions. She wasn't even a pure-breed, damn it! But she was picking up way too much, and he realized she had been since the first time he'd met her. How was she able to sense so much?

That jungle of knots he'd been fighting became sharp and slicing. Not only did it seem like Loren had a connection with this woman, Steven seemed to have some sort of interest in her as well. And that was just not going to happen. Not if Loren had anything to say about it.

# CHAPTER SIX

SHERIFF LANGSTON'S contemptuous scowls cut into his face, his gaze zeroing in on where Angie rested her hand on Mark's arm, restraining him from expressing himself further. Her lips thinned at the air of aggressive disapproval she recognized in both the Sheriff and Loren. *What is wrong with these people?* They should be thanking her for keeping Mark from going over the desk at their indifference for her safety. She'd witnessed the heated burn of anger in his eyes in the room and didn't think it would take much to bring it to the surface. The last thing she needed was to have to bail Mark out of jail for being belligerent to the local cops.

She turned to Loren, telling him point blank, "I'm ready to go speak to the council. I had to the last time. I'm sure this will be the same." She expressed the last for Mark's benefit. None of this was like she had expected.

Sheriff Langston nodded and stood from behind his desk. "I'll let you know if I find out anything about the shooting."

"I bet you will," was a low mutter at her ear.

"Fine," she said, ignoring Mark's irritation. She spun on a heel and strode out of the Sheriff's office, breathing in draughts of fresh air to ease her racing heart and clear her mind. Loren lagged behind, the door separating them when it slammed shut with a heavy barred, locking sound.

"What is with these people?" Mark demanded. "There is no way that was a bad shot, loose bullet, or someone mistaking you for a deer."

She faced him, trying to be rational about it. "Honestly, I know that, and you know it, but to show it wasn't someone firing by mistake will be next to impossible to prove." She pushed loose tendrils of hair away from her face, the breezes flowing over the mountain finding her with ease. "Would you like it if someone came into your neighborhood and claimed someone tried to kill them? In LA anything's possible, but this is a small town. Everyone knows everyone. We're accusing someone of attempted murder. Without a face or something other than a missed shot—"

"Two."

She sighed rather than choosing to argue about it. "Two missed shots into the ground. The charge isn't easy to swallow. I wasn't hurt, and we don't have a bullet as proof."

Gentle hands framed her face, and again she saw the indignant fire in his eyes, the urge to protect her, to fight for her. Bits and pieces of the man he'd never allowed to show before were right on the surface. "All I know is what I heard and what I saw when I got out of my car." He released her stare, but not his hold, staring beyond her to the Sheriff's office. "I don't know what they are doing in there, but you need to be careful. I don't trust them. They don't trust you, either."

She remembered Loren's expressions and Sheriff Langston's unending disapproval. "You might be right," she admitted. Sheriff Langston was a broad man, like Mark. Unable to think of one reason for it, she could have easily been intimidated by his glares and the depth of mistrust she found in him. But why? What did he have against her? The obvious level of suspicion made no sense to her. Not when someone had been shooting at *her*. And were the two men watching her like she was some sort of spy?

"Look, Angie, let me take you to LA," Mark quietly pleaded with her. "Let's get you help. Someone can. I just know it."

The door behind them popped open with a hard whoosh, stealing her chance to answer. Loren strode out, more grim faced than he'd been when they'd left him inside with the Sheriff.

"It's time," he said, stalking past the pair.

"See?" Mark said, lowering his head so she could hear him.

"Let's at least see what they want to know," she cautioned. She was fighting for a little calm herself. None of this was going as she'd hoped, nor the way it had the last time she'd been there. The council had welcomed her. She knew that wasn't the case this time. When she rested a light touch to his hand, Mark flipped his and wrapped hers in warmth, sharing strength with her as they followed Loren farther down the block. "They may not allow it without the proper channels being taken, without the museum being here to oversee what is done." *To make sure I don't find something I'm not supposed to.*

"I'd be fine with that."

Angie didn't answer, not wishing to continue it into an argument. She knew he'd be tenacious enough to try to win, too. The chance to leave had long since passed her by, now that there was a chance to find the talisman. She needed this one last escape and maybe that one last hope she refused to name. Even if she died with nothing but dirt under her fingernails from scaling those cliffs in the canyons, then she would die doing the things she loved to do the most. Mark didn't understand, not yet. He only knew she needed help, and wanted to do whatever it took to get it for her. Angie was out of options. That was the only truth in her life.

Just ahead, Loren held open an ornate wooden door tucked into an alcove of an old wooden building. A warm scent of herbs reached out to her through the doorway mingled with the breeze outdoors. Confusion gave her the slightest pause. This wasn't where she'd met the council before.

Once inside, she noticed it was a large single-room structure with high beams and a central fire pit, with a large grated hole in the ceiling with what appeared to be a separating cover or flap directly over the pit itself. The wood around the smoke hole was blackened with soot, and the walls showed age. There were several mats around the cold pit. She followed Loren's path when he avoided walking on the mats. He stood where he stopped. Herbs and flowers hung from the rafters, while drawings marked and decorated several segments of the walls. She was in a holy tribunal house. She almost felt out of place in her jeans and simple T-shirt, her sneakers scuffing the hard-packed dirt of the floor.

"This is incredible," she murmured in awe, lingering in amazement over the wards and drawings on the walls. Strength, honor, and several more that she immediately rattled off in her mind.

"This is our common house, but ceremonies and discussions are held here also. Unless we need more room, we hold our town meetings in here."

She nodded, asking, "Wouldn't a room in the courthouse work better?"

"This is the traditional way," he replied, standing on one side with her and Mark. Really he stood well away from Mark. No doubt the two men did not like one another.

A clicking sound drew her attention to a door in the farthest wall across the expanse of the pit. Three men entered from the hidden doorway. The first happened to be Sheriff Langston, which took her by surprise. He hadn't been on the council before, nor did he say one word to her when she was filing her report. He was followed by River, a chilling, cold reaction rearing up to rake over her nerves like the fangs of a snake. She didn't understand it but recognized a warning when it crawled up her spine. She didn't know the third man who entered.

Of the three, only the Sheriff wore his hair in a precise cut. The other two wore it long and tied with a single leather strip, the severe manner exposing their features in stark contrast.

The trio stopped opposite of her and Mark. Loren took a step to the side. The air seemed to come to a grinding halt, and her lungs burned as each met and held her stare. Not one of the men showed a sign of welcome. *Crap. Here we go.* She silently pleaded for Mark to keep his cool and to not say anything. She didn't doubt just how hard that was going to be, considering the day she'd already had.

"We understand you wish for permission to hike into the canyon to search for the talisman," the one in the middle said, addressing her. He had piercing, coffee black eyes, with shots of silver strands through his hair.

*Well so much for being polite.*

Mark's stance tightened next to her at the icy tone, but Angie squeezed his hand to keep him from making an outburst. She should have come alone but knew he'd have never allowed it. Mark had never dealt with the monochromatic vision men like these had for the world around them. The land and its possessions were no one's, and it was their right to keep it that way. She respected that belief and wouldn't fight them for it, but their choice wouldn't stop her either. The search was all she wanted. The talisman, if it were found, would remain with the tribal elders.

"I know a lot of the land is protected animal preserve. I wasn't aware I needed permission to hike into the canyon." A game of cat and mouse. She could do that. "The museum has rights to the original sites. Those are my destination."

Barely a hint of acknowledgment hit his dark eyes at her sidestepping reply.

Loren's voice suddenly sheared the tense silence. "Why isn't the rest of the council here?"

It was the first indication something wasn't exactly balanced about their meeting. It confirmed her impression that they were trying to set her off-kilter by meeting on their turf.

"Grace should at least be here," Loren stated, a surly glare directed toward the other three.

River shrugged in a dismissive way. "She was unavailable."

*Unavailable or not even asked?* Angie wasn't that stupid.

Displeasure rippled on the air between her and Loren at River's response. She fought to keep most of these new realizations off her face. That had happened more times since they'd met than she cared to count, and she had no idea why it was happening. She'd been acutely aware of him in the Sheriff's office, the same as she was now.

"This is not the way," Loren barked. Then he surprised her by stepping in front of her and rattling off a long string of dialect language she didn't have the chance to interpret at the speed he was speaking.

"Croma, you know I am right in this," was his final statement. She finally was able to put a name to the third man when he replied in the same language.

Loren snarled in answer, but Croma snapped a hand upward, gesturing with a clear order. Silence fell like a stone between them all.

"Ms. Merrick, I apologize. We have been rude, and that wasn't our intention. I am Croma, one of the head councilmen for our town, and I understand you already know our Sheriff, Steven Langston." His hawk-like gaze never deviated from her, watching her for any hint of deception, she was sure.

She nodded, not falling for the olive branch of welcome for an instant.

He began to ooze concerned charm. "We are very interested in your research, as we were before, but must show caution because so many have followed since the original excavations to try to find anything of our ancestors to sell for profit. We do appreciate that you have at least come to us to tell us of your plans. Many do not give us the same courtesy." His lips formed a derisive tight-lipped mockery of a smile. "You arrived this time without the backing of the Natural History Museum. It has caused some...apprehension. Forgive us for being heavy-handed in your welcome."

Mark coughed to cover a snide grumble of opinion. She squeezed his hand in warning, then dropped it when three sets of eyes immediately turned on him. "I appreciate your concern, but I assure you, this is strictly a personal visit."

"So you aren't here to find the talisman?" River asked. He crossed his arms, frowning. He hadn't done anything else since he'd walked in.

She returned his gaze, unafraid and unwavering. Not that she'd let it show if she were. "I am, but it is more for the search than the find. I respect it's sacred to your people. *If* I find it, I would honor the tribal wishes before my own, as we did with the original pieces that were found. I am not a treasure hunter." She knew with every bone in her body what her chances were and would never waver on that conviction if it were found.

Loren's gaze sliced across his shoulder, those enigmatic amber eyes meeting hers unflinchingly. She felt it again, an almost infinitesimal sense of understanding that sprang between them. Something that said he could be an ally. He nodded for her alone.

Loren believed her. Well, that was welcomed. She was certain he was the only one who did.

"Why have you come to look for it?" Croma asked. The one in command with the bearing of a captain on his ship or the ruler in his world. "If it hasn't been found, we would prefer it stayed that way. It has calmed down since the original finds. Something of that magnitude turning up would only start the rush all over again."

She let out a slow breath, flipping through an assortment of answers to give him. When nothing seemed to fit her feelings, she gave them the truth. Her gaze collided with three sets of untrusting, unbending wills. Three against one, on their turf, in a place where they believed the tribal unity would be on their side.

Her secret was she didn't feel that way at all. There was strength flowing around her, decades if not centuries of souls who had occupied this exact same room before her, buoying her. The unease she had tasted at her entrance had since dissipated, while the ancient symbols of power and ageless wisdom covering the distance in all directions empowered her. That put the ball in her court.

After a few contemplative seconds, she told them, "It is for myself. A last connection with a culture I devoted extensive study and a lifetime of personal obsession."

Her health issues were none of their business, but they could verify the rest with nothing more than a background check on any search engine on the internet, against every archived file. She was listed on anything to do with the Jahehn. After more than a decade of personal and professional interest and study on the extinct people, she was the best acknowledged expert.

Steven nodded, seemingly willing to accept her reasoning, even if no one besides him believed her argument. Croma looked at both men at his side. River remained unconvinced, not conceding when Croma looked at him.

"Are you finished?" Loren bit out. He was indignant on her behalf. She had officially won him over.

"They are free to do as she plans," Croma relented with a snapped nod. "Stay, Falcon. I have a few words for you."

Loren leaned close, lowering his voice. "We'll leave in the morning, early. Be prepared."

Angie barely had time to verify the time before Mark dragged her from the meeting house.

"Jeez!" He sneered when they were both outside and far away from the council. "Could they have been bigger assholes?"

Angie didn't disagree when he tucked her into his side, guessing at how much he'd hated standing there, listening to their superior attitudes.

"I wanted to punch the one on the right. If I didn't know any better, he'd as soon see you fall off a cliff as ever speak to you again."

"River?" He nodded when she mentioned the man's name. "Why do you think that?" Maybe having Mark with her had a benefit. She couldn't focus on all of them or all of their reactions at one time.

Mark squeezed her close. "He was staring daggers at you any time you weren't looking at him. I don't trust any of them. Like you need their permission to go hiking on park lands." Disgust clearly layered his complaint.

He continued to guide them both until they reached the main street to stroll to the hotel. Mark had always been so even tempered at work, through everything from their friendship all the way through her divorce. Seeing this animated side of him was new to her. The protective, emotional side of Mark fascinated her.

"Was it just me, or did they seem nervous that I'm looking?" Angie wondered.

"Yeah, I got that feeling."

"That's what I thought. They didn't come right out and deny me or say not to look."

The pair crossed the street, the motel visible further down in the small town, when Mark asked, "Makes you think they know something about it, then, doesn't it? And if they do know where it is, why wouldn't they want it found? What a phenomenal relic for the history of their tribal ancestors."

"That's true." She slipped her arm around his waist, finding a belt loop with little effort. She wiggled her fingers, fitting them to his side. It was a perfect hold. "So if there's something about the talisman that would keep them from wanting it to be found..." Excitement made her feel giddy. "Are you thinking what I'm thinking?"

"That there might be something special about it?" He rolled a shoulder, reaching into his own pocket for the key card. "I'm not going to say I believe any of the old myths surrounding any of the Jahehn, but they apparently believe something about it. Something that may be incentive enough to shoot at you to keep you from finding it."

"But the only person I told before now was Loren, and seriously, I followed him out of the diner. It couldn't have been him." The feeling went much deeper than that, inside where she felt connected to him on some level. It hadn't been Loren Falcon.

Mark closed the room door and locked it, drawing her up to face him. "All I know is since you've been here, someone has shot at you, the Sheriff is this close to calling you a liar or eating you for lunch, and the council..." His voice lowered to a scathing level, detesting what he'd seen. "They all but put you on trial for even being here, for wanting to hike. They are hiding something. I'm positive of it."

Angie thought the exact same thing.

# CHAPTER SEVEN

LOREN WAITED FOR the door to shut firmly behind Angie and Mark before whirling to face his father and the other two, guardians like himself.

Outrage fueled his voice. "That was completely uncalled for! She doesn't have long until her final merging, and you treat her like this?" He paced to keep his fury in check, appalled by their disregard of tribal laws.

"She isn't one of the people," Croma, his father, pointed out.

"She is, and you can't deny it! Just because she isn't listed and wasn't introduced to the council does not mean she can be dismissed. She is still one of us."

"Loren," River snapped. "She is not one of us. She's a bitch half-breed who slipped through the cracks and is now after the talisman for her own gain. Do you have any idea what that kind of exposure would do to us?" He all but snarled the words. "She's a liar and a thief."

"How can you say that? She's devoted her life to the tribal history. She didn't take one grain of dirt back with her that she didn't willingly leave to the decision of the council when she was here with the museum. She has a true empathy for the people. She's a female with the calling and too close to merging to be put through this."

"She won't survive. She's had no training," Croma warned him.

"And you do not have the council's permission to help her," River added, not giving reasons for his decisions. "You need to make sure she doesn't survive." He crossed his arms over his chest, inflexible. "She is a threat to the whole community."

*Murder?* That froze Loren from his pacing. "You want her silence so badly, you'll condone murder?" He had to have misunderstood, shocked by what they were unanimously ordering. Loren was there to make sure his people *did* survive the merging, not die from it. He just couldn't help them when the wolf brother overcame the physical body. The two had to merge and combine equally. This was all wrong.

Steven and River both started to speak, but Croma raised a commanding hand, bringing immediate silence. "You know the law, Loren. No one is denying that. We are not condoning murder, but the talisman cannot be exposed. I will agree with you that she is one of us, but it is our place to protect the tribe and everyone in the community. She has chosen the others instead of her own people. She brought the *notse,* and we know too little about either of them for her to live. If she knows to come hunting for the talisman, if her research is as thorough as it seems to be, then she knows too much."

"That's my point!" Loren snarled at his father. He took in the expressions of the other two men. "No one has her level of knowledge of the community ancestors. She chose him because she doesn't know what she is, and we do not have the right to find her guilty for that alone. She *is* one of us. She should be protected regardless. I think all of us are missing something and condemning her to death before we know what that is. This is not the way our people have survived." He smacked a fist into his palm in emphasis.

River was the first to speak out. "Regardless of her knowledge, she can't be allowed to live. She will expose us."

"You do not know that," Loren said, daring to sound confident even though he couldn't swear he was right. It was nothing more than a feeling he had, something unknown that he shared with her, giving him confidence to say it. Whether his father or uncle believed him or not, he refused to dismiss what he knew as a certainty.

She was Jahehn. What they were ordering went against everything he knew.

River remained adamant and unbending. If Loren could talk to his dad alone, he might be able to convince him, but not with his uncle's influence right there. Steven would follow Croma's choice but might possibly listen to reason. He simply didn't have a chance, three against one. This was why Grace should have been present. They needed more of the council, but suspiciously, they'd kept it between them. Injustice at the unbalanced meeting clawed at him. All because she'd never been introduced to the council, they were treating her like an imposter, or worse, a criminal to their tribe.

Anger seethed beneath his efforts to stay calm. Her appearance meant that at some point, someone had gone against the tribal laws and fathered a bastard child. Was that what they wanted to hide? Was her father now in their town? Were they protecting one of the council members? Children were revered, each generation proof of their success in remaining secret and under the radar.

Children were taught by their parents from an early age who they were, how to carry on their lives and be part of the tribe, one of the people, as well as how to blend in and fit within the world at large. Angie was an enigma that broke every rule and law Loren had known since he was barely able to walk.

Sweat broke out across his brow. This was bad. If anyone like Angie was discovered... Any adult of age going into the merging could do far more damage than this researcher could ever hope to do. Their entire world would be blown apart. It was a miracle in itself that her own need for knowledge and her research brought her right to the only people who could help her. And if her father had bred more than her, more than Angie, who could it have been? The single worded question—who?—gnawed at him until he thought he felt the hole in his stomach become real. And he hated that feeling, because he was glaring at one man who'd had opportunity.

Loren's own father, Croma. It explained the recognition sensation between himself and the blonde from the very first moment.

He breathed deeply to confine that insidious worry. Right now, he had to stay focused on Angie and her situation because ultimately, she might or might not be the catalyst to their end.

And someone wanted her dead.

"What about the gunshots? Was it one of you?" he demanded. Returning rage made his throat raw with fury, because the need to protect her was apparently stronger for him than any of them. Each of the men standing before him could be guilty of firing a weapon at her.

All three glared at him in varying degrees of anger and annoyance, though Loren didn't back down. The truth of the matter was, if they felt this strongly about an outsider's knowledge, knowing the pain involved with merging and tying his hands from helping, then any of them were marksmen enough to make a killing.

"That's an accusation I will not answer," Croma said, loathing echoing in his words. His eyes narrowed to slits at his son. "I will not allow physical harm to her."

"But you want her dead."

Croma nodded with a stiff head movement, unable to deny it. "By merging. You said yourself she thinks she's dying. She should be dead within the week."

"This is bullshit," Loren spit out, completely repulsed by his father's nonchalance. This was not the way of the people. It was not what he'd been taught to uphold. Or what his place was in all of it, to let life be lost without regard.

"Your guardian place can be revoked," River warned him.

Loren aimed a vicious glare at River. What were they trying to hide? Who were they protecting?

"Not by you." Did River know? Did all of them know? River and Loren had never got along. Even though River was Loren's mother's brother, there had always been friction between the two men as Loren matured. His adamant stand against Angie by binding him to silence seemed to be more a perverse pleasure rather than a protective gesture to the council and tribe.

"Take her into the canyon. The *notse* too," Croma said after a very pregnant, stretched pause and a deep breath. For the first time, Loren saw the weight of the decision on his father's shoulders, but it wasn't enough to make the man relent or change his mind. "When she has failed, then the threat will be gone, and we can put all of this behind us."

Steven nodded, seconding the decision. "It is better this way, Loren."

"For whom?" he bit out, disgusted all over again. When silence was his answer, he spun for the wooden door and wrenched it open, slamming it shut behind him.

# Chapter Eight

Secluded in the hotel room, Angie stared into Mark's face, relishing the sweeping of his hands creating waves of sparking need on her back. She soaked up the feeling, letting it fill her, heating her blood until her skin felt tight. She pressed into his length, absorbing every inch of him against her front. His tenderness never evaporated. The caring heat in his warming gaze never abated.

His lips parted, and she wanted to kiss them. Although kiss was probably too tame for what was running through her thoughts. She wouldn't apologize for the new awareness humming along her nerves. Now when she was seeing him clearly, really physically experiencing him, she had to admit she liked what she'd found. She refused to think about time or pain or dying. This was now.

His gaze darkened with a controlled hunger and turmoil-laden thoughts. "Please tell me you aren't comparing me to Neil. I would never treat you like that." His voice was pain mixed with desire, and it caught her off guard. When he didn't move, waiting for an answer, she realized he was serious.

"No." She straightened in his arms to see him better. "Why would you think I was?" Angie wasn't ready to tell him what she was thinking, but she hadn't expected that.

Mark slid down the door behind him to be better aligned with her. The friction between their bodies sent another wave of heated shivers coursing through her. Her heart thudded like a hammer into her ribs. He'd held her for only a few short minutes, and she was so turned on, she was almost afraid it would all disappear. Each deep breath rubbed her breasts against his body, sending tingling shocks into her core.

"Your expression. You were thinking of something. You get this gleam in your eyes. I've seen it so many times." Tender lips caressed her temple, nuzzling against her, kissing her everywhere. He knew her too well. Knew her every thought, her every want and need. Just because she'd never seen it or sensed it didn't make it not true.

Lifting a hand, she framed his face, her fingers reaching for the bottom of his ear, teasing it. "No, I was thinking how wonderful it feels to be right here, just like this."

The earthen color of his eyes burned molten and hungry, desire flowing like a speeding electric current between them.

"Really?" A quiver rode his chest. The pulse in his neck beat faster. She imagined running her tongue up the side of his neck to nibble on the ear right in front of her. She craved to feel, to please, hopefully as much as he did.

Angie nodded, then licked her tongue across her bottom lip, watching as he latched onto its slow progress.

He groaned, and the sound sent a shock to every nerve, every muscle in her body until it sat like a hungry hunter low in her body. She squirmed, unable not to, forming herself against him completely. Braced by the solid strength of his thighs, along with the hard heat of Mark's chest touching hers, she ached. His eyes shut, and his head fell to the door behind him.

"God." He moaned.

His arms tightened around her, and suddenly clothes were too confining everywhere. Mark shifted, the length of him burning into her. Hot, hard, and sexy.

When he opened his eyes, their sultry need rocked her. "You're making it hard to stay sane, much less honorable. I don't want to add this to your problems. You're more important to me than sex."

A hungry groan gusted through a stiff jaw when she answered him by sliding her palm upward, curling it delicately beneath his ear.

Angie had never seduced anyone, never been consumed by a raging need like this either. Sex with Neil had been normal, pleasurable—but not intoxicating. Every touch from Mark sent lust roaring through her body; every brush of skin made her want more, crave more, searching for it.

"I'm not asking for honorable, Mark," she told him, giving in and doing what she'd been imagining for the last ten minutes. She licked a path from his pulse to his earlobe with her tongue, discovering drugging warm velvet and male strength, animalistic desire at its rawest. The shock struck her clear to her toes at the contact. The clean, musky taste of him added fuel to the flames. He was as addictive as chocolate and twice as mind-warping as tequila. "I'm asking for right now." A shudder racked his frame when she repeated her torture, punctuating her words with a teasing caress. At the pinnacle, she stopped to nip his earlobe between her teeth, then soothed him with her lips.

Her hand drifted down his shoulder, and her fingers flared across his stomach in appreciation, finding the taut expanse for the first time. A solid wall of muscle and skin. It clenched repeatedly under her fingertips. She didn't stop her exploring there. Falling lower with a silken touch, she brazenly cupped him through his jeans. He felt amazing in her palm, hot and full enough to fill her hand. The proof of his desire drove her blood pressure and hunger skyrocketing.

A growl erupted, filling the tiny room. Mark snapped straight and carried her to the bed in caging arms. Files and pages flew out of his way when he swept an arm to clear it. He laid her on top of the bedspread as though she were a precious gift. Lips as hot as brands found hers, delving and devouring her until she was writhing beneath his solid chest where he propped over her on flat hands. Warm skin and thick hair slid beneath her fingers, pulling him closer, tighter, demanding more.

Mark's intent fingers deftly removed her clothes, his lips following, dropping searing kisses as inches of skin were revealed. She gripped at the closest fistful of cloth and yanked, the hem of Mark's shirt popping free of his jeans. Stripped from his chest, it went flying, forgotten. Her nails scraped gently down his abdomen in awe. Exposed muscles rippled, clenching and shaking beneath her questing fingers. A six-pack to envy.

"You're incredible," she whispered. She caught the appraising fire in his stare, spearing her through to the last sane thought she had.

When she tried to speak, he swooped in and claimed her, obliterating any words before she could utter them. Angie sank into the kiss, loving the driving, then gentle pressures he used. The trailing touches, then the path he wove with his lips and tongue down her throat until he reached the swell of her breast.

"I've imagined you so many ways, Angie. Sweet and sultry," he whispered between fiery caresses, his breath hot and panting over sensitive skin. "Demanding and playful, just like you. Just like this."

She arched when his lips wrapped around the tip of one breast. Bliss flared across her vision when the hot slash of his tongue over the peak plunged her deeper into euphoria. His fingertips teasing her other breast had her crying out and moaning shamelessly, pleading for more. The sensual rolling and tugging matched the pace of his tongue on taut flesh.

Sparks sizzled like embers thrown from a fire. She locked her arms over his head, holding him prisoner. Her thighs tightened, then quivered. Her spine bowed as the pulse of her own blood raced through her body.

He increased his attack on her senses. Hotter, harder, and her reaction was explosive, carrying her over the cliff's edge into an undiscovered land of passionate release. Lightning roared through her body, making her feel liquid and boneless.

She gasped, sucking in oxygen as he curled around her, keeping her pinned to Earth with the comforting length of his own frame. Her fingers danced over his shoulder as he dropped a languid trail of sipping kisses up her neck.

"That was incredible," he murmured. "I'm going to enjoy learning this side of you, Angie." A devilish grin appeared on his lips. "And I have many, *many* fantasies to share with you."

Her heart thundered in her chest as she shook with ripples of pleasure. "I hope you plan on starting today."

"Today and tonight and every minute I get to spend with you." He rose on his palms until he hovered over her, his chocolate gaze imprisoning her.

The warmth of skin slid along her arm when she curled it tighter over his shoulder. "Show me."

His fingers toyed with the snap of her jeans, and that hungry grin reappeared on his lips. "I plan on it." The snap came free with a twist.

Her jeans were tugged free, leaving her burning in need when his gaze found the powder blue underwear she wore. Tender fingers removed the strip of fabric when she raised her hips. He stared at her for a smattering of seconds with pure adoration in his expression.

"Your turn," she said, anticipation making her voice husky.

The tease of skin as he undressed for her was tantalizing and agonizing at the same time. She knew Mark wasn't conceited about his body, but right then, he did know how to take pride in it as he removed his jeans and underwear with a slow show for her benefit. Her heart thudded as he exposed himself to her—warmed, smooth skin and one full erection.

She actually felt her lip quiver. Angie felt alive, more alive than she had in months. She felt beautiful; the proof was in the heat of his gaze. A wantonly playful thought crossed her mind.

With a hand she beckoned him closer. She rested a palm on his thigh, caressing the tight muscles beneath her touch. Her splayed fingers barely covered the expanse in her view. Enjoying the light dusting of golden hair on his thigh, she slid within the vee of his legs and cupped him. His head reared back and hissed air filled the room. His entire body was rock solid and pulsing.

Daring herself to take what she wanted, she leaned forward and licked him. A low growl was his answer, the sound falling to her. Emboldened, she swept his length with her tongue, quivering in anticipation to the newfound desire and electricity whipping between them.

"Angie," he ground out, his fingers twisting into her hair.

His plea fell on deaf ears. She thought she'd known what it meant to give and receive pleasure. Feeling his skin dance beneath her lips like molten silk made her feel powerful. Stronger, deeper, and so intense, she thought she'd explode.

His hands loosely encircled her arms, bringing her up until their mouths were fused. With a tenderness hot enough to melt her, he lowered them to the bed, his long, hard body blanketing hers.

Those sparks he'd ignited grew to wildfire proportions, teasing with small strokes, taking her over the edge of sanity one agonizing, tortured inch at a time.

Labored breath rushed passed her ear as he stilled, driving her crazy. She whimpered and moved beneath him, needing something and needing it now.

His withdrawal was slow. Lips trailed down her neck to nip at her shoulder, returning to leave a blazing trail until he found her mouth. He rocked against her, plunging, to swallow her growing cries.

Energy exploded in brilliant colors when she found her release, so deep and so consuming she felt weightless. His arms tightened, holding her closer, holding her together as she shattered in ecstasy. Seconds later, his own voice filled the room, chasing hers as he followed her into passionate oblivion.

"THE SUN'S SETTING," Mark said, coming into the room after leaving to buy dinner for the two of them. She knew he'd also picked up his car from where he'd left it earlier. A single-strap bag hung on his shoulder, a bag with boxed containers in his other hand. She blew a few strands of loose hair away from her face, twisting the thickness to lie behind her in a rope, the braid long gone. Relieved to see him, she offered a smile. He leaned in and found a kiss.

Her lips curved against his when he released her, warm and lingering. The man gave great kisses. He was melting her to the consistency of warm butter pretty easily with them either way.

"I peeked, but I didn't open the curtains or the door." She had been watching for him, worried, making sure he was all right but not letting it show on her face. It wasn't that much of a stretch to think someone would hurt him now, too.

Sitting in the middle of the bed, she indicated the photos and drawings of the Jahehn caves and campsites in front of her with a wave of her hand. "I've put these in some order." The pages on the floor had been reshuffled with those from one of her other boxes of documents. "I have another two boxes' worth to try to find something, some clue to their nervousness about it being found, and maybe where it could be."

He placed the food on the table, to drop his bag to the floor. "Then it's a good thing I did come," he said with a teasing purr of humor. "You can't read a map sideways. I know you won't remember all the details. It's been too long since you catalogued everything from the first dig."

Angie stuck her tongue out at him but didn't argue. Sadly, he was right. She was horrid at reading maps. She was always making scenic detours if she wasn't well prepared.

Symbolism and Native American mythology and etymology were Mark's expertise. It was one of the reasons they'd worked so well together for so long. Her research blended with his specialty, and her obsession fascinated his need to know more about North American tribes and the way they communicated. She chuckled lightly, surprised to realize how seamlessly those two studies had merged together over the years to suit them both.

With a cautious eye, she grabbed a fry from her takeout, eating it slowly in case it was all she would be able to stomach, while she reviewed notes splayed out before her.

"You know," she mused, tapping one of the photos before her a moment later. "They were such a complex society, I'm really surprised others haven't jumped all over this to try to find out more. Like this one." She showed him a page with numerous shapes and sizes of a moon crescent. "Obviously they understood the changes of the world environment around them."

He wiped his hands on a napkin and reached for the photo, nodding. "I'd say they understood their environment as well as could be depicted in that time frame. They didn't have a written language like modern Homo sapiens, but they were able to communicate fairly well between their branches. Looking at this, it's very similar in style to the Olmec language and the Mayan hieroglyphs of the pre-Columbus European invasion."

She felt reenergized reliving their lives, delving into their world again. Studying another stack, she said, "By these, it looks as though they believed in the animal hierarchy in a way that they could connect with themselves. They had totems similar to many of the current and past tribes. It's almost as if they revered them. They really felt a kinship with the wildlife." Many of the photos were from the canyon, but there were just as many from Canadian sites, too. She palmed a notebook and sat on the edge of the bed, flipping pages one at a time, eyeing the individual drawings. "I know several of the tribes even today have the same connection, but deciphering their drawings and their ritual structure, the Jahehn somehow communed with the wildlife. At least, to them they did."

Angie paused a few pages in. "Here's the talisman shape again." She traced the interlocking circles with a finger, noting the information written with it on the page. "This was found in the cave we dated those bone splinters from." A frown pulled her brow down in thought, and she searched over her shoulder to the other loose pages. She held them together a moment later. "And here it is again in this canyon. It was only one of three caves we were able to get into because of the time limits."

"And funding."

A muttered grumble escaped. "Yeah, that too. And the distance between them." She stared at the two images, thinking to when they had found those glyphs. "I wonder what else could be in those caves."

"Spiders, rocks," he suggested, giving her a grin. She smiled at his teasing.

This was how it had always been with her and Mark, talking about the history surrounding them. Only now it felt...better. Stronger.

How long had she missed his most obvious facets? He was the perfect complement to her own work. He understood her in a way Neil never had. She peeked up from the photo, watching him through her lashes as he ate. How long had she taken him for granted?

When she had wanted, craved, needed just a little sign of understanding from Neil, Mark had always had her back, and had been her rock in the hardest of times. A repentant sigh escaped and he cast a glance her way.

"What was that for?"

Angie gave him a lopsided smile. "Just realizing how selfish I've been, and how badly I've mistreated your knowledge. And you."

He cleared his throat, but his gaze never wavered from her expression. "So what does that mean?"

"It means... I'm sorry. I've ignored so many things right in front of me, and now I'm running out of time to make it all right."

His hair whipped as he snapped his head in argument. "There's nothing to apologize for. You didn't know there was anything else around you. You were in a committed relationship. I was the one who needed to find a way past it." He stopped, and his gaze deepened to a molten heat, hungrily sweeping her form. He leaned forward until his face was barely a few inches away from hers. "But now that it has changed, I'm going to take full advantage of the opportunity."

"You are, huh?" she challenged him, feeling her temperature starting to spike at the lazy, sexy way he watched her. Damn, he could make her melt into a mass of womanly nerves in nothing flat.

"As often as possible," he warned, that devil's grin popping up just before he stole a kiss from her lips.

He straightened into his chair and said, "You never did say why finding this talisman was so important, especially with the council not wanting it to be found. You could always back off and leave it alone."

She heard the hopeful note in his voice but she couldn't do what he wanted. Her shoulders hunched beneath the weight, while she blankly stared at the pages in her hands. "I wish I could. Honestly, Mark, it's almost like I feel driven, like I have to find it."

He propped himself against his chair, giving her his full attention. "Why would you feel like that?"

She picked up her feet and crossed them before her on the bed, circled by pages of information on the culture she'd spent her life researching.

"You were almost right when you first got here." Chills made her skin prickle, but she pushed them away. "I am searching for the talisman because of the legends that we've deciphered from the syllabic language hieroglyphs."

"Which one?" He leaned on his shoulder, crossing his arms and ankles, listening to every word.

Her voice barely worked when she spoke again, because she was finally admitting, really deep down acknowledging that her one last chance to live lay somewhere out in that canyon, if she were even remotely lucky. If it still existed. The one fact she had denied for weeks had become the real truth after all.

"There are writings that it had healing properties," she whispered, the room so silent she heard the thud of her own heart. The rustle of the curtains as the air conditioner swirled the air drafts through the room seemed loud. "It's the only chance I have left."

He burst upright. "It is not the only chance you have, Angie!" Mark leaned forward, his elbows on his knees, refusing to let her escape as he reached for her hands. "This isn't like you. I know there's a way to help you. There has to be. You can't really believe in this, in what you're saying. Maybe there's something psychological, and the shit with Neil compounded it."

She shook her head, already positive of at least this one answer. "No. This was going on long before he started to drift away. Well before Ilene."

He eased the pages from her hands, then tugged until she was sitting on his lap, her head cradled on his shoulder. He carefully pulled her hair from her face, her only protection from his searching. "Angie, there has to be something. Damn it! You can't be dying. Maybe going into the canyon will help, but you can't believe this artifact is going to do what you swear doctors themselves can't do."

She swallowed the rush of tears when his arms encircled her. "I have nothing left to hope for, Mark."

He pressed his cheek to her. "Maybe you just need something to live for," he breathed. Silence sat long and heavy in the room. Even the near silent kick of the room air conditioner turning off didn't cut through it. Mark shifted, pulling her in as tight as he could. "If this is what you really need to do, then all I can do is make sure you're happy doing it."

The final note of acceptance in his words brought the dampness full-force into her eyes. He rocked her, holding her as she clung to a last, impossible hope.

# CHAPTER NINE

"YOU HAVE GOT to be the most focused woman I've ever run across," Mark uttered, keeping the sadness tearing his world apart out of his voice. He rubbed his cheek to her hair and found the spring peaches scent that always reminded him of her. She smelled like one, and she tasted just as sweet. Sheer feminine honey on his tongue. Closing his eyes to the memory of that afternoon, he swallowed the want that holding her created. It took nothing more than the curved warmth of her body, and he craved her beyond anyone else he'd ever known.

He yanked his wandering thoughts to the problem at hand.

Something that could almost be a laugh came up from where she was pressed into his chest. "That's a kind way of saying I'm obsessed."

"Only mildly obsessed," he returned with a teasing note. He knew she was laughing. The delicate shake of her shoulders gave her away. He'd much rather see her smile than being so deeply mired by what she faced. He refused to accept that her situation was hopeless. He'd given her his word, but he'd made a promise to himself as well. The only thing they seemed to agree on was he would make her happy no matter what.

Mark had to do some fast talking to get the time and even faster scheduling to find someone to cover his class at the college. It had taken work to convince Mr. Singleton he had an emergency and had no choice but to leave. He was willing to do anything for the woman in his arms, and if that meant risking everything, it was a choice he'd gladly make.

Her breath flowed over his shirt, warming his skin beneath her lips and cheek. "I've never told anyone else. You're probably the only person who would understand how close I feel to these people, the connection I've carried for the Jahehn." She shifted, and he listened. "To Neil, they were my job, what I did for the museum while I was at work, but they've always been more than that to me."

He brushed his hand down her arm, soothing her, realizing how rare it was for her to be this open. Angie was a strong woman. Having her sit on his lap talking, sharing, was something he sensed she really needed. He wasn't in much of a hurry to have her change their situation either.

"I remember you had done research on them to add to your thesis, so you knew about them even before you were hired."

She dipped into his shoulder, a light blush appearing.

"I'm surprised you remembered. I found the first hint of them mixed with the Cheyenne writings. The whole muddle was lumped together because early Europeans didn't distinguish the different tribes as being separate peoples, so the information went back to the late fifteen hundreds with the early settlers' accounts, as sketchy as they were. The real facts about the Jahehn were construed to be ancestral to those tribes, and there wasn't that much information about them to begin with. When I got the archeological position at the museum, I almost died in happiness, and suddenly my pet project had a lot more interest and a lot more support to research. Their research of the native populations was what drew me to the museum, and finding an ancient culture that could have rivaled the Mayans if they'd survived was an unbelievable find. For me and for the museum."

Mark reached for one of the closest pages, studying the marks and drawings. "They did have an incredible language base. The depictions are so real." Her fingers trailed up his arm, and she stood, reaching for more of the pages. She sank down to the bed, crossing her legs beneath her. She spread the pages out, fanning them across the bed, and he moved his chair closer.

"See, here," she said, pointing to a line of drawings that could be translated to be read as a cohesive line of thought if the reader had understood the Jahehn language. "I think they had a real strong affinity with their natural environment. This was dated at about 200 BC, but..." She paused, and he watched as she drew a slow breath, sliding him a slanted glance from beneath her lashes. "I believe they've lived more recently than anything we've found and catalogued."

"Weren't there signs they lived until around 700 AD?" he asked, studying the photos. "I remember there was a certain point, and then they just seemed to vanish."

"Right." Her eyes were bright, excitement in their depths. "According to the writings I have, and this is all theory, during certain years a ceremony was held, and the talisman was an integral part of it. They believed the talisman could heal. Okay, fine, that's one to argue, but I think the Jahehn also believed in reincarnation, that they could control it to a degree, and the talisman was an important part of their ceremony." Her fingers flexed. Then she placed them on her lap, wrapping her hands around her wrists. "I also don't think they're extinct."

He jerked to sit straight, stunned worry hitting him hard with her words. Maybe she was a lot sicker than just what he'd seen and thought. "That's quite a theory."

He heard an exasperated sound bubble from her. "I don't expect you to believe me. They're just my ideas on it. I know I'm just as likely wrong, but if someone else had taken the last thirty years to study them as intently as, say, the Romans, more might be known, but they didn't. They've been hidden among the tribal histories for hundreds of years. It's almost as if they didn't exist at all since they were so easily overlooked for so long, except I know they did."

"Reincarnation? Like life everlasting?" Mark continued to watch her expressions, the urge to ignore her pleas growing. She couldn't really believe— Could she? By her expressions, her gaze flitting over the photos before her, she believed every word she said.

Her hand wavered over the photos. "I can't swear to any of it. I only found three places where the historical designs made any connection to references. One of them was within their last known burial ground, which happens to be in the canyon."

"But you don't think they believed in immortality, right?"

Her answer was quicker, more assured. "Not at all. They had ceremonial burial sites. Treasures. Afterlife offerings. They knew what death was, and it all links to the talisman. The same talisman the council doesn't want found," she quietly finished.

"Reincarnation, huh?" He scratched at the side of his chin, trying to remember where she had found this insight in their histories or if she was painting a mirage. Watching her fingers dance over the photos, he knew there was really only one thing he could do for her. She needed help. He'd been right on with his first decisions to see her get that help.

Her voice tugged, bringing his attention to her instead of the way her fingers traced the images in the photos.

"I believe in it. I always have."

"You do?"

She nodded, a slow movement. "I also believe in mental ability, seeing." His skin prickled at her tone, a deep, shared secret.

He tipped in the chair, staring at the pale cream ceiling panels overhead. "But you want to try to find the talisman on the improbable chance that it can help your problem, because you feel an affinity with the tribal ancestry of this culture." His air left him in a frustrated whoosh. "Do you even realize how that sounds? It's an insane chance. You know that, Angie. Your problem is not going to be cured this way. This is you sticking your head in the sand, and I can't let you do that. I thought I could, but I can't."

He glanced over when he saw her lips thin.

"You gave me your word. I'm not leaving." Pain and anger flashed in her eyes when she lifted to meet his stare. "Mark. I *am* dying. Just because there's no reason for the pain, I know my body, like knowing you have the flu before you actually have a temperature. I know what happens every time I seize. I can't even describe the pain. I can tell you they are getting progressively worse, that they are coming closer together. And one of these times, the pain is going to be so bad, I'm not going to survive it. That's my truth."

A single tear tracked from the corner of her eye, and he was powerless to help her. She moved from the bed, kneeling next to the chair. She reached for his face, capturing him, the misty leaf green of her eyes imploring him. "I know what you're thinking, Mark. I've seen that same expression just as many times."

"Can you blame me?" he ground out. His hands fisted as he fought the impulse to throw her over his shoulder and force her to go to LA. The tumultuous heave of his stomach rocked him, and he shuddered. "Honestly, can you sit there and tell me this isn't all some wild fantasy? You're looking for a piece that has been missing for millennia if it even exists." Needing to feel her beneath his touch, he reached for her. Searching her face didn't alleviate any of his fears, though. "I saw that seizure, Angie. This isn't the way to help you."

"Do you want to know what the doctors have told me, Mark? I'm a healthy twenty-eight year-old woman with great blood pressure and no physical anomalies. Not even a hint of sugar or cholesterol. I'm healthy to a T. That is what the doctors have found after months of testing, X-rays, and pints of blood. So either you stay and help me look, or leave. It's your choice, but I'm going to at least try to find it." Liquid eyes beseeched him, her voice anxious with her next words. "Because looking is the only thing keeping me sane right now."

"Damn it, Angie," he groaned, tugging her onto his lap, to wrap her into his arms. "I'm not going to leave you." Misgivings filled him with each breath. His chest ached with them. "If this is the way you really feel, then..." He exhaled, fighting his own common sense. He knew there had to be a way. He just didn't know what it was. "I'll do it your way." *Until I can think of something better.*

"LOREN."

The call of his name and the sound of steps coming from the shadows froze him with his hand on his truck's door. Tension rippled across his shoulders, preparing himself for the next few minutes.

"What, Steven? It's late." He had an early morning to gather Angie and get them all out of town, and it was hours past dark. He was exhausted from trying to dissect the council's decisions with his brother, who was just as enraged at their decree to let her die by merging. Andrew hadn't made it to guardian status yet, so he wouldn't have been invited to the sham of a council interview. Hours later, they had come no closer to deciphering why they didn't want her to survive.

Loren watched the man who had once been a close friend approach. Not in uniform, his appearance at this time of night didn't bode well.

Loren glared into the darkness. "Waiting? Didn't you get enough of that game when we were younger?" His hand fell free from the door handle. It had been a while, but coming to blows was just as likely as it had ever been since Steven's sister had disappeared.

Steven's expression hardened, anger making his eyes snap with electricity. "Believe me, hitting you is the least you should be worried about. This is about that woman." He sneered his opinion vividly, mentioning Angie. He was probably hoping to get a reaction out of Loren, who was just too tired to accommodate Steven.

"What about her?" Loren asked, mustering boredom easily enough.

Steven crowded him, his black eyes glacial in the shifting moonlight. "She better not survive. You owe me this for Brelynn."

Loren's jaw stiffened along with every muscle he had, readying for the attack. They were inevitable once she was brought into the discussion. Steven's interest had flipped on Angie apparently. "I owe you nothing for your sister. It was her choice, and always has been." He inched away from his truck. He needed room to defend himself. The anger was coming. It was only a matter of time.

Steven's pain was snarled through every word. "She left because you denied her. You banished her."

The stillness of the night surrounding them made the sound of his heartbeat harsher, each pulse punctuated by the sound of his breathing, one drawn breath at a time. Steven had never forgiven Loren for his sister's vanishing act, a situation Loren had never been guilty of, but try explaining that to an older brother whose sister had been missing for months that had lengthened into years. Loren had found that he couldn't, and Steven didn't want to hear it. But he still tried.

"I didn't banish her. I never made her promise herself. I never claimed her either."

Steven's teeth ground together. "You didn't have the balls to do it, Loren. You left her no choice when you went into the Marines, and stayed there. You left her, and she had to face the truth, alone. You came home the fucking hero, a year too late. She left in shame." His face twisted into an angry snarl, a look Loren had seen too many times and hated because there wasn't anything he'd done to create it. And nothing he said could fix it. A deep-seated anger Brelynn herself had fed by mailing a letter out of the blue, laying the entire blame at Loren's door, never to be heard from again. Destroying a friendship that had lasted most of their lives.

"You think I planned my tour that way?" Disgust threaded through every word. "I had no choice! It's the military, Steven. They have their own rules. But you wouldn't know that because she never told you the truth!"

The hit came hard and fast from out of the dark. His head snapped on his neck, and he grunted as pain burst across his jaw. In the next instant, he was plastered to the hood of his truck with stars streaking across his vision like runaway comets. Steven pinned Loren down with the weight of an arm crushing the nape of his neck, the solid strength of the six-foot-three trooper behind it.

"Consider this your chance to redeem yourself. She dies, or I take up River's vote to have you removed from council and from status," he bit out. "He can't do it, but three votes and cause can. Defy the council's order, Loren." The last was a grated dare. He shoved once more, smacking Loren's face to the hood before letting him go.

"This is low, even for you, Steven." He swiped a thumb to his throbbing lip, wiping the blood away. "Is it because she's a half-breed? Or because she has chosen from outside for her mate? That has never been acceptable to you, has it?" Loren taunted. He narrowed his eyes, focusing on the man before him. Waiting.

"She is nothing!" He sliced the air with a hand, trying to make him flinch as the breeze flowed over Loren's cheek. He wouldn't give him the satisfaction.

"I don't think you believe that. You admired her as a woman before her friend touched her. You know she is one of us, and you hated seeing that."

Steven bared his teeth but didn't deny it.

"She will survive." Loren was adamant about it now. He stood straighter. Too many people had too many reasons for why they didn't want her to live. Somehow he'd figure out how to do it so he wasn't cast as a traitor from the tribe. Laws were meant to be broken. He'd find a way.

"If she does, then you've sealed your fate. I will see you stripped and dishonored the way you should have been when Brelynn disappeared." His eyes narrowed to slits, raging with his vehemence. "You've had your father to protect you, but if she survives, even the winds themselves won't be able to save you." He left Loren standing next to his truck, bleeding and angrier than he'd ever been about his position on the council and within the tribe.

Too many people wanted Angie dead. It was not the way. It went against everything he knew about his people, and all they held sacred, including his purpose.

Steven wanted revenge, but what about his father and his uncle? What was it about Angie that they didn't want known? Was it the exposure his father feared, or something more?

Furrows filled his brow, his pounding jaw making him aware they were all serious. He slid into his truck and smacked the steering wheel with clenched fists, his plans moving forward faster than he'd wanted.

# CHAPTER TEN

MARK SAT AT the small motel table, the leftovers from their dinner gone, stacks of photos and his own notes in front of him instead. A breathy sigh reached him from where Angie lay on the bed sound asleep. She looked so relaxed, so beautiful, her hair pulled to the side, her form wrapped in a sexy thing she'd laughingly called a nightshirt. It was the sheerest excuse for a nightshirt he'd ever seen. He was realizing that beneath her take-control façade she showed the world, Angie was a feminine delicacy. It had taken a lot of restraint to not slide under those sheets with her, even if all he did was hold her.

He rubbed his eyes briefly, then focused on the images before him. The pale light of the small room lamp arced around him, just bright enough to see. The coming morning was going to arrive early and ugly, but he'd deal with it then. Right now, he had more important things on his mind. Studying the pictures on the table, he resolutely pushed the image of her only a few feet away out of his mind. He was mostly successful. He'd be going to bed soon himself, but something she had said had stuck. He needed to refresh his memory on the writing and language nuances to try to figure it all out.

Almost all of the native cultures had held, at some point, a correlation to their natural environment wrapped into their beliefs, whether they expressed it in their totems, life symbols left behind at their encampments, marks on their weapons, or in other ways. Studying the Jahehn photos and the notes Angie had collected over the years, he noticed the tribe had a very strong affinity for different animals, many of them depicted in recurring patterns. Was this where she thought the reincarnation came into play? He moved the photos around. Was it possible they had believed they could 'return' as animals?

He straightened and rubbed a tired hand across the back of his neck, massaging the kink brewing. A glance at his watch confirmed the reason for the tightness. A brisk tap at the room door snapped him around. He glanced once to see if the interruption woke Angie. When it didn't look like it had, he stood, frowning at the person on the other side of the peephole.

He swiped the key card off the dresser and silently removed the locks. With the door shut tight behind him, he faced the other man.

"You can trust me or not," Loren said without a pretense of friendship in his tone. "But we need to leave, now."

"Why? It's only a few hours until morning. We can leave then." Mark crossed his arms. Angie was exhausted. He wasn't feeling much better.

Loren shook his head, running a hand in aggravation down his face. Mark spotted the shiner on his chin, the swelled lip more noticeable when he pivoted into the distant beam of the parking lot floodlights. "Because she's in danger. Do you need it plainer than that?" The impatient growl surprised Mark. He reached into one of his pockets and held something in his palm. "I found this where she said it had happened." The wasted slug from a rifle glinted dully.

Mark's chest shriveled at seeing it, bringing that afternoon into sharp clarity and making it real. He wanted to take her home. Right now. "I knew someone had shot at her," he said, trying to hide his disturbed irritation, replaying the Sheriff's dismissive attitude. He stared at the man before him. "Why?"

"I don't know." Disgust and muffled, tired anger were apparent in his tone. "None of today has made sense." Loren slid the bullet into his pocket. "Get ready. I'll be here in an hour. Leave your room lights off. We should be ahead of whoever made that shot by morning."

"How do I know I can trust you?" If she was in this kind of danger, it made more sense to him to get the Sheriff, someone, involved, not run out in the middle of the night.

Loren paused as he was spinning to leave. "You don't, but I'm the only chance you have at keeping her alive. Someone in this town wants her dead. If you want her to live, then you have to trust me." There was a keen hardness in Loren's gaze, an urgency that glittered. But there was still something there that he couldn't trust. Knowing something and not telling. Mark wouldn't let his guard down.

"Fine. *We'll* be ready," he replied, making it clear he wasn't going to let her leave without him. A single nod was his answer. He watched Loren stride away, vanishing down the block until an engine sliced the late night calm. Headlights never did appear.

Silence returned, the sounds of crickets and the scrabble of cats echoed from somewhere in the dark. He made a sweeping search before going inside, careful to stay quiet.

Standing over the bed, he whispered her name. He hated to do it when he knew how badly she needed the sleep.

Puzzled, she blinked up at him. Then she sat up. "What is it?"

"We're leaving. Loren will be here in an hour."

Her eyes became green pools of questions, but she didn't argue. His tone conveyed the urgency when he couldn't explain it. She tossed the covers and rolled off the bed to her feet. And just that fast he lost his voice and much of what he had been thinking about.

Her lush breasts were visible through sheer, cream-colored fabric, and her hips were lovingly wrapped in the hem of her top. Lace curved downward to her thighs, matching the wisp of material covering the treasure between her legs. Lust struck hard and fast, and suddenly his jeans were way too tight in too many places. He'd never believed one woman would have this strong of an impact on him, had never expected to feel the way he did, but he couldn't deny the way he wanted her.

Tawny rose nipples puckered as he stared, and her breathing had grown shallow. Her lips parted, and he watched the tip of her tongue reach for her upper lip. He couldn't stand still any longer.

Mark's fingers threaded into the loose fall of her hair, tilting her up to his kiss. She melted into him, and he found her lips. He swore it would only be a kiss. The feel of her rocked him, blinding him to everything else. The press of her created a burning hunger he was finding to be insatiable around her. Pressure from her fingers at his waist urged him to pull her a little closer, parting her lips and finding the warmth of her, savoring the sweet friction.

He groaned when she deliberately rubbed against him. He released her reluctantly, but she refused to return the favor. Reaching up, she formed her hands around his head, tugging him to her, mewling with whimpers of desire.

His hands wound over her hips, lifting her easily, sending heat whipping through his blood, hotter and stronger with every breath. Long legs curved around his waist, and he hardened behind the crease of his jeans, painfully full.

Excitement, anticipation, and hunger fed the frenzy. She wiggled against him, her breasts jutting into him like brands. His breath slammed out of his chest when she rubbed the heat of her core over him, just as needy, her underwear damp with her desire.

He trembled, fighting with his jeans, releasing his erection from its confines. Her eyes burned with passion when he stroked himself, teasing her wet sheath, guiding the thin band of material out of his way. Angie shook with each sensation, swarming over them both, rocketing their need higher.

He captured her mouth as he entered her, swallowing her cries and feeling her shudders of ecstasy. He closed his eyes, filling her and withdrawing with torturous long strokes. She shook, wrapped around him. He held her steady, never losing his stride as their excitement roared out of control. He curled a hand around her, taking more of her weight and she answered with a deep, throaty purr.

"Like that?" he taunted, watching the flush on her face, watching the way her eyes dazzled and danced with passion, wanting her to find her pinnacle and soar past it.

"Mark," she ground out, striving to reach her fulfillment with each long stroke. Her body quivered, her sheath claiming him as he plunged into her, burying himself inside her hungry heat. Sparks flew across his eyelids with each motion. She met each upstroke with a grinding thrust that drove him insane, holding him like a fist of silk.

She gasped and moaned. He lowered and nipped at the top of one breast, her squeal striking him in places only she could find. He was almost at the end of his endurance, needing his own release, so close to heaven. Then he shifted and filled her once more.

Her entire torso tightened like a strung bow, taut as the detonation flared over them both. The intensity of it rattled him to his bones when he found his release, pushing deeper, caging her tighter, her answering cries and arms capturing him, not wanting to let him go any sooner than he wanted to relinquish his hold on her.

His body flexed with adrenaline-filled pulses, tingling nerves. Air rasped through his lungs as if he'd run a marathon. He lowered his forehead into the curve of her neck, her soft scent and the sweet feeling of their ebbing passion leaving him languid. Her fingers danced with delicate flutters through his hair, and he sipped kisses against her skin.

The muscles in his legs quaked. "I don't want to drop you," he finally said, breathing in that sweet peach scent he loved about her. They also needed to get ready to be picked up. Glancing at his watch, he noticed they'd shot a lot of their hour. *But what a way to do it,* he thought with a grin. He did his best to hide it. When he was almost sure he'd wiped his expression clean, he told her, "We still have to pack."

A feminine sigh was heard near his ear, and he rose, looking at her. Tenderly, he brushed kisses to her eyes, trailing down her cheeks until he found her lips again. There was still a taste of desire on them. It surprised him when he twitched, eager to explore it all again.

"Okay, I know we don't have time for more," he said, regret in his voice, warning her, "I'm going to set you down now." *Or we'll be in trouble, in more than one way.*

Her fingers slipped free, and he eased her to her feet. She seemed unnaturally quiet, barely meeting his gaze when he tipped down for one more kiss before he pulled his pants up.

"Angie?" The grate of his zipper raked the growing tense silence.

A blush ripened her cheeks. She pulled a hand through her hair, sweeping it over her shoulder. "I'm sorry." She seemed embarrassed or surprised, evading his searching. "I've never... I've never behaved that way before," she finally admitted.

He cupped her face in his hands, confused at her reaction. "Like a passionate woman?" He was trying to ignore the fact that she was essentially naked except for the little bit of lingerie she wore.

Consternation made her quirk her upper lip. "No. I attacked you."

"I'd let you do it again in a New York minute, too." His grin was back, full force.

"Mark!" She groaned, rolling her eyes. He loved it when he flustered her.

"Believe me, you didn't attack me. That was incredible, and I'd love to hit rewind and do it a couple more times, but Loren will be here in less than thirty minutes." Her lashes remained lowered, hiding a lot from him. "Don't start regretting this, Angie," he whispered, his lungs burning with the new worry smacking him.

"I don't! I just... It's..." Her eyes glistened as they filled, and she swallowed. She blinked, and the tears threatening disappeared. "I'm going to change. You can tell me while I get ready why Loren felt it was necessary to leave at two in the morning. Do you have what you need?"

He nodded once, trying to stamp out the knot of fear her hesitant words caused. "I'll manage." He hadn't packed with the intention of camping or hiking, but he'd be all right. Her skin beneath his palms was smooth, the softness lingering long after she'd left him for the bathroom to change. Silence filled the room as he filled boxes to lock in her car.

Once her backpack was filled and stocked, it was only a matter of waiting.

SUNLIGHT COLORED the horizon a bright Indian yellow as the three marched in a line into the depths of the canyon. After a short argument in the beginning, Angie had relinquished her pack to Mark. She now walked between the men, with Mark at the rear of the line.

Loren had them moving steadily, but now with more light, it was easier, and he picked up the pace. He hoped to get that much farther from whoever was watching the pair behind him. Loren knew where he was, though. They didn't. He kept an eye on them to ensure they'd be able to keep up with the little sleep they'd managed. They'd both done well, and neither had argued with his demands for leaving in the middle of the night. There was little doubt by the way Mark bored Loren's back with an unrelenting gaze that he was the reason. Loren knew Mark didn't trust him, but the other man didn't disbelieve the need to get away either. Loren was thankful for that much. He wasn't sure what she was up against, not completely. He knew only the council was wrong.

He'd parked his truck deep in the passes. It would take trackers time to find the right exit and gully to follow. Loren prayed he had time to think of a way to help her. As of yet, he had no ideas on how to approach her merging.

Angie didn't have council guidance, no training, and if everything she'd told him was true, then she really did think she was dying. Which would make convincing her that much harder, and she was so close to her merging. Loren knew it as clear as the ringing of a church bell on a Sunday afternoon. Getting her out of town was the safest thing he could've done for her.

Every atom of his self-conscious mind screamed at him to tell her the truth, to warn her— something—but the council had bound him. It wasn't as though he could approach a stranger and divulge their secrets, but the council had taken it a step further, tying his hands as effectively as if they'd used actual chains and shackles. Giving away the truth was exactly the thing Steven hoped for, what the other man needed to have Loren banished for good.

The only reason Steven hadn't won his arguments over his sister's disappearance was because Loren was the firstborn to the most respected and oldest guardian family on the council. On top of his lineage, his place within the tribe was sacred, for more than one reason. It had eaten Steven alive that he couldn't strike out when Brelynn disappeared. Guilty or not, Loren had been blamed when she'd vanished, and he'd never been forgiven.

Loren wiped sweat from his brow, marching on, aware of every step the two behind him made. He felt Angie's anxiety in ragged waves. He didn't have to look to see the wary caution on Mark's face. When he'd arrived at the hotel, his terse greeting had been for them to rest for the hour it would take to drive to the passes. It was the only rest they would get, and Loren knew it.

He dreaded the coming questions, since he didn't have the answers they wanted.

Not that he didn't have a few questions of his own. Like who were Angie's parents? What had really brought her to Inglewood? Was she hunting for the talisman, or did she have a more desperate reason? Was the tribe in danger from her or her friend? Was River right, was she hoping to expose them? It wasn't easy to displace the accusation. No one could remember the last time an unknown had arrived unexpectedly right before their merging. Even if her training hadn't been overseen by the council, parents still prepared the children as they matured. Loren frowned, knowing she hadn't had any training. Angie was an anomaly across the board.

The fact that he sensed her so easily still confused and bothered him. The only reasoning was somehow, somewhere, they were related, and picturing how that could be, and what it meant to him, created a rare rage within.

Loren's father had been faithful to his mother. He'd never doubted it. Until now. So faithful, his father had never remarried when she passed unexpectedly one winter. Croma had raised his sons, and Loren didn't believe he'd ever once regretted doing it alone. Angie changed that belief in glaring Technicolor.

Conscious of his footing on the worn animal trail, he refused to dwell on it. He had to believe his father wouldn't have disgraced his mother, even if the possible proof walked only a few paces behind him.

Croma was the eldest guardian on the council, Loren's uncle just a few years younger, his mother's older brother. Loren grimaced, forcefully obliterating the circling thoughts. He refused to consider it for longer. Angie simply was, and that was the end of it. The more he thought on it, the more the riddle made his head hurt.

"How long will it take to reach the caves I showed you?" Her voice slowed his steps until they both stood with him. Tree limbs overhead offered some shade as the rising sun warmed ground-level air drafts. Branches shook and rattled as life awakened, and the morning scurry of life began.

"They're about fourteen hours straight in." He pulled a towel from one of his leg zipper pockets and wiped his face. Mark popped open a canteen and handed it to Angie before drinking. She smiled gratefully, sipping, then handing it over.

Her gaze was piercing now. That challenging, green color landed right on him. "Want to tell us now why the rush this morning? I had less than two hours of sleep after an incredibly weird day, and he had none." She tilted her head to include Mark.

"The truth?" His throat felt dry even after he took a drink from his own canteen.

"I'm following an absolute stranger into the woods. I think I deserve some answers."

He found the damp of his sweat in his hair when he slid a hand through it. Her eyes narrowed, waiting.

He opened his mouth, but her next words stopped him cold.

"And don't bother to lie. I can tell when you do."

He gaped at her, and "shit" slipped out before he could catch himself.

Her lips twisted in displeasure. "Yeah, I'm not exactly crazy about it either. So start explaining, or I'm not moving another foot."

Loren glanced beyond her to find Mark pensively watching. They both meant it. "Let's take a break. I'm sure we could all eat something."

She nodded and followed when Mark accepted as well. He led them until they reached a shaded outcropped clearing, finding a place to rest against large trees. He offered fresh snacks he'd brought along, aware the dried packs wouldn't last long, but they'd get them to camp. He could hunt for something more substantial then. He was also fairly confident they wouldn't need food for too many days if he was right about Angie.

When the granola and fruit was eaten and he wasn't blessed with more distractions, Loren leaned against a tree and watched the pair before him. What could he tell them? How much could he trust them? If it had been just her...but it wasn't. He flipped a stick he found near his feet out of his fingers. It didn't alleviate any of the frustration winding through his gut at the moment in the least.

"So why the push last night?" Mark asked. His features softened when he tilted to look at her but hardened just as quickly when he faced Loren again. "What made you change your mind to help?"

"Someone in town wants her dead." *Actually a lot of someones.* But mentioning that wouldn't have gone over very well.

She froze beside Mark, the bluntness of his words apparently taking her by surprise.

A delicate eyebrow arched. "Wasn't that what I told the Sheriff? The shots? Someone trying to kill me?" The bite of sarcasm was hard to miss. Loren shrugged, unable to solidify a real answer.

"But why?" Mark leaned, stretching an arm over his raised knees, holding Angie close with the other. "Who would want to shoot at her, want her dead when she's been in town two days? Who is threatened by her?"

She scrubbed her hands down her face. "Why waste the shot? Give it a couple of weeks," she mumbled, misery in every word.

Mark drew her closer, resting his chin on the top of her head. "We'll figure this out. I told you we would." Mark sought Loren's gaze one more time. "Someone wants her dead, and you believed her when the Sheriff was unconvinced. Why?"

Tension formed knots in his shoulders. "It's complicated," he answered drily.

"Try me." Mark's tone flattened. His hold on Angie was more protective than comforting. Loren was beginning to suspect the *notse* was a worthy mate for her. Too bad no one else saw him that way.

Unable to stay locked into the battle of wills with her eyes boring into him, Loren relented as much as he could. "I was ordered to ensure she doesn't survive her illness." He knew his father and the council had in fact condemned her to death. Fury still seethed inside of him because of their choice.

Drops of sweat reflected the sun's rays as blood leached from her expression. "I don't understand." The words were weak and thready, the shocked sound making Loren cringe. What they'd ordered went against everything he knew, every law he'd been raised to uphold and revere. Mark's anger echoed his own when his barked retort filled the air.

"You brought her out here to die! That's sick, man." Mark leaped to his feet. "I knew I should have listened to my common sense!" Mark reached for her then jerked her to her feet with a single pull, wrapping her into his embrace. "That's it. I'm taking you back right now. No more of this insanity over the talisman. Whatever is wrong with you can be cured." He gripped her shoulders until she was looking right up at him, her eyes wide with surprise.

Loren stood slowly, watching them carefully. Mark wasn't finished.

"People have shot at you, and instead of doing something about it or getting the Sheriff to do his damn job, you convince me to follow this jackass out here. I saw when they shot at you. I don't care who it was. I'm not going to let you die."

"Mark," she tried, her hands on his chest, beseeching him.

"I don't care, Angie. I wanted to keep you safe, but this has gone far enough. If you're sick, then we'll get you help. What I am not going to do is let this asshole lead you out into the wilderness so you can die because someone ordered it, shot at you, or by any other way. I'm not."

Loren flexed and made up his mind. It was up to him to do for her what should have been done from the very beginning. The council was wrong. He *knew* it. Watching her, it didn't matter that she was an outsider or that she'd chosen from the others for her mate. She was still one of the tribe, and she was running out of time.

Tension bunched his shoulders until it crawled up his spine like a snake, making itself at home around his neck as he made his decision. Going against the council would guarantee punishment, but he couldn't deny his instincts or the need to help one of his own regardless of the outcome to himself.

Accepting his choice and his fate, he faced them. "I didn't bring her out here to die," he said with calm steel, getting their attention. "She's not dying."

# Chapter Eleven

Mark's hands slid from her shoulders when she ripped herself from beneath his hold. Her eyes narrowed to slits, slicing Loren to the ground. It took four paces to stand in front of him, and not nearly enough to calm the rage roaring through her at being patronized. Bloodless fingers fisted into his shirt. She jerked him down to her level.

"Do. Not. Just do not."

"Angie," Mark pleaded, reaching for her elbow. She ignored him, her gaze locked on the man before her.

"Do not stand there and think," she ranted, her voice so low with rage, it rumbled like a growl from her throat. "I don't know what the hell is happening to me! I have been in pain for a year." She pulled him down closer, silently daring him to blink. His eyes widened into deep amber pools. "I know what it means to die."

"A year?" Sympathy and something that almost resembled shock flitted across his features.

"Yes," she hissed. "So don't think you have any idea about what I've lived with, lived through." She shoved him away from her. Fury colored her vision, making her world red. She sought air in long draughts, seeking an inner calm that wasn't where it should have been. Mark's arms were welcome when he wrapped her up, tucking her against his caring body.

Loren's agitated movements caught her attention out of the corner of her eye. He plowed a hand through his hair, muttering, pacing a step or two, and jerked to a stop. He looked right at her, a wild, awed look, then shook his head. "This doesn't make sense."

"What is there to understand?" she jeered, her voice cracking because her chest hurt, twisted from the inside out. All she really wanted was to curl up and cry like a baby. Not that it would help.

"A year is too long." Loren stopped pacing.

"Well, no shit!" she snapped. "I shouldn't be in pain either, but don't tell me it isn't happening. I can't ignore it, even if there's no excuse for it."

"No, you're wrong—"

A shudder racked her frame. Mark held her tighter in answer.

"Loren. Just stop. I don't want to hear it. I've heard it all already." Defeat made her sag into Mark's embrace. Exhaustion, heat, and the facts that wouldn't go away weighed her down like the reverberation of an oppressive death knell, one only she could hear. "Let's just keep going, okay?"

"Angie," Mark whispered from over her. She shook her head. She was tired of fighting it, tired of explaining it, and just tired from the lack of sleep. She was physically worn down and knew that if she had another episode soon, it would likely be her last. She couldn't keep fighting them. It was a losing battle.

She took comfort in Mark's tender touch against her neck, the gentle massage of his fingers soothing her. What did Loren think he could do to help, anyway? Shake dust over her head and make it all right again? She pressed her forehead into the chest supporting her a few seconds longer, starved for his comfort, for his attention. For his affection.

She forced herself to lean back, to look up at him. "I know you think I'm crazy and that there's a miracle, but there isn't. I've accepted it. Right now, I just want to believe I have the time to do this." She reached up and palmed his distraught face in her hands, pleading. "You said you would stand with me on this. Please, don't back out now." She brought him to her until he hovered over her lips, her voice dropping, his brown eyes growing dark with his internal war as she bored into them, searching for some sign. "I need you for this, Mark. I do. Please?"

Relief made her blink to hide what his answer meant to her when he acceded, nodding gently. Angie knew what she was asking of him and hated herself for it, for demanding so much from him, but couldn't stop herself from needing that support either. She brushed a quick kiss to his lips, then let him stand straight.

"I'm ready when you are," she informed Loren.

They marched for hours into the afternoon, only breaking for short rests, then heading northward again. The going was slow as Loren found trails and paths that forked and wound along the canyon floor. The long silences gave her ample opportunity to think. There wasn't a shortage of topics.

Someone had shot at her. Who would want to kill her? Was it really meant to just frighten her? Why? She knew she was going to die. Why bother with shooting her? She frowned, low-lying limbs adding to her frustration, disturbing her thoughts.

Okay, so Mark was right. She was turning morbid over this. She pushed branches out of her way, paying more attention to Loren's path. Regardless, she couldn't ignore the facts.

Shadows blanketed rocks and shaped the ground as the sun traveled overhead. Tiny dust devils swept across their path as air drafts ran down the side of the canyon nearby. Her steps followed Loren's on autopilot.

Did someone in town recognize her and hold a grudge for the original dig? It had been said several times others had come searching for items to sell. Did they blame her for the treasure hunters going into the canyon? Maybe, but it wasn't as though she was *telling* people to come here. Hunters would have come once word got out about the site whether her team took the items to the city to place on exhibit or not.

Loren was the only person she'd told her purpose to until meeting the council.

Focusing forward, she studied the expanse of Loren's shoulders, trying to remember everything she'd told him. She honestly believed he wasn't the one who had shot at her. Unless he'd left and raced for some unknown perch to watch for her, it wasn't plausible. And why shoot at her, then defend her in front of the council? Studying him, she didn't know him, didn't exactly trust him, but something stopped her from taking the plunge to believe he would try to kill her. She *felt* something when he looked at her, something almost protective, and there was still the sensation that she knew him somehow. She wasn't wrong. It hadn't been Loren.

So if it wasn't about the dig, about the exposure, then why? Was it because she was searching for the talisman? The council didn't want it found, but she could understand their concerns. Not only was the tribal site in jeopardy, but the wildlife would be also. The canyon was a noted haven for wolves. She'd never heard or seen one while she and her crew had been there before, but there was nothing to say they weren't there now.

She dropped her gaze to pay attention to her footing once more. What was she missing? It felt like the puzzle piece was huge and she should see it, but it just wasn't recognizable.

It was late afternoon when Loren finally signaled they would stop for the night.

"We'll be close enough to reach the caves about noon tomorrow," Loren explained, shucking his backpack and stretching. He turned away and pulled out supplies.

"Is there anything I can help with?" she asked. Mark set her pack down with a mild groan. Loren shook his head.

"I'll hunt tomorrow when we set up camp again." He was staring blankly at the packages in his hands rather than looking at her when he answered. "We can get to the caves the following morning. They're farther up the face and a lot harder climb than getting there."

She nodded. In other words, rest. They still had a long way to go.

THE FOLLOWING MORNING she was slow to get moving, a stiff start from sleeping on hard ground. Loren didn't say anything when she had the most difficulty getting her feet underneath herself. Sleep hadn't been easy to reach. There had been too many thoughts plaguing her.

The sun was past noon when he stopped them. She barely registered the landscape beyond the fact that there were trees, rocks, and a lot of both around her.

"I'm so lost," she muttered, shaking her head. Map or not, she'd never find her way back if she became lost.

Loren sat on his haunches, already digging items out of his backpack, and pointed to her right. "That way is east, that is west." He hooked a thumb over his shoulder. "And if you want to go back, go in either direction until you hit the canyon face. You'll eventually come out at the neck."

She sank down to a flat spot on the leaf-strewn dirt, shaking her head. "How far did we come?"

He grinned. "Now you want to know? Why do you think I didn't mention distance, only time?"

"I'd throw something at you, but I'm too tired." She allowed her head to drift until she found the tree and closed her eyes. Muscles were screaming, and she hadn't even been carrying the pack. "So fourteen hours from the pass?"

"Yes."

She heard Mark settling, propping the backpack nearby. "I'm taking a stab in the dark, but twenty miles."

"Almost right. Eighteen. You can make some time in the flats on the animal paths."

"Oh gawd." She groaned. She slid a look at Mark, and except for sweating through his T-shirt, he looked fine. "I am not out of shape. How dare you not even look out of breath?" she told him, annoyed that he looked so good when she felt like a wrung-out washcloth.

Loren grinned over his shoulder at her disgruntled tone, but when she turned toward him, he turned away. Tension knotted his shoulders, twisting muscles as he stared straight ahead.

"You should have an easier time of it on the way home," he told her, a neutral inflection to the words, apparently absorbed in what was in his hands.

She didn't have the energy to argue the point. Maybe some of it was downhill or something, and maybe she'd actually still be alive to make the return trip.

Loren stood a moment later, palming a small rifle, then brought a knife out of his pack, sliding it into a leg pocket. "Rest. I'll be back with something to eat for tonight." In seconds, he faded through the trees out of sight. She envied him the ability to vanish into the shadows, like he belonged in them, a part of them.

Fingers on her chin turned her. Brown eyes studied her. "Are you okay?"

"I think so." Exhaustion was creeping up on her. The only energy she seemed able to muster was to get comfortable against the tree in the shade and sit.

The misgivings Mark felt were plain on his face. "We'll take a break then set up the tent. Sound okay?"

"Sure."

Her eyes slid closed, unable to look into his and see the doubt, the certainty that he'd made the wrong choice following her into the wilderness for this insanity. She was beyond worn out, that was all. It was a long hike on very little *real* sleep. She desperately wanted to believe she wasn't that close to running out of time.

He dropped a kiss to the top of her head and began to empty the backpack of their tent and supplies.

ANGIE HELD PAGES of notes in one hand and a cup of coffee in the other, sitting cross-legged in front of the fire the following morning. Breakfast had been simple, with leftover rations, powdered eggs from Loren's stash, and nuts and dried fruit from hers. She had to give him credit. He was a master chef cooking over a campfire. Even the coffee was flavorful. He'd walked out of camp to check traps he'd set the day before for their dinner tonight. When he returned, she'd be ready to start the climb to the first cave face.

Smoke curled in wispy spirals upward from the dying campfire. The strong acrid odor of pine and elm filled her nose as much as the coffee. Birds chirped and rushed from tree to tree, chasing insects through the branches. Spying a few, she was amazed when they didn't collide into each other or the tree itself on their Kamikaze style flights.

"Any ideas on where to start?" Mark asked, returning to the campsite. There was a stream a few hundred yards further up the path. He looked damp and completely delicious in the early-morning sunlight after washing the wear of the last three days away. He flung the towel in his hand over the top of the tent and sank down next to her.

She tapped the photo in her hand, then stretched behind her shoulder, pointing upward to the mouth of the closest cave. "This is right over there. I have a few notes about wall markings and drawings inside. I'm hoping they're still there and haven't deteriorated."

He nodded in answer. "I went over some of the legend records before we left. I can see some of the points you were talking about now. The reincarnation was undoubtedly deep in their beliefs. The sharing of animal spirits that took them from one life to the next. I also know it's not possible."

She tipped her chin into her chest, refusing to look at him, knowing what she'd see. Not exactly condemnation, but definitely doubt, and it killed her inside a little bit. "Logically, I know it too, but for now can we just look?"

He pressed a kiss to her temple. "We're here, and I haven't dragged you out by your hair yet, have I?"

She couldn't help when her lips lifted at the groused tone. "No, you haven't. I know you want to," she said, a quiet murmur between them.

"You have no idea," he replied on an expelled breath, standing to reach for the coffeepot on the stones.

The sudden howl of a wolf split the air, carrying through the trees. She gasped, scanning the shadows within the trees. "That sounded close!"

They both watched, listening for more, for any sign of how close it could be. She set the pages and cup down, standing next to Mark. Tense moments passed. Silence stretched like a tuned wire on a piano, her nerves humming with the same taut strain.

He rolled a shoulder and sat back down. "Were there any that close before?" She took her place next to him, shaking her head.

"Not that I remember. I knew wolves were protected in the area, but—"

Her words were sliced off with a cry of alarm. A large, gray wolf charged into the campsite from the nearest edge of trees, taking them by surprise. Mark shoved her behind him, blocking her with his broader body. Snarls were punctuated by snapping jaws, the wolf rocking back and forth, gauging. It lunged for Mark, then made a stand a few feet away. Very slowly Mark scooped up a handful of dirt. "Run when I stand."

*The hell I will!* But she kept silent, not wanting to distract him, feeling his body bunch, preparing to spring forward to scare the animal away. In a fluid motion, he tossed the dirt in the animal's face and leaped to his feet, yelling and shouting.

"Run!" Long teeth clicked when they missed his arm by scant hairs. "Damn it, Angie! Run!"

Searching for anything that could be used as a weapon, she eyed a thick branch meant for the fire and grabbed it. She swung it toward the wolf. Mark yanked it out of her hands and shoved her out of the way again. He lunged at the animal, forcing it to retreat, but only a pace or two.

She hunted for another branch, anything to drive it away. Without warning, the animal sprang for Mark, knocking him to the ground. She screamed. It lunged for his throat.

Angie froze in horror as the animal fought to wrestle past Mark's upheld arms. Jaws closed just an inch from his face. He fisted his hands, striking at the animal to defend himself. Scratches pooled with blood on his arms and down his neck from razor-sharp claws.

As unexpected as the first, another wolf exploded from the tree line. Before she could raise the branch clutched in her numb fingers to stop it, the beast barreled right into the wolf attacking Mark. The impact knocked it clear as both rolled into the dirt. Weathered leaves and dirt spattered as they rose and faced each other. The only thing she could think was that the pack had gathered. They had no guns, nothing that would fight off the strength of pissed-off wolves.

Midnight black, the second wolf rushed Mark's attacker, pushing it farther and farther until its pacing created a barrier between themselves and the wolf that had attacked Mark.

Angie's trembling fingers found Mark's shoulder by luck and jerked him until he started to move away from the pair challenging each other. The wolves charged each other, colliding with ferocious snarls and raging jaws. The crash clamored above every other sound, driving silence into the trees all around them. With Mark holding her close, she watched the scene unfold, unable to do anything but watch and breathe. She didn't dare run. What if they decided she was better game? What if there were more waiting in the shadows?

Jaws clacked as they bit in challenge. Dust rose in dry puffs as paws marked the ground beneath them. Claws an inch long gouged dirt for purchase. Long teeth found then lost vicious holds on thick pelts, until the midnight black wolf toppled the attacker again to stand over it. The victor was clear, and the loser whined pitifully.

Mark pushed her behind him again, prepared to block if either of the two wolves looked in their direction again. She did without argument but stayed close.

Oddly, when it allowed the loser to rise, the midnight black wolf lowered its head and snarled, herding the other wolf toward the trees. The darker gray slunk away, its tail between its legs. It disappeared into the dense trees of the woods.

The coal black coat moved like dark water at midnight over solid muscle when the remaining wolf shifted to one side to cast a look at her and Mark. Just a quick glance. Then, without another sign, it whirled and raced after the first wolf, the trailing sound of a howl wafting to them from deep in the canyon.

# Chapter Twelve

Mark blinked, watching the second animal vanish into the woods, until there was nothing but silence and the occasional chirp of birds checking to see if the coast was clear.

He plopped to the ground with a groan of adrenaline-delayed shock as his legs gave out. His arms were scratched everywhere, and he knew he had something on his neck. It burned. He considered himself lucky to even be alive. The remembered image of focused eyes and teeth the size of small steak knives aimed for his face forced a chill to his skin. That was definitely one of the last things he would've expected, even out here. Didn't wolves usually avoid humans? A tremor shook his shoulders. He tipped up, finding Angie standing nearby with a thick branch in her hands, intently watching the shadows for anything. "They're gone, baby," he managed, amazed at how calm he sounded.

"You don't know that." The slightest drag of her fingers on his neck sent an electric shot down his body. "You have a bad scratch here. You need to be treated."

The crunch of heavy steps rushing toward them grabbed their attention. She cocked the branch. The sigh of relief was loud between them when Loren reappeared through a gap in the trees. The branch Angie held hit the ground with a soft thud.

"Are you two okay? I heard the wolves but was too far away." Thin lips and twitchy movements were the only outward appearance of his anger. He tossed the gutted rabbits he carried over the peak of his tent's roof, then hunched down in front of Mark. Anger deepened his expression.

Angie did the most graceful collapse to the ground Mark had ever seen from another person. Her head sank to rest on his shoulder, carefully avoiding any of the scratches on his arms and neck.

"I don't know what happened. We were just talking, and then the howl. A couple minutes later, it was here." She shuddered.

Mark dragged a thumb down her cheek. "You were brave, but next time, run. I don't want to see you getting hurt."

Loren was crouched in front of his backpack, pulling out medically marked tubes.

"Is it gone?" Mark asked, idly stroking Angie with his hand, trying not to think about the scratches that burned or why the wolf had attacked or how close he'd come to losing to it.

Loren's gaze locked on Mark. Anger simmered in their depths, a raw heat that took Mark by surprise. Almost amber red, his eyes seemed to reflect the sunlight around them. Golden and wild. Something poked at Mark's consciousness, but Loren's voice broke the spell.

"They won't be back."

"Was it a rogue wolf?" Angie asked. "What about the second one? Why would they do that? Are we safe here?" She rolled her head against his shoulder, as confused as he was over the attack and the interference of the second wolf. "I've never heard of a wolf attacking like that, much less being chased away." Disbelief and worry rode her voice. "What if they have a pack? They could be close."

Loren crouched with them, then began to clean Mark's scrapes and cuts. "We're safe. It's rare for them to come within ten feet of a human."

"I don't get it," she murmured. "There weren't any in the area before."

"There have been some spotted, but I wouldn't have expected them here." Loren's jaw tightened as he spoke, swiping antiseptics and creams over the last cuts on Mark's arm. He looked furious, in fact, avoiding both Mark and Angie. He handed over the wipes and the cream. "This is for your neck."

"I'll do it," Angie offered, releasing Loren from the task. He jerked to his feet, gathering his hair with a thrusting hand, snapping a black band over the length. Hadn't it been tied when he'd left? Mark dropped his gaze and found Angie studying the scrape, giving it tender care.

"Are you okay?" he asked quietly.

She swallowed and gave him a brave smile. "Yeah, just shook up. It happened so fast." She lowered her lashes, hiding from him, and just that fast, he wanted to kiss her. Had to taste her again to keep away the demons she feared. She was beautiful, with pale cream skin and long blonde hair that he really wanted to use in some of his fantasies.

The rough sound of a tent zipper a few feet away reminded him they weren't alone. A slow breath centered his thoughts along with the feel of her fingers on his. The scents of the camp and the sounds of the world around him reminded him too. He turned and nuzzled beneath her ear, stealing the moment anyway.

"There. All done," she said a little breathlessly when she leaned away to stand. Her eyes glowed with a sensual spark. A slow, wicked grin formed on her lips, and he knew he'd been completely busted in his thoughts.

She handed over the medicinal supplies. She leaned for the pages that had been scattered on the ground, wiping leaves and dirt off them. Mark helped her while Loren worked on finishing the rabbits for their dinner.

"Here. I think this is all of them," he said, handing them over. "Hey." He lifted the pages between his fingers closer. "Here's that symbol again."

"For the talisman?"

"No." He swept a hand over his T-shirt in absent thought, dusting his clothes off. "I saw this the other night, after you'd mentioned the reincarnation idea. It kept reappearing in the notes." Looking at the eye shape of the pattern, he said, "It makes me think of my grandmother's stories about spirits and how she always said the soul was merely the eye to eternity, because it never really dies." He followed the line of carved markings in the photo with a finger. "If I used her logic and the communication techniques, this could have been a retelling of one of their afterlife stories. The Jahehn really felt communed to their totems." He tapped a shape. "See? Doesn't that look like a wolf to you?"

"Only if I don't have to see one up close again," she mused with a wry glance toward the trees.

He gave her a knowing grin, sure he didn't want to see one up close and personal like that either. "They were very spiritual. I saw several of these shapes with animal totems in the notes."

"I haven't had a chance to go through all of them," she admitted. "I was looking for the talisman carvings."

He chuckled, kissing her lightly on the forehead. "Not surprised." He handed over the sheets. "Better not lose those."

"Just how many languages have you studied?" Loren asked, pulling a pack onto his shoulder, obviously ready to lead them to the cliff face and caves.

"Roughly fifteen with nearly eighty dialects, plus the Olmecs and the Mayans." It was hard not to smile as Loren's jaw loosened in surprise. So what if he held pride in his knowledge? It was his own specialty, the work he enjoyed. Not many could say they liked what they did for a living.

Loren shook his head, grinning. "Man, you'd be dangerous around here. Every one of the seniors would be testing you."

"I'd welcome it. My grandmother used to toss stuff out at me just for fun. Mom did, but she stopped when I could turn it over and stump her knowledge."

Loren's grin remained, but something in his eyes hardened, became assessing for a beat, judging, and almost challenging. Then he turned away. Mark peered at Angie, but she hadn't witnessed the exchange, so he shrugged it off as imagined.


HOURS PASSED AS the sun ascended and moved across the sky, Angie climbing to one cave, then another on the cliff face. Mark followed her, keeping track of her, her notes, and keeping pace with her determination.

*The soul is only the eye to eternity.* His grandmother's age-roughened voice, one of the few memories of his childhood that held no bad feelings, no pain, and no shame continued to run through his mind for the rest of the day. She had always told him there were things out there he wouldn't understand and would never be able to control.

When he realized the abuse his father was giving to his sister and mother, he thought she'd meant he'd have no way to control it, because he couldn't help. He'd never quite understood, and she passed away before he did. He hadn't thought much about her since then, because he'd spent the rest of his growing years learning that his father hadn't been the norm.

What if she were right, though? What if there were things he couldn't understand and had no control over in his life *right now*?

He hadn't told Angie these beliefs, because he was scared for her and didn't want to give her more false hope, but he believed in an afterlife, reincarnation, and mysticism... All of it, actually.

Secretly, he believed his grandmother was behind his father's heart attack. She'd promised that one day he would pay for hurting her daughter and grandchildren. She knew she couldn't physically stop him. He'd laughed at her. Threatened her for being too old, a senile old crone who believed in things like spirits and justice paid to those who deserved it. It was hard to miss threats of curses or drunken boasts when only walls separated them from his young ears.

Mark had never told anyone about his grandmother, pocketing much of her wisdom and sometimes unbelievable knowledge down in a cavernous wedge of memory. Yet the more they talked about the Jahehn, the deeper they dug into the interpretations of the wall paintings, carvings, and designs left behind by their ancient civilization, the more her voice whispered between his ears. And the more he was compelled to examine what was right in front of him.

Reincarnation.

Sharing the same space.

Animal totems, animal spirits, and walking between two worlds.

"Hey, you all right?" Loren strolled into the cave they were currently searching at that moment. He'd gone ahead to study the coarse path along the cliff to ensure the caves Angie wanted weren't inhabited and were safe to study. Sunlight streamed into the cave opening behind his lean frame. The cliff edge sliced into open sky, silhouetting his frame, lighting him from behind.

Mark blinked and reached a hand toward the wall to steady himself, suddenly dizzy, looking at golden eyes, and seeing what he knew he shouldn't. "Yeah, I'm fine." His throat felt like he'd swallowed glass.

*The wolf.*

The black wolf had looked right at him, two golden, sun-fired eyes. That wolf had saved Mark, had protected them. And he was staring at exactly those same eyes right now.

Loren's eyes.

Things began to click into place. Years of language analysis and studying of the Jahehn writing with Angie, breaking the language code they had used. The Jahehn believed in a lot of things that until five seconds ago, he'd written off as human ignorance the same as Angie, but now he wasn't so sure. And it was that insane possibility that prodded his disbelief now. "You're not Cheyenne," Mark said, every second he scrutinized that impenetrable gaze making him more positive.

Loren's attention zeroed in on him from where he'd been watching Angie ahead, intent on her notes and deciphering. "Of course I am. Inglewood is governed by the BLM." His derisive tone inferred that even an idiot would have known that.

Mark shook his head, meeting the stony stare of the man before him. His heart raced, a sign of what he was daring to believe. It sounded as loud as a runaway train. Things were falling into place, and he was unsure he wanted to believe, much less if he could. It wasn't rational. It wasn't feasible. It *was* insane.

But he knew that stare. *The wolf looked right at me.* He sucked air into his lungs, calming his erratic heart and his wild imagination. Could delayed shock from that morning make him see things that weren't there?

He'd examined the native languages for years, the Jahehn among them, and recognized common threads. He and Angie had endlessly discussed those same drawings and their meanings over the years, deciphering the stories left behind, weaving legend and theory together to create the picture of the people, of the tribe. Stories about earthly gods, guardian animals, and shamans who had the elemental forces of nature behind them. There wasn't any way Loren could be Jahehn. They were extinct. But the triangle was almost there. The wolf that hadn't attacked them, that had protected them. The Jahehn. The history.

He steadied his stance, clawing through his disbelief to make the connection, his gaze never wavering from the annoyed glower of the man in front of him. What he was thinking was the fantasy of fiction, of Hollywood. Not a small mountain pass town buried deep in the Rockies. Yet if he looked at it just right, focused on it as if nothing else could be the truth, it was as if a panel of mirrors aligned and suddenly the whole picture, the idea, became real. He couldn't find one argument strong enough to shatter the picture.

Loren broke the spell, blinking first, and turned to walk away.

"It's not possible," Mark choked out. Loren froze, just a heartbeat, his jaw clenching, then releasing, a single hesitation that Mark caught. And latched onto with the eagle eye of a sniper waiting for his one shot. His throat hurt from sucking in harsh breaths. Loren shook his head, the sharp movement silencing him.

"I am Cheyenne. Check the records, *notse.*" Scorn ripped the quiet of the cave apart. He tried to walk around Mark, dismissing him. Mark blocked him, leaning into him with a shoulder, not giving an inch. Angie was absorbed and oblivious, but Mark still kept his voice lowered.

"Where were you?" Mark refused to budge when Loren tried to circumvent him to avoid the question.

"Checking the traps. Food goes a long way out here." The coldness of his tones struck something in Mark's mind. He sounded evasive.

"Why would one wolf attack and a second stop him? Wolves do not protect humans."

"How the hell should I know?" Loren sneered. "Consider yourself lucky that you lived." Loren pushed at Mark, but he refused to budge under the pressure. It would take a hell of a lot more than an impatient shove to move him.

"Who was it?"

Loren barked a derisive sound. "Who? What the hell are you talking about? They were wolves."

"You know what's wrong with her. Tell me again she isn't dying," Mark demanded.

Loren pressed closer, meeting his glare with one of his own. Tension rocked the air between the two men. "I don't have to tell you shit."

"Wrong," Mark snarled, standing nose to nose with Loren. "She's dying, and you know why." He wasn't buying the smokescreen. Angie may have focused her time on the tribe, their culture, and more recently, the talisman, but Mark knew equally about their legends and ancient writings. He'd assumed they were descriptions of the Jahehn and their commiseration with sharing characteristics of the wolf—speed, loyalty, the pack mentality—as many of the tribes had done through the centuries with different animals of their environments. It was a safe assumption. They couldn't share the same physical space. That's what he'd believed.

Until now.

He didn't think he was wrong, but for once he'd be thrilled if he were. "You brought her out here because the council *expects* her to die." Anger was growing, a tight, venomous curl that spiraled upward. "Because they know what's wrong with her. And so do you."

Time dragged as Mark waited, knowing he couldn't be right, but that didn't stop him from listening to his gut.

"What is wrong with her?" he bit out, enunciating each word through a jaw that burned, locking the real words he wanted to use behind his teeth. "Tell me, or I'll tell her the truth."

Loren barked a scathing laugh. "She won't believe you. She doesn't want to believe either."

"So that removes any guilt for you, because she doesn't know?" Fury sparked in Loren's eyes, and

Mark knew he'd hit a nerve. "No one else has ever figured it out, have they?" Loren's jaw ticked once. Mark pressed again. "Is that why someone shot at her? Why you rushed us out of town? So she can die out here and no one cares, no one gets exposed?"

"I don't know why someone shot at her," Loren conceded. "I brought her out here to protect her."

"Bullshit!" Loren and Mark both looked back down the cave length at his outburst. Angie wasn't in sight. She'd moved on without them. "I don't believe you."

"I told you you'd have to trust me. I do know someone in town wants her dead. I don't know who."

"And in the meantime you just wait for her to die out here. That's a fucking load of bull, man."

"Damn it! I don't want her to die." Torment raked his expression, and drawn air raised his shoulders, a small concession. "By law, I can't tell you. The council bound my hands as it is."

"They want her dead that badly?" Shock subdued his anger with a sickening rush. Continued numbing silence was his answer. "Why? Because of the talisman? Because she's here? Because she has whatever you do?"

"That and more," Loren answered.

Mark froze, the ramifications knocking the breath out of his lungs. "Shit," he muttered. "You are Jahehn." Loren's glare returned. "That's why you were told to make sure she dies, because she's a threat to the people in that town, isn't she?"

A breeze whistled past the opening where the two men stood, punctuating the strung out silence. "You both are. By law, I shouldn't be saying anything to you about it. You're *notse*."

"An outsider," Mark murmured, fully aware how insulting that was supposed to be. When

Loren's glare intensified, he said, "I told you I understood the languages. I know enough of most of them to get me into trouble." He crossed his arms. Having come this far, he wasn't giving up now. "You didn't answer the question. What is she going to die from? What is killing her?"

A war of wills, two gazes locked with neither giving. A glance from Loren into the cave where she'd walked, and he relented. "The merging."

Mark swallowed. That did not sound good. "What's the merging?"

Frustration furrowed his expression now. "I can't tell you," Loren bit out. "It's more than our laws. It's a protection borne over the millennia. I can tell her, but the council bound me to silence. I break that order, and I'm a traitor to the entire tribe. She is one of us, but she won't want to believe it. She wasn't raised to expect it. But understand this—it can kill her. I can't tell you, not like this. You're not one of the people."

"But her time is coming?" Mark guessed.

Loren nodded, sympathy now apparent in his strained features where before there'd been nothing but secrets. "Soon. Very, very soon."

Mark took a step, looking but she was still somewhere down beyond where he could see, around a corner, or engrossed in a wall. He fought to control his voice. "How did she... I mean, is it..." He didn't even know how to phrase it. Knowing her, it seemed ludicrous, but finding that amber fire of the wolf in Loren's eyes, it struck his disillusions clear. Loren and the wolf were one and the same. He had no doubt.

Loren rolled a shoulder. "She's a half-breed, and she carries the spirit. It's rare enough in the women. That's one of the reasons they don't trust her. She's experiencing the calling, yet no one knows who she is."

"I know it's not her mother. She's the spitting image of Kendra. They could be sisters." Which meant Angie slipped through the cracks, and there wasn't much, if anything, known about her birth father.

Loren nodded, not arguing with the obvious.

"You had said you could help her. Did you mean that?" The fury he'd felt not five minutes before was now being shaped by an ice-cold fear. If she was suffering from this "merging," and it could kill her... The thought of her dying because of her...breeding, heritage, whatever, was tying his stomach into a colossal knot. She really was dying, and he had no control or any idea of how to stop it from happening. Dread coated his throat until it burned as much as the fear in his blood chilled his heart.

"It's my place," Loren admitted, albeit with an apparent twinge of regret. "But my help may not be enough. It's dangerous, and she's had no training."

Mark absorbed that. "That's why they expect her to die, to fail, isn't it? She doesn't survive, and the threat of her looking for the talisman, looking for anything to do with the Jahehn, is wiped out."

Saying nothing was louder than any answer from Loren. Scorching heat rose from the inside out. "She can't die," Mark whispered, desperation knifing him until he feared he'd see blood if he only looked.

"Will you be able to live with what she is?"

Mark's gaze jerked to his, anger unfurling like a whip on his tongue, ready to strike at the patronizing question. Loren's expression was calm. Deadly serious. A fear even worse than the ice coating his veins filled his soul. That was when he realized she would be forever different. She was and wasn't human, whatever she was, and things were not going to be the same on the other side of all this.

Taking a breath, he finally relinquished a step to give space. He replied, "The only way I can't live is without her."

# CHAPTER THIRTEEN

ANGIE TILTED her head, admiring the sparkle of the distant stars in the night sky through the branches. Their bright beauty amazed her. The only stars she'd ever seen in LA wore designer gowns. These were far more breathtaking. The dying glow of the fire crackled a few feet in front of her where she lingered at the lip of her tent. She'd tucked one of panels to the side to sit and think. She certainly wasn't sleeping.

Loren was out cold in his own tent, perfectly at ease in the wild. He'd had no trouble whatsoever rolling over and calling it a day. Mark lay behind her, sound asleep, making her envious with his state of blissfulness.

She hadn't been so lucky. Fatigue mocked her, and sleep was eluding her. She'd had no luck playing find the needle in the haystack. Since there would be no sleep, she let her mind wander over the reason she was awake. The talisman was out there; she knew it. She needed more time to work through the markings she had, and the few new ones she'd found deeper in the caves. Unfortunately, time was one thing she didn't have.

Her head yanked up when a wolf howl drifted to her from a distance. It sounded much farther than the first one had been but it still made her heart race. A few leaves rustled overhead; otherwise, silence returned with just the quiet soughing of the breeze through the leaves above. Tension leaked out of her as time passed and the howl didn't repeat. She hugged her knees a little closer, her worn and comfy sweats and a halter exercise top her pajamas out in the woods.

A muffled snore from behind her confirmed Mark was still asleep. She wasn't sure as to what or when, but something had happened between Loren and Mark. It wasn't what she'd call a friendship. Maybe a truce? Mark had quit staring daggers at their guide, and Loren had quit frowning every time Mark touched Angie.

She rubbed her chin on her knee, trying to figure out the male mind. She'd probably have better luck discovering the moon was made out of cheese first, she mused. Mark had barely left her side all evening, watching her, simple touches that said he was there. When he'd finally decided to go to bed, she was almost thankful to be alone, but that hadn't lasted. He'd pulled her in with him and fallen asleep with her resting on his chest. As though he didn't want her out of his sight.

A tender smile lifted her lips, but there was no one to see it. Okay, she could admit to herself—it was more than just like. But she refused to allow herself to fall for him. That luxury in her life was gone.

A sigh of regret slipped out before she caught it. She searched the stars. For what, she didn't know. Maybe an answer? Hope? She'd even be happy to have an explanation before she lost the battle. Or even a few that had nothing to do with dying. Like why she had been shot at? Or why the council was so against her taking this trip? Crossing her ankles, she wrapped her arms around her legs and stared off into the darkness.

Lost in her thoughts, she didn't catch the whisper of noise until a body loomed out of the shadows, tall and broad slipping into her vision without warning. She startled, trying to backpedal into the tent.

"Sorry. I didn't know you were awake," Loren said, raising a hand in apology as he came closer to the fire's warmth. His voice was low between them. It rumbled in the quiet with the effort to calm her. "I would've warned you."

She let out a small laugh. Even relieved, it sounded shaky. "It's okay," she told him. "Just thought you were asleep, too."

He shook his head, sitting down near the banked fire. "Couldn't sleep."

"Me, either," she said, offering a commiserative smile. "Sleep isn't always possible anymore."

He gave her an assessing look, his amber-warm eyes unblinking as he stared right at her. Maybe even right through her. "Why?"

She shrugged. "The pain mostly. It's almost constant now."

"Is it bad?"

She smirked, trying to cover a cough. "What's your definition of bad?" She rolled a shoulder, then dropped her chin to her knees again. "I've got used to a lot of it, but the nonstop is new. The last few weeks, I guess."

He shook his head, sitting forward, poking at the fire with a stick, absently making the flames leap. They sat like that for several minutes in thoughtful silence.

"Sometimes pain leads us to bigger things," he murmured, still staring at the fire, his hand moving in slow and steady circles with the stick, stirring the coals.

There was wisdom in those words. Too bad it didn't apply to her. "Yes, but in this case, it's not leading me anywhere. There's no reason, no illness. Just pain unlike anything I could describe. I don't have any idea how to stop it either."

"Are you sure?"

She stopped following the hypnotic motion of his hand and looked at him. "Positive. If I knew, don't you think I would have stopped it by now or found a way to treat it?"

A small shift of the shadows around his features made it seem that he'd nodded. "You strike me as that kind of person, yes." He resumed stirring the coals, sparks racing on the rising heat drafts like tiny fireworks into the night. The glow warmed the side of his face that she could see, showing the hollow of his cheekbone and the sharp contrast of his eyes to his hair.

"Who did you get your eyes from?"

The corner of his mouth lifted. "My mother. She was a lot like you. Stubborn, proud." He glanced up, and her heart leaped to her throat when she found her gaze locked within his. The energy between them was unsettling. As though she should know him. That was still there and still confusing. He swallowed and, with a rough toss, flipped the stick into the coals to be eaten by the fire.

Standing, he muttered under his breath. "This isn't right." He crossed to her and sat down. "Look, I can help you, but it's complicated."

"Loren, don't start." She searched deep into his eyes and was surprised at the earnest light in them. It took a moment to regain her thoughts when the warmth of those eyes seemed to convey an honest sympathy for her. "I appreciate you bringing me out here, for not picking a fight with Mark, and for defending me in front of the council, but there's still no answer to what's wrong with me. It's not your problem, either."

He cupped her chin to make her focus. The way her nerves popped whenever he was close to her was unusual enough. It wasn't sexual, she knew that, but it *was* something. Instead he held her, leaning close to whisper into her ear.

"You can transcend the pain," he told her. "The spirit brother is strong in you. I can see it. I can feel it."

Leaning away, she created a gap between them. "You can't be serious? Just what did you do on your walk tonight?"

Sparks of heat reflected off the golden amber of his eyes. "I can help you."

She pulled free and his hand fell away. "Loren, I'm dying. Don't mock me."

"I'm not." He trapped her in the glow of his golden eyes. "You only have to believe."

"Angie?" Mark's murmured voice, deep and drowsy, reached her clearly from within the tent.

"Good night, Loren." She patted the dirt from her feet and sweats, then slipped inside the tent. She pulled the zipper down, hoping she'd be able to fall asleep.

Mark's hands were warm, sliding up her arms to bring her down to lie with him. His lips were seeking, brushing hers before he wrapped an arm over her, folding her against his chest.

"You okay?" he mumbled, half asleep.

"Yeah, just restless."

His fingers drifted in lazy swipes along her side. "You're in pain." He said it like he knew.

"Were you eavesdropping?"

"Not intentionally. You were only four feet away."

She groaned. "You were supposed to be asleep."

"Couldn't. You left."

She shook her head at him. His fingers found her braid and played with the end. It seemed he was always finding reasons to play with it, not that she minded. She stretched out more, blanketing his chest to rest on the top of her hand over his heart.

"I've been thinking," he said.

"Why does that worry me?"

He chuckled. "Because you know me. But what if he's right? What if there is a way?"

"Mark." His name was an exasperated, groaned sound. "What did you two talk about today? Do you hear yourself?"

"You know there's more out there than we can explain," he told her, his voice low enough to rumble past her ear but not beyond. "You believe in a lot of things most people don't."

"So if I believe, it'll all go away?" She pushed up onto her palms to peer at him in the darkness. "Do you hear yourself? I've been praying for months. I *believe* I'm healthy because that's what every doctor has told me. I *know* I'm dying regardless."

"But nothing proves you're dying," he stressed, looking up at her. He lifted a hand when her eyes narrowed in answer to that. "No. Hear me out. You know you're healthy. You know you're not having a breakdown. What if it's something you have no control over? Something you don't understand? The spasms are bad, but what if they aren't killing you? What if they are doing something else altogether?"

"Like what?" she asked, humoring him.

"What if the Jahehn weren't extinct? What if you're right?" he asked, looking up at her.

She shook her head, an adamant denial. "They have nothing to do with me, or with what's wrong with me. I know they are gone. That's why they were overlooked in the natural development of the native tribes. Nothing to tie them to a more current family or tribe."

"You didn't think that two days ago."

"That was me being fanciful, unrealistic. Maybe even a bit hopeful," she added, watching his expressions, feeling exasperation at his persistence. "You know, something really big." Regret was hard to hide with him watching her so intently. "I know I'm not going to be that lucky, not now."

"I've read those legend notes, the deciphered cryptology of their language. I think you were more right than you know. They did exist, and still do."

"You're wrong, Mark. They vanished, and considering the factors—hard winters, migrating herds, a small core population—it's not that hard to envision. It's survival of the fittest."

"I'm not going to take that personally," he muttered, sliding a palm beneath his head. He stopped playing with her braid too, and oddly, she felt the distance between them more than the loss of his touch for it. "I know they were your project, but I read them too, and I think you're very close to them, drawn to them for a reason. I think it might have something to do with your father."

Silence fell like the ringing void after a sledgehammer's strike on steel. "Mark, Daniel is the only father I know."

"But I still think the real reason you're here isn't because of just the talisman," he countered. "I think you were drawn here."

She flopped down, sprawling across him again. "I don't think so. Look, let's just say it. I was looking for an escape. If the talisman exists, great!" she said with forced enthusiasm, her eyes widening in faked happiness. "But the chance of it being here, slim to none." Her expression fell flat, completely devoid of hope. "The chance of it being able to cure me?" She snorted, rolling to his side. "Nil. There, are you happy? You got me to admit it."

"Damn it, Angie," he groused. "You are the most stubborn, tunnel visioned woman..." A deep breath made his chest rise next to her. "I know what I'm talking about. What I meant when I said I read the notes was two nights ago in the hotel." He sat up. "You said something that night about the animal totems, about the communal belief they held that they were one with their animal spirits."

"No, I said they felt a deep communal and spiritual bond, like Christians feel for God, or the Buddhists for Buddha. You didn't hear what I said or read it right."

His frame stiffened beside her. "I know the language nuance, Angie. I know it sounds crazy, but it's there if you look for it."

She shook her head. "No. I know you don't want me to die. Hell, I don't want to die. I can't tell you that enough. You are reading it wrong."

"I have as much background as you do," he pointed out to her, although it was a dry reminder. "I haven't been nose-deep into them for as long as you have, but I do know the language and definitions of those carvings. It's there."

"Fine. What's there? Since I'm obviously not getting it." She sat up too, facing him over the sleeping bags, crossing her arms in front of her.

"The Jahehn aren't extinct. They are alive and well, and the reason you're having spasms is that you're one of them."

Her jaw dropped at the same time laughter bubbled up. "Oh God," she choked, trying to catch her breath. "Mark, you are so wrong. Do I even look native for heaven's sake? I'm so blonde, I glow. Mom's Swede through and through."

He shook his head, but his mouth thinned. "It's the legends, the totems. They were more than totems. What's happening to you is—"

She stood up, infuriated that he wouldn't drop the subject. "You know, Mark, I really thought you knew your stuff. Make-believe turns into reality around the age of eleven. There are no Jahehn left. Even if it were possible, why would they stay hidden for centuries?" She pointed to herself. "I would like to meet them because I've spent so much of my life studying them. I know that's not going to happen. It's completely unrealistic, but if I sit here and all I think about is how soon I'm going to die, I will go insane."

He snarled in his throat, standing too. "I know what I saw today."

She stopped laughing, finally noticing his restraint and the flare of anger in his eyes. "Mark, you're wrong. You misread whatever it was you saw. You have no idea what's been happening to me. The doctors don't know. This has nothing to do with the jackass who ditched my mother. This has nothing to do with the Jahehn. They are seizures. People die from seizures."

"Angie." His shoulders flexed, and he glared at her. As though he wanted to toss her over a shoulder and make her see reason.

She took a step back, as much as the tent would allow, her hands on her hips. "I thought you understood the Jahehn language. I thought you understood me. I was wrong, because you don't."

"I understand more than you'd like to think. You have to believe, or it will kill you."

"It *is* going to kill me!" she cried, waving her arms in frustration. "Damn it, Mark, you don't get it. There are no Jahehn left. There is no reason I was drawn here other than my own curiosity."

He leaned forward. "You're wrong," he told her flatly.

"I thought you knew your linguistic history," she challenged him.

He frowned, shaking his head slowly. "That's below the belt, sweetheart. You think you know everything there is to know about this culture, don't you? So no one else can possibly know more than you, isn't that right? You don't know enough to realize you're one of them."

Her mouth fell slack, the bite of indignant anger right behind it at his scathing remarks. "Get out."

He yanked up one of the sleeping bags, bunching it into a tight fist. "I know what I read and what I saw. It's there. I believe it, but unless you do, you *will* die." He flipped open the tent flap, silence and darkness on the other side. "You can't see it. You can't see past the moment you think you're going to die. Maybe you should try looking at why you're really here, rather than just because you want to find the talisman, or because you think you're dying. Because honestly, Angie, I'm tired of fighting harder than you to keep you alive," he added before he stomped out.

She ripped the zipper downward, able to hear him spread out the sleeping blanket nearby. She collapsed to her own bag, crossing her arms to frown at the panels before her. Had she stopped fighting?

No. She hadn't, but she had accepted that she had no answers.

He was wrong. There was nothing about her that was any way Jahehn, or any other kind of native gene pool. Knowing her luck, her real father was some college grad turned scientist or something, since her mother hadn't been academically inclined. Mom had been a hard worker her whole life, supporting an infant baby until Daniel had come into the picture. Even then it had taken her a long time to make the relationship equal being young, with a new daughter, and unsure of what curves life would throw at her.

She had no clue what he was talking about. What could he have seen that she'd overlooked all these years? What was in the notes and the writings that would make him think they hadn't died?

She believed they weren't extinct, true. Silently apologetic that she'd become defensive over that point, she shrugged her shoulders. She regretted telling him that little secret now, because he was using anything as ammunition to convince her she wasn't dying, and that was just underhanded. Stretching out, she rolled to her stomach to rest her chin on top of her hands.

Her theory was they'd lived more recently than any of the found records would lead most to believe. It didn't make her one of them. The residents of Inglewood were Cheyenne descendants, with a few immigrants tossed in for color. If they did still exist, as she believed they did, there were too few of them to be separated out of the tribal family list as a separate people. Chances were just as good that if they still existed on some level of community, they didn't even know they were Jahehn but had been integrated into the full tribal order over time and no longer had a sense of being Jahehn.

For some reason that possibility saddened her. They had been such a strong community, a culture that loved, warred, celebrated, and lived. She'd studied them, had written theories on almost every find, had learned about them, yet she still wanted more.

A sigh slipped out, and she turned to rest a cheek on her hands, her eyes drifting shut. Sleep wasn't very kind to her, but she managed a scattered doze here and there, ignoring the warmth of her body. It was constant, like the fatigued muscle aches after a hard workout, except she felt that way every day, no hard workout required. Eventually, the scraping of the branches overhead lulled her into sleep.

# CHAPTER FOURTEEN

ANGIE WAS AWAKE when nighttime dark warmed to morning gray. After palming a few essentials, she cautiously lifted the zipper to the outside world, finding Mark asleep near the fire and Loren's tent closed tight. Not a sound came from either as she slipped from the circle of their camp. Turning for the stream, she ambled along the path she'd walked with Loren the day before, guiding her so she'd know where it was. The night had been long and restless. The aches remained. All she wanted to do was sleep, a deep down, incoherent sleep—for about a week.

Placing her towel on a low-lying branch and unwinding her hair from its binding braid, she stripped, then almost cried out at the ice-cold temperature of the water when she stuck her foot in. Gritting her teeth, she stumbled across the rocky bed until she reached the dip in the stream Loren had told her to look for. When the water reached to just above her knees, she crouched down until she was covered. After a few breaths, with her eyes closed, she was able to forget the water was as cold as glacial runoff.

She scrubbed her skin until it glowed pink, then rinsed out her hair, the long tresses flowing behind her on the stream's current in a golden wave. It felt good to be clean, although hot water would have felt so much better on her tired body. She promised herself that for her next life, she would own a hot tub. She'd earned it this time around.

Feeling the swirl of the water against her body, she relaxed. Cold or not, the water felt heavenly, decadent. There was the gleam of the sun as it peeked over the horizon, glinting on the water and warming the trees, a show just for her. She was alone in a natural paradise, and the moment filled her with wonder. This was the kind of beauty she'd never seen in LA. The sound of peaceful silence that was so profound, only the lapping of the stream broke it.

Birds woke to the warmth of the sun. The chirp of squirrels in the boughs, scampering back and forth, reminded her what nature was supposed to look like.

As clean as she could get, she carefully picked her way to the edge of the stream, taking a few minutes to dry herself and dress, then brushed her teeth. She wrapped her dripping hair up in the towel to tie when she reached her tent.

With full morning lighting the ground and sky, she knew she'd been at the stream for quite a while. She stretched, feeling invigorated and pleasantly at peace. A few minutes to herself seemed to be just what she needed. A couple of feet down the path was as far as she managed before she was stopped stone-cold dead in her tracks.

A hiss followed by a shaking rattle had her swallowing hard, freezing like she'd been staked to the ground through her toes.

*Oh shit!* Her voice shook even in her own thoughts. The snake must have been asleep when she'd walked by earlier, the nighttime air keeping it sluggish. Not so lucky on the return. Leaves shuddered barely two feet to her right, and the whip of the rattle disturbed more of the deadfall as it screamed its warning: *Trespassers beware.*

She spotted it with little effort when it tightened its coil. That did *not* look like a good thing for her. Didn't rattlers strike from a coil position? She forced air into burning lungs, her heart racing with a new kind of fear, never losing sight of the large, deadly head swaying from side to side, sizing up its invader.

"Oh, God," she whimpered. Whimpering sounded like an absolutely justifiable reaction, at least to her. "Go away." It sat there mesmerizing her with its slow up-and-down head movement. The twitch of the rattle told her it'd heard her and she needed to shut up. *You got it.* She was not about to piss it off any more than she had.

"Angie?" Loren's voice floated to her, and she closed her eyes in thankfulness. She had trees on both sides of her, not thick, but she was definitely not about to take a flying leap for safety.

The depth of the rattle intensified at the new pitch of voice and approaching steps. She closed her eyes and prayed. *That wasn't me!* But somehow she didn't think the snake knew the difference or cared.

She stayed as quiet and as still as she physically could. So long as she wasn't moving, the snake wouldn't feel threatened. She knew they sensed heat as much as scent, so if she could keep her blood pressure down, the little fanged beast at her feet wouldn't think she looked particularly tasty for dining on.

"There you are," he said, spotting her. Her eyes widened as the snake showed how much he didn't want more company. "Hell. How long have you been there?" he asked, freezing as soon as he heard the sound.

"Couple minutes. I was hoping it would lose interest." The rattle grew until the leaves it had been hiding under were completely dislodged. It was good and pissed now.

He lifted a finger to his lips. She barely nodded. And, of course, the movement loosened the towel on her head. She bit her lip to not squeak with fear. Her tranquility had been completely destroyed.

Her heart thudded as Loren edged closer, picking up a long branch with a forked end on his way.

"When I tell you, move. Straight forward, don't look down."

The snake, however, wasn't going to be anyone's capture and swung to watch Loren's approach. She swallowed and carefully acknowledged that she understood with a shallow nod.

"Don't move!" he warned in a rush, keeping his voice low, his eyes pinned on the rattler when it whipped in her direction. "I need it looking at me."

She followed him from the corner of her vision, his approach slow and calm as he angled himself to the snake. He didn't even look like he was breathing heavily, his entire attention on the snake on the ground. Holding out a hand as a target, he kept the snake's focus as he lined up the branch.

His moves were seamless, like the fine artwork of a fire brigade, every muscle working with each movement to create a measured approach, slow and easy as he stalked the snake. He neared until he was standing closer to it than she was, the branch in his grip hovering over its head.

The snake and Loren seemed to be in a staring contest. She never saw him blink. The reptile barely moved. With a stab of his hand, he pinned down the hissing head with the forked end. She never saw it drop.

"Go!"

A starter's gun couldn't have been more effective. She sprinted until she heard him catching up to her. She stopped, collapsing to her knees, shaking and shuddering with unharnessed fear.

His hands were strong and comforting, helping her to her feet. The towel fell free from her hair. He snatched it midair in his hand. A second later he was wrapping his arms around her heaving body.

"Shh. It's okay." His hands were warm, enfolding her into his hold. "You're safe."

She dug into his chest, crying with relief. "Thank you." He pressed her closer, his hands stroking her, sweeping upward through her hair to distract her. She gulped air until the urge to cry was gone. She'd promised herself she was done crying for anything.

"You were brave and smart. He probably would've lost interest and left. He was just grumpy because he hadn't eaten yet. It takes time for them to warm up, then start to hunt."

"I guessed he was still asleep when I went by the first time."

He nodded, his cheek rubbing against the top of her head. "As early as you left, very likely."

"You were awake?"

Loren chuckled, the warmth of his body soaking into her stretched nerves. "I wasn't even in the tent. I saw you leave."

"Oh." That kind of caught her off guard. "You were watching?" She felt embarrassed now, thinking of the time she'd spent in the stream.

"No," he said, his voice sincere. He offered a little space between them. "I was running."

"Out here?"

A cocky, playful grin lifted his lips, lightening his gaze. "Always do when I'm in the woods. It's hard to pass up the chance. It helps me to think." He gave her the once-over, searching. "You all right now?"

She smiled and he dipped to buss a chaste peck to her cheek. A ghost of a touch of skin that shocked her. It comforted her, too.

IT WAS A KISS that Mark caught, though. It was impossible to miss how Loren held her, with Angie completely wrapped in the cage of his arms. Mark's feet dragged to a stop before they noticed him on the trail between trees and shadows, his heart beating with a crippled rhythm at the tableau. All Mark saw was the kiss in slow motion. Loren stood straight from where he'd leaned over to reach her pale skin and rolled the towel in his hands to loop over his neck. They were speaking quietly. He couldn't hear them, but he saw the interest in Loren. A particular expression Mark had hoped he'd only imagined the few times he'd caught Loren staring at her as though deciphering a puzzle.

He'd tried to ignore it since he'd confronted Loren the day before. Angie needed his help, and Mark wouldn't keep her from it. Angie was getting comfortable around him, trusting him more as he'd spent time with her going through the caves or discussing new discoveries.

His assurance in his own skin said plenty. The way he carried himself, in total command, answering to no man. It made Mark feel eleven again with the memories of his father's hate. Trying to find a way to protect everyone when he couldn't grasp what was wrong with himself to cause the amount of hate he'd inspired. Once again he'd been found lacking.

Except this time the pain was excruciatingly personal. It sliced deeper than any rejection he'd ever felt from his father, hotter than any hit he'd ever endured because of the old man's drunken rages. This pain struck his heart and kept going.

Loren was the man who could help her, who knew to the letter what was wrong with her. She would be better with someone who understood her. She'd refused to listen to him. Doubts had plagued him since she'd spoken those words of denial. Maybe he'd been wrong all this time, believing what he felt was love. Wouldn't she have believed him, had a *little* faith he could be right if she felt the same? The only women in his life who'd really loved him had been family. Maybe there was a reason for that.

He spun before they spotted him, retracing his steps to the campfire. Sitting, he found a cup and filled it with coffee Loren had made, staring at the hypnotic dance of the fire. Her laughter reached him well before they reappeared. His knuckles brightened to white holding the cup, his teeth grinding at the sound, knowing she was laughing at something Loren had said. If he'd had any sign that she'd listened to him the night before, he'd be introducing Loren to his right fist, but that didn't seem to be the case.

Her glances at Mark were fleeting, buried under golden lashes as she ducked into the tent to drop off her bathing necessities. He felt the sting of her evasion acutely. Nothing he'd said the night before had got through. And she was still mad at him. She didn't say one word to Mark.

Fine. Somehow he'd find a way to keep her alive. And the only man who could was crouched across the fire from him, stoking the flames hotter to cook. That's all he'd ask, and then he'd leave.

"You swear you can help her?" Mark asked, using his unpracticed and rusty Cheyenne for the first time in probably five years.

Loren stiffened, then nodded. Mark had surprised him. "I'll do what I can," he replied. "She's very stubborn and..."—he paused, glancing at the tent—"unprepared. Uneducated. I'll do what I can, but if she doesn't know and won't listen..." He frowned, stabbing at the fire in irritation.

Mark swallowed the hot coffee sitting on his tongue in a gulp at the penetrating sadness on Loren's face. Loren didn't hold much faith in her. He didn't expect her to live.

"If she knew what she was facing," Mark offered, hoping.

"She doesn't want to believe. I heard you last night. I'm forbidden from interfering," Loren stressed, poking at the fire, stirring the flames higher than needed. He stopped, then tossed the stick into the circle of stones. The strain of his words hung on the air like the thick smoke from the fire. It reached everything. "She's going to enter the transition knowing nothing."

Mark's eyes closed as he felt the blood run straight for his feet at that news.

"You can't tell her?" He didn't bother to find the words in any other language, dropping back into English.

"No."

"How close is she?" Mark feared hearing the answer. His stomach burned with every moment that Loren hesitated, the snap of the firewood splitting the strained silence between them. He could hear her moving around in the tent several feet behind him.

"Today. I can feel it in her. It is coming."

He swallowed the curse that burned his throat, wanting to rage at the heavens, to anyone to keep her from dying. The rasp of the tent zipper from behind him had him on his feet with a lurch. "Angie." His heart had taken residence in his throat. She'd changed clothes and had tied her hair out of the way. He ached just looking at her. No matter what she felt, Mark loved her with everything he was. He glanced once over his shoulder and discovered Loren was watching. Mark's heart broke, but he had only one real choice. With him gone, Angie could find what she needed. For now and for a future.

"I can't take this. You've given up," he accused, glaring when her mouth popped open, tired of her refusals to listen. Her jaw snapped shut. Sparks flared in her eyes. He didn't have to take any more of her insults either. The memory of her words fueled his anger because he'd never faced anything that hurt this much before in his life. "No, don't bother. I'm going back. Stay here with Loren." He heard as the other man stood behind him, but didn't stop, knowing what he had to do. "You won't listen to anything I've said. If you're going to die, then you can do it without me, because I can't stand to watch it."

He stomped past her into the tent they'd shared and grabbed the small shoulder carry-all from the camping gear, quickly stuffing it with his clothes and things.

He didn't look at her but stared right at Loren once he stood outside the tent opening. "I'm leaving. You can do what you need to do. Make sure she gets back when you're done out here, all right?" Determined, he managed to keep his voice even, knowing Loren would understand why he was leaving. And what he wasn't saying.

"Mark?"

Confusion and shock ran rampant in her gaze at his sudden change of heart. No, staring into the spring green of those eyes, he didn't doubt it for a second what he felt for her. It just didn't look like she shared the feeling. He felt his heart shred, bleeding and burning inside his chest in flagrant agony.

"Goodbye, sweetheart." He didn't dare touch her. He'd kiss her—long and passionately—and he needed to leave. If she was hitting her merging today like Loren thought, then he needed to give him the room to help her. He was only tying the other man's hands by remaining. The memory of her sprawled across her desk, the slicing pain he'd seen in her eyes and the tears streaking her face, haunted him until his gut cinched itself into a pretzel. He prayed Loren did know and could help her, because Mark knew he couldn't.

Steeling himself for the coming moments and deepening pain, he faced Loren. "Spare a canteen?"

Loren fished one off a branch. "You want supplies?"

"Just what you can spare. I'll eat when I get there. The trail is due south?" Mark asked, putting the protein bars that Loren handed over into the mini pack. Then he slipped the single strap over a shoulder.

Loren motioned in the direction they'd come from. "Follow the animal trails until you reach the gully we came through. Regardless of where you hit it, it will lead you back to the highway. You'll have to hitchhike back to town."

Mark shrugged, unconcerned with the pending days he'd be short of food. "I'll live," he said, allowing a last look to drink her in. The distance to get to town really meant nothing to him at this point. With a final prayer, he turned and walked out of Angie's life.

# CHAPTER FIFTEEN

ANGIE STOOD FROZEN, uncomprehending what he was doing. Mark vanished beyond tree trunks, and she realized he meant it. He was going to leave her out there. Her best friend had just deserted her because she wouldn't fall for a line of hocus-pocus mythology that didn't exist.

Her mouth popped open, but no sound emerged. Her throat gurgled with the angry yell that she wanted to shout at him, but her heart was unable to voice it.

"Bastard," she whispered instead, furious that he'd left her with a near stranger to die alone! She whirled on Loren. "What the hell did you two discuss yesterday? What kinds of stories did you tell him?"

"None. I didn't have to," he said, crouching once more to continue cooking, pulling the pan from his stock to place on the rocks around the fire. "He was able to read them fine on his own."

She planted her hands on her hips. "He believed them, Loren! Why didn't you tell him you were pulling his chain or something? That the legends he read were wrong?"

"Because I wasn't pulling his chain, and he wasn't reading them wrong," he told her dispassionately. "I'd have preferred it if he had." He added water to the pan and stirred in canned beans, completely disregarding her confusion and anger. Mark had deserted her, and Loren was absolutely unemotional about it.

"Fine," she ground out, plunking to the ground. With a cup of coffee in her hand, she shoved the fact that Mark left out of her mind. "When are we going to search the next cave?"

"We're not."

She choked in shock. She lowered her cup, coughing to clear her throat. "What?"

Loren's shoulders rose with a deep breath, and he swept his hair back. "We won't have time to worry about them today. Mark sacrificed being here so I could help you. He's unbound me by not staying to witness what's coming. I can help you. There's not much time to prepare you."

"Oh great," she said, her scathing tone matching the toss of her hand. "What is with you two? There is *nothing* to believe!" She wanted to shriek, though kept her voice lowered by sheer force of will. "The legends are *theories* for heaven's sake! I wrote them."

"You wrote them because you recognized them, didn't you? They meant something to you?" He continued to stir the contents of the iron pan, his questions almost an afterthought.

Her mouth popped open, but after two seconds of stunned silence, she snapped it shut again. "Mark told you that, didn't he? Isn't anything private anymore?"

Loren's expression showed very little, his concentration on the pan and the food he was preparing for them. He tasted it, then set it aside, grabbing packages to add to the beans to make a stew of sorts.

"He's made it clear he wants you to survive. Don't you think you owe him the same to at least try?"

She dropped her forehead to her hands, massaging her temples with stiff fingers. "You don't get it, Loren. Every doctor I've seen has found nothing. Not one knows what is wrong with me."

He stirred the mass in the pan, and it thickened. It actually smelled really good.

"I do."

She groaned, massaging harder.

"Mark recognized it. I recognized it. You're the only one who is fighting it." He looked up, absolute blankness in his gaze. "If you continue to fight it, it will kill you. It is the brother's way."

He plated the breakfast stew for the both of them and sat to eat.

"You should eat. You'll need the energy later today." The silence was only broken by the sound of the fire and the scrape of his fork on his camping plate.

"I don't believe this, Loren," she finally said.

He sat straight, chewing, giving her a thoughtful look. "Not believing will kill you. You need to listen, and until you're ready, there's nothing to discuss. You only have a few hours to accept it and learn what I can tell you. Don't take long." He returned to his plate to eat.

She reached for hers, even though she wasn't sure she'd be able to eat a bite. Her recent record with eating had been unremarkable. "Why now? Why didn't you say something when I met you?" she asked, looking for a hidden agenda, something to call him a liar. He had to be as delusional as Mark. She knew what she was facing.

"I was ordered to silence, physically bound to not help you in any way by the council. They see you as a threat, an unknown with an in-depth knowledge and interest in the Jahehn. Only one person has that much historical knowledge in our entire community, and she's earned the right to it. You endanger every person in town with what you know. I was ordered to let the transition finish the job that you had already accepted, that your illness was killing you."

She swallowed the lump of food in her mouth, as tasty as a coarse wad of mud with those words. "You're insane. Do you know that? The Jahehn are extinct. Even I know of Inglewood's Cheyenne reservation background. I researched it as much as the Jahehn because they intertwined so often. If Croma or whoever told you to bring me out here to distract me from finding the talisman, fine. It worked. I know they don't want it found. Fearing future treasure hunters will come and disturb a balanced wildlife sanctuary, or for whatever sick reasons they have. I get it, but you don't have to tell me you buy into the same idiocy as Mark. I knew he was off on the legends." Anger added scorn and disappointment to her accusations.

He finished eating while she ranted, barely acknowledging a single word. He drank deeply from one of the canteens. Setting it aside, then wiping his mouth, he asked her, "Did you feel that way when you first tried to break the language code? Did you think either of you were wrong then?"

*Well, no, of course not, not then,* she thought. But time and acceptance changed perspective on a lot of things in life. "It was new then. Nothing seemed like it could be wrong. There was nothing to negate the findings."

"And now none of the legends seem probable?"

The answer was on the tip of her tongue. Of course none of them were probable. It was the look he gave her that made her swallow the immediate answer. He believed in them. Mark did too. She put her still full plate down, thinking carefully before she answered.

"I think I've outgrown the amateur wonder of finding them," she admitted. "Rationally, I know the difference between wanting to believe and knowing logically how they can't be real."

He pressed his fingertips together, resting his chin on the steeple they created. Staring into the fire, he asked her, "And that's safer for you, isn't it? Not believing means they can't hurt you. They can't desert you."

She sucked air through her nose at his rationalization, and her eyes narrowed to pinpoints. "You don't know anything about me, Loren. Don't look for explanations to what I believe."

"I don't have to. It's all in your history." He tilted on his neck, staring unblinking right at her. "And because I see something that no one else has, and if they did, it only compounded the reason they wanted you gone. Or dead." He paused, considering. "You are *taka-ja-meh*."

She gasped, her lungs aching following the harsh single thud of her heart. "You think I'm a returning soul? A real reincarnation?"

He nodded. "It makes sense, at least to me, after spending the last two days with you. It also means you're important to the tribe and to the council. And whoever shot at you knew that and was threatened by you. *Taka-ja-meh* are revered by the council for numerous reasons."

"I didn't exactly get that feeling from them."

He cracked a smile at her prim tone. "You are an unknown. An outsider, and untracked. That we know of, a situation like yours has never happened.

The laws are there to prevent it. You did say you never knew your father."

"No, I didn't know him. Mother never told me much about him. I think she was ashamed that the relationship wasn't deeper, when she thought it was. When she found out she was pregnant, that was it. She did tell me that once he knew, he vanished." She shrugged. "So he was a loser, and she thought they were stronger than sex. We all make mistakes. I've never blamed her or the man she slept with for anything. I'm here. Daniel is my father, the one who matters."

Loren nodded, although discomfort and an echo of pain crossed his features when he told her, "I'll have to ask Croma. He or Grace might have an idea of who your father was. It could be very important."

"Why?"

"Because there's more to happen if you survive your merging."

It hit her then. Her vision faded to gray for a brief instant. She'd completely listened like she believed him, because he'd got her to discuss the man who had impregnated her mother. And worse, she'd admitted some of her darkest secret pains.

"I can't believe this." Outrage turned every word bitter. She leaned closer, wanting to strike out, but held herself taut. "That was low, using my parents to get me to listen, much less think any of this is real. I am not a returning soul. You suckered me good, using something that would catch my attention. I have no Cheyenne ties. I have no Jahehn blood. Want to know why?" She didn't give him the chance to answer. "Because they don't exist in today's world." She lurched to her feet. "That was really good. You really had me going there. There's a whole town of Cheyenne descendants in that pass." She tossed her hand in its direction, ignoring the way he stiffened where he sat. He stood with her, yet she couldn't make herself stop, refusing to feel intimidated when he towered over her.

"Look, I understand. Bureau of Land Management did a number on all the native peoples. The government and the white man. I don't blame anyone their resentment of a culture that invades and, even worse, does it under the guise of goodwill when they only intend to conquer and take over. But you don't have to pretend you're a hidden race of people. There's an entire town thriving in that pass. And it's Cheyenne, not Jahehn."

She whirled to walk away, but his hand clasped her arm.

"If you walk away, I can't help you with the little time we have, Angie. You think you're dying? You think you've suffered? You haven't even come close to what the brother can do to a body when the merging is off balance. He can tear you apart from the inside out. The brother spirit is relentless and will challenge and test you until the pain you've suffered is nothing but a memory by what he *can* do when he feels you are not worthy."

The cold steel in his voice brought her up short.

"I don't want to die, Loren," she whispered, more than a little scared at the intensity in his voice and in his grip. The pressure of his hand fed that fear.

"I don't want you to either. I want to help you."

"This makes no sense."

"If you live through it, it will make complete sense. It's the only way you'll understand. You have to accept it and want to merge with the spirit."

His unblinking stare glowed with a reddish heat from the sun's rays, and she swallowed, feeling the pulse of her blood tick beneath her skin.

Silently she nodded, agreeing to listen for the moment.

"The town, our ancestry, is camouflaged to look like we're Cheyenne to protect us from discovery. There are other bands, small ones, and no one but the tribal elders know the connections. I am not Cheyenne. You and I, we *are* Jahehn. There's the brother spirit and the soul spirit. I sense you have the energy of both. That is enough of a reason for someone in town to not want you around all by itself." She sucked in a hard breath, but he continued as if he'd not said the most shocking thing she'd heard in her entire life. "Are you willing to listen, to learn as much as you can? To accept the merging and become one of the tribe? It's not an easy process, and painful as all hell."

"Of course it is," she muttered. "Like I haven't seen enough of that." When he pinched her arm in rebuke, she murmured, "Sorry." She wasn't mocking him, not intentionally.

"Then I will coach you." He released her. "When the brother spirit comes to you today, remember what I tell you. It's the only thing that may save you. You've been fighting him for a year. You're on his homeland now. He won't accept anything less than your full transition or your life."

"Oh, God," she whimpered. "Why didn't the doctors find this before now? Surely a mutation—"

A sharp head shake silenced her. "It's not a mutation. It's spiritual. There's nothing but a promise made in blood between you and the spirit brother. It's a bond that has survived hundreds of years."

Breezes shook the branches overhead, sunlight streaking through them in fine arcs to split the earthen shadows with golden color. She inhaled, filling her lungs as reality weighed down on her. There was no avoiding this. And only one way to reach the other side.

"Usually the entire council witnesses the merging. There's ceremonies and offerings to the brotherhood of wolves for sharing with us."

"Wolves?" She staggered back. That was the first time he'd mentioned that!

"Mark nailed it on the head yesterday." When she continued to gape at him dumbfounded, he added, "You thought he was wrong. He's smarter than you give him credit for, Angie. I think he knows you better than you'd like to admit." He turned from her then, cleaning up from breakfast.

She snarled at his hunched form. "That's really none of your business."

Once done, he sat, ignoring her irritation. She watched as he pulled a pouch from his gear, lining herbs up near the fire.

"You know what you've told me is insane. There are no such thing as shifters in our world."

"Because humanity doesn't believe in the spirits that once shared our earth with us. They were real, but humans prefer to ignore them. The Jahehn have respected the bond with the spirit world and will never break the vow. I believe you can survive the change, but you have to want to. You have to believe in it as well. It is painful. But it's an honor to share the spirit, and the pain reminds us of that shared honor."

"It never goes away, does it?" she asked, filing the knowledge away.

"No, every time we take the shared form, it is there. The first one is unavoidable when he calls. No one can avoid his test. You will always have the choice after that. No one can force you to merge after the first time."

"You... You are one of them?" she asked, refusing to acknowledge the twinge of weakness in her stomach. She shouldn't be asking at all, but what if he was telling the truth? What if all these years she'd been following her own legacy? *Becoming* her own legend? It was almost more than her brain could absorb.

Loren tilted, thoughtfulness in his answer. "The wolves yesterday?" She encouraged him when he hesitated, yet feared what he would say at the same time. "The black wolf didn't attack either of you because that was me. I know who the other was, the gray one, and he was punished for interfering. I don't doubt he returned to town to report that we'd arrived and you still lived." He lifted amber eyes. "I wasn't here to see either wolf or their color. Not in this form. I can tell you the entire fight, bite by bite after I knocked him off Mark if you want to hear it. I can tell you which way he went, that he has brown eyes and in any form, he's an ass, because I know him."

"You?" It was a croaked whisper. The fine hair on her arms and neck stood, and she wanted to deny him but was terrified he wasn't lying. When he made no effort to refute her, her stomach completely froze into a solid void of cold.

Trembling, she sank to the ground next to him. It was her first concession to really listen to what he was going to tell her. "What happens first?"

"The first thing to remember is that while you have to share, you are in control. Nothing will harm you, and you're protected here." He pulled several knotted bunches of herbs from his pouch and rubbed dried leaves between his palms, then sprinkled them into the fire, murmuring as he did. The bittersweet essence of the herbs quickly filled the air over the fire.

She listened to the deep cadence of his voice, the rhythm of the language rolling off his tongue like a crooner's musical seduction.

He repeated the herbal incantations a few more times, then stood, reaching for two blankets out of his tent. "These will have to do." He spread one out on the ground and handed her the other. "When it is time, go to your tent and undress. Wrap this around you for the final blessing before the first pain strikes."

Her hand hesitated, her throat tight with uncertainty, the blanket hanging in front of her, daring her. Challenging her beliefs and her disbeliefs. She almost dropped her hand, logic over myth. Seeking Loren's expression, his calm acceptance waited for her decision. When numb fingers finally gripped the coarse weave, she realized the concession she was making. Turning from her, he searched for a long stick and burned the tip off. Dragging it around her and the fire with the charred end, Loren created a circle emblem scored with symbols that she recognized from her records. The confident way he worked spoke volumes about his knowledge. It also quickly destroyed the chance that he wasn't telling her the truth.

Who else would know those symbols? Why would this one man unless he was Jahehn? They made no sense to anyone other than the tribe.

She stared at the blanket, trying to comprehend what was coming, and fearing it. Is this what had been ripping her apart for so long? Was she truly Jahehn? She tried to swallow but realized her mouth had gone bone-dry.

It took her a few minutes to realize he'd finished and was sitting again. He studied her. He held his chin with curiosity in his eyes. "What I'm wondering is what your totem spirit is going to be. It's strong in our family."

"Our family?" she squeaked, confusion raking her like a battering ram, over and over. "What do you mean?"

He shrugged indolently. "One of two things. You're either my sister or my cousin. I won't know until someone admits to being your father."

Her world spun off its axis—again. How much more could there be? "Are you serious?"

There was no denying the grimace of anger, something that only Loren knew. Angie felt out to sea and was quickly losing sight of land. "I've felt it since the first meeting that you were one of my clan, but it's been...hard...to picture you as my father's daughter."

Immediate understanding rushed through her. This was at least one question answered. "Is that why I've felt..." Her thoughts tumbled as she tried to put them into order. "Sensations from you?"

His grin was kind and much more understanding. "Essentially. It's a recognition ward. You'll probably feel it when you meet my brothers too. The closer the blood bond, the stronger it is."

"Wow," she breathed, overwhelmed at the idea. "Suddenly, I have family everywhere."

Loren's expression tightened with a new seed of worry. "You need to go get ready."

She didn't question him, rising and dashing for the tent. "God, please don't let me die," she prayed once as she stripped in a flurry of shaking hands and erratic misses.

She tugged the blanket around her. As a last measure, she unbound her hair. Twisting the blanket in her hands, she joined him by the fire.

"This feels so weird," she muttered, standing, shivering with fear and indecision. "And you've told me nothing."

"I will help you as much as I can," he told her, his voice soothing. "You would have been trained had your family known, had either of your parents known." With a sorrowful glimpse, she realized he meant it. "Since your mother was not Jahehn, your father has quite a few things to explain." His lips thinned when he stopped speaking. "I can only guide you from here forward. There isn't time to detail your training."

"Cliffs Notes?" she queried with a prayer of hopefulness. The grimness in his expression told her the answer plainly.

She watched his every step when he began to chant. Every pace as he walked and murmured, dusting the fire one more time with an aromatic concoction she couldn't begin to dissect. Her heart rattled with the harsh staccato of steel rails beneath a speeding train. She clenched her jaw when her teeth almost clacked with the jarring tempo.

He stopped before her and put his palms to either side of her head, speaking in some tongue she didn't understand. She almost called it quits right there, feeling foolish and stupid for believing in something that couldn't possibly be proven as truth. But something kept her knees locked and her feet frozen to the ground.

"When the transition starts, relax as much as possible. Allow your mind to open and welcome the merging. Your physical self will change, but not the mental. You will still be Angie, though you will share the spirit's ability in form, and it will share with you."

She closed her eyes and deepened her breathing. Panic wasn't going to do her any good. "Why is this the last one? Why did it not work any other time?"

Concern and confusion crossed his features. "I don't know. It might be your lack of knowledge or a block to withstand the request. Not knowing may have been your saving grace for as long as you've been suffering his calling. There's a vibration when you're close to the merging. You're so loud right now, you could shake windows loose. It helps us prepare the one being called well in advance. When the first sensing of the wolf brother appears, training begins in earnest."

Training she never received. "Oh." She dropped her gaze and obeyed his motions to sit on the other blanket. She settled at the center, pulling the clutched blanket tight over her shuddering shoulders. Angie tried to focus on one thing at a time to keep from losing her nerve. "You said the brother spirit was wolf." She licked her lips to hide the quake in her voice. "And the soul spirit, if I had one, would be different."

"Yes."

"Do you have a soul spirit?"

He crouched by the fire, resting on a knee, almost as if he were counting the seconds as they ticked on an invisible clock. "I do. Mine is the falcon. And yes, it hurts just as much to call on him."

She felt the grin fighting to form at his humored tone. He was trying to comfort her. She'd never felt more alone in her life. "Does this have to do with the shaman legend?" Angie asked, taking a chance on the histories that she'd deciphered, testing her own knowledge and the merest probability of being right.

Her heart pounded when he nodded. His answer gave her a lightheaded feeling, but she focused on him and didn't allow herself to crumple where she sat. It was a tough fight, but she won.

"Yes, that legend is true. One of the ancient fathers was attacked while hunting. He killed the lion with a solid strike to its side, but he was almost killed in the process. His throat had been nearly crushed by the cat's attack. He lived but had lost his ability to speak."

She watched him, encouraging him to continue, wanting to hear the real version.

"The merging of the wolf spirits happened not long after that. It's rumored how that happened. Especially over the years, even the most sacred tales become a little warped."

She laughed, albeit shakily. Fingering the blanket edge, she said, "I can imagine. Please, tell me the story."

He rubbed a thumb against his lower lip in thought. "It has been passed down that this same ancestor went on a vision quest at the prodding of the tribal shaman. He had lost his status in the tribe because of the injury. He was still physically strong, but the injuries were much harder to overcome then."

"He couldn't communicate?"

He grimaced, sadness weighing heavily in his voice. "Not well, and he wasn't able to be on watch because he couldn't warn. He had no wife, so there was no family to rely on."

Sympathy struck hard and deep for the man who'd lost everything on the chance of a bad hunting encounter. "And he wasn't considered marriage material." Loren's expression said it all. "So what did he do?"

"He sought the shaman and asked what he should do. He was told if he went into the deepest mountains, he would find his voice, but he had to be willing to see it when it appeared because it would not be apparent through his eyes." He dropped his hand, stirring the fire coals with a protruding stick. "This warrior had fallen within the tribe and had lost many things. Belief in what he was still living for was one of them."

She tried to ignore the first niggle of heat and pain on her neck, concentrating on the story instead. The stiffening of her spine didn't go unnoticed, though.

Loren reached for her, but she shook her head. "Don't stop. I have a few minutes." If she had to kill for them, she would get those few minutes to hear this legend.

After a tense, watchful pause, he continued. "He walked for more than a moon's return—a full moon, no weapons, no food, and no water. He traveled over mountains and through the canyons, following nothing but the shaman's order to search for his voice. He walked until he collapsed."

Loren stood to circle the campfire once more, this time sprinkling herbs on the symbols he'd drawn. When he finished, he came and sat with her on the blanket. She turned to face him, to have his face to focus on as the heat crashed over her.

The timbre of his voice filled her ears, and she watched the motion of his lips as much as heard the story. "When he awoke, wolves had gathered. He knew fear like he'd never known before. He was weak, defenseless. He'd never survive if they attacked. Yet an amazing thing happened. They didn't attack him for being an invader in their hunting territory. They howled. Songs like he'd never heard."

Her eyelids fluttered closed, and she automatically gripped the hand that found hers as the heat intensified, rolling in all too well known waves over her body. "What did he offer them for the gift?" She knew enough to know it had been nothing less in the mythos of the story.

"He said nothing. He couldn't, and the wolves gathered wouldn't have understood. He searched the ground and finding the sharpest rock, gouged pits out of his chest and off his legs." She envisioned every word, seeing the blood bond that he'd offered them for the gift of their song. "He bled for them, swearing his life to them. His fear had been eclipsed by a new belief, and he knew what he had to do."

"Tell me," she choked out, knowing the ending was near, but she had to hear it herself. She had to know.

"The largest male approached the fallen warrior until he stood nearly at his hip, sniffed at the blood, and howled, a cry that carried to the four winds. When the pack joined him in salute to the warrior's offering—and this is where the spiritual starts—this wolf, strong and proud just like the warrior who'd lost everything, bared its teeth before the warrior in pact. Something happened in that moment that has never been explained."

She felt the grip of his hand in hers, focusing on his skin against hers as much as his voice to stay above the building pain.

"When the shaman had told him to believe in the voice when it came to him, the warrior had believed it was the wolves themselves which had found him. It wasn't. The voice he needed was their song, a song that animal or man would recognize, and there was only one way to sing."

She gasped as heat burst up her spine when she was unable to forestall its rage another wrenched second. "They shared one body." Her jaw clenched around those few words.

"Yes."

"Beautiful." The word burst free, ripe with pain.

"It really can be. But it is deadly if abused," he warned. The strain she found on his face through the slits of her eyes was evident as the merging began. "Many believe that wolf, the alpha of the pack, was a god on earth in wolf form, and he claimed the warrior and his blood as his eternal vessel. That ancestor became the shaman of the tribe and spent years sharing his teachings and reverence of the wolf pack's ways. The clan became immersed in the gift, and that spirit is with us today, guarded and protected because that was the vow. Some of his bloodline have learned to embrace their totem spirit of our wild ancestors also."

"So the Jahehn were shifters of the wolf and their totems?" Wonder built inside her, side by side with the engulfing pain that was knifing up and down her spine. She arched into it, feeling the familiar spasms, the known waves of crystal sharpness, clawing sensations of bone and muscle as though she were being shredded from the inside out. This time she felt the request in the pain, a pact formed from centuries past, and recognized it for what it was and how it was meant.

Tears leaked from her eyes as the pain fireballed. The spasms she'd suffered up to then were only the precursor to what was going to happen now. That realization didn't make her feel any better after already living through so many and for so long.

"Don't fight it," Loren warned her, except miraculously she heard it in Mark's voice.

His image hovered on her eyelids, and she desperately clutched at it as fear rose on her tongue. The concern he'd shown her, the real want to help her when she'd done everything she could to push him away.

Trying to protect him from being hurt, she realized she'd only been trying to protect herself. She didn't want to cause him pain. Didn't want to desert him. It was a lie. She didn't want to be hurt.

She clung to Mark's face, Loren's hand, like a lifeline. Could she do this? Heat encased her, drove into her. She cried out as the fire mushroomed. As if a flaming army hiked up and down her body from the inside, leaving destruction and suffering in its wake. With the legend still echoing in her ears, she opened herself up to the whispered voice in her mind, hearing the howled song of the wolf pack in the ancient legend, and felt a growing sharpness merge within her, a sound she'd only vaguely heard or acknowledged in the past, not knowing what it was she'd carried all this time. Their song reached through time, joining hers, filling her with their strength.

The rising agony made her arch, dragging the scratchy thickness of the blanket over her skin. The next scream formed on her lips but never emerged. Her throat had closed as she suffered the same injury of the warrior of long ago. She panicked, clawing to fight it, to not succumb to the blackness crashing around her. Breathing became a harsh exercise as her world vacuumed to that ancient injury.

The soothing melody of a chant fell over her, and she struggled to reach it. Heated waves of lava rolled over her, scorching every part of her until she feared she'd incinerate on the spot. There wasn't a part of her this time that didn't feel the shifting of her own skin as the wolf brother laid claim to her body.

A new pain erupted from her hands, shooting up her arms until it raced past her shoulders, more ruthless than any other part of her. Even her feet and toes screamed at her in agony. She clawed at the blanket and dirt beneath her fingers, fighting to embrace the merging instead of fighting the pain completely.

Every muscle and bone cried out with renewed pulses of torture, and black edges crept into her vision. She wouldn't survive. The blinding pain was unbearable. It was crippling. Death had finally come for her. Another rocket-hot shard sliced her in half, and the screams poured out of her.

She continued to hear Mark in her mind, comforting and tender with every breath, encouraging her the way only he could. The blazing hand she'd felt began anew, pummeling on organs and bones. She felt herself beginning to lose the fight, at the end of her endurance.

"Hang on, Angie! Open to the spirit!"

Steady hands touched her, reminding her she was human and she was the one in control. It was the only feeling that separated her from the bone-splitting torment. Ultimately, she couldn't deny the timeless plea.

She released a gasp for life and plunged forward into the unknown. The sensation beneath her palms immediately changed. The drag of claws felt awkward, the tension of her touch different as skin and bone realigned.

Sensations bombarded her from every angle and direction. Scents, sounds. Everything she touched caused her to moan in renewed, exhausted agony. Her skin felt as though it had been heavily burned, prickled and dry, then raked with sharp tines over and over until it split in a burst from toe to finger.

The ache in her jaw amplified, and any movement of her mouth or tongue brought up another unavoidable whimper.

Bones popped and ground, the sound echoing inside her own head a thousand times, snapping like dry twigs. It happened so fast, yet the agony of it all made it feel as though it took an eternity. She wasn't sure she was still alive even after it was finally over.

Blackness enveloped her senses, and she collapsed completely to the ground. Whispered words were the only reassurance that she had survived the merging.

The last murmurs disappeared in a deep silence as she simply let go and let the clan claim her. She had taken on the spirit of the wolf brother and accepted her place in the tribe. What was left could wait.

# CHAPTER SIXTEEN

SHUDDERS RACKED her body. The gray veil over her mind was slowly dissipating like a thick morning fog melting beneath a raging sun, heavy tendrils that weaved and wavered as she woke, revealing a truth she couldn't name. She felt her mind recoil with the rush of knowledge. She was Jahehn. The merging was a success. She still breathed, even though it didn't feel like anything she'd ever experienced before. Muscles twitched, but...they weren't hers, exactly.

Scents bombarded her with each inhale. Odors of wood smoke, male sweat, and everything surrounding her from the wool scent of the blanket to the earth and trees. She kept her eyes closed. There was so much to take in, so much assaulting her at once, it was overload without even moving.

"It's okay, Angie. You're alive."

She cracked an eye open. Her first reaction was to snarl at the shape before her. She stopped when she realized it was the wolf part of her reacting, but she couldn't blame that side of her for being upset. Angie would have more than a few choice words for those who'd left her unprepared and deemed her unworthy too. The agony of the merging had been a hell on earth type of pain. The seizures she'd suffered had never come close to this.

Loren hovered over her, then knelt to the ground with her. She felt the weight of the blanket slide free. Feeling exposed, she shivered.

"Take your time."

If she'd been in her own shape, she'd tell him where to shove his advice. Instead, she breathed.

"You don't have to rush this, Angie," he murmured over her, talking soothingly. "The pain will be there, but not like this." One eye cracked open again. "I know you don't believe me. I don't blame you for not trusting me." Regret furrowed the sides of his mouth when he frowned.

He waited on the edge of the blanket, giving her space. "There's no reason to not let you have the training you need now."

*Now?* What the hell happened to *before*?

"Sharing the spirit is a real gift, especially for the women. Only a handful at a time seem to receive the calling. Not all survive. You were incredible, brave."

She heard awe in his voice, and a new respect.

"I don't think I've seen a woman embrace it that well in my lifetime."

If he was trying to make her feel better, he had a long way to go. So what if it was a gift? She usually liked gifts, but this one had a lot of downsides, least of all the *excruciating* pain the council had known she'd experience. A rush of anger at the men who had decided her death by merging made her growl, and her legs twitched, unfamiliar paws reaching out.

Her entire length froze at the unexpected sensation when they dragged on the blanket beneath her. Damn! This was going to take some time to get comfortable in her own skin. Staring at long, hair covered limbs, she realized her thoughts were right on the money.

"Easy," he said. He hadn't moved to touch her, just watched her. "One step at a time. Usually the council is witness to help with this part, but..." He seemed to withdraw for a moment, taking a few moments to focus on her again.

*You should feel ashamed for them!*

"It will become natural in a few minutes," he explained. "The wolf within us is ancient and has patience. It's usually us who have a hard time adapting."

*Really? You don't say?* The sarcasm was quick off her tongue today—almost her tongue. Definitely a fast pitch out of her thoughts.

"The reversal will hurt, but not like the transition. Take the time you need to find your legs."

*What? My sea legs?* She growled. Ooh yeah, she was on a roll today.

He scrubbed a hand down his face. "I know it doesn't mean much now, but I am sorry I couldn't help more. You needed training, preparation, and there just wasn't time. Your family would've filled in the gaps once they realized you were receiving the calling. I know you didn't have that."

Nope, not even close. She realized it was her father—the real bio one—behind this transition. And did she have a few *choice* words for him!

Which meant Mark had been right.

*Oh God.* She wanted to whimper but held it inside. Still lying on her side, panting as apparently only a wolf could, she realized the mistake she'd made with Mark. She had to find him. He had a few hours on her, but she could catch him. She lurched to her feet. And froze.

With unavoidable hesitation, she followed the length of her new body with her gaze, marveling at the sleek shape from her shoulder to her tail. *Incredible.*

"Easy."

She turned to him and glared.

He lifted his hands. "Give yourself a minute."

This time the growl was self-explanatory, and he blinked.

"I deserve that."

*You don't know what I think you deserve. Bastards!* The whole town's worth. How could they have done this, left her to suffer when she was one of them?

She lifted her nose and found his stare. They had a lot of apologizing to do, but first she had to find Mark. She had been so wrong, so many times. Her stomach—it felt like hers, but it was too hard to figure out at that exact moment—clenched with worry and self-aimed anger. He was gone, and she was the reason. She had a sinking feeling he'd never want her after the awful way she'd treated him. She winced inside for every unjustified accusation she'd shot at him and how little she'd listened to him. Somehow he was right on target when she couldn't see past her own nose. Admitting that stung.

His had been the voice she'd heard when the pain had been too much. His face was the one she'd clung to when dying had been tempting instead of succumbing to this side of the transition. When fear of the unknown had almost undone her will, the idea of Mark holding her during her worst moments had kept her from giving in completely.

Her head sagged. She owed him so much. She had to find him. And...as a wolf, she could. The animal would know, would be able to track him! Excitement made her tremble. She could do this. They shared. One body, one voice, but it was still her. She was thinking like Angie, but the wolf's senses were real. Sight, sound, smell. The wolf was reading them all, teaching her with every breath.

"Angie?" Concern in his voice had her glance in his direction. "Are you okay?"

She spread her front legs and felt the strength and power in her chest, the way the animal's body contoured. She had the urge and followed through before she realized what it was the wolf wanted. She tipped back her head and howled. Loren's smile was ecstatic.

Too bad he didn't realize she wasn't sticking around to share in his wonder. She trotted past him into the tent, dropped her nose, and began searching. Scents infiltrated her mind, one by one, separating each until she found Mark's.

"Hey!" he cried when she shot right by Loren going the other way. "Damn it, Angie! You can't do this."

*Stop me,* she challenged him without looking back or slowing.

"Angie!" he shouted, leaping to his feet and rushing after her. She ignored him. Mark had a head start of hours. She had her work cut out for her.


LOREN QUICKLY LOST her in the trees. Four legs could outrun two any day. She was mastering the symbiotic relationship in leaps and bounds. He bit back his own frustration as her pale coat vanished out of sight.

"Damn it," he gasped in annoyance, slowing to catch his breath. "Don't do anything stupid, Angie." He didn't think she would, but there was so little she knew about the wolf and the laws. She'd have to be instructed and quickly, before she had any chance to make the mistakes training warned the tribe against making. Right now she was vulnerable and didn't even know it.

MARK LEANED AGAINST a tree, drinking sparingly from the canteen after eating one of the bars Loren had given to him. Several hours later, the sun was on the downside of overhead. He'd get as far as he could and try to reach the highway by afternoon the next day. He really didn't know how far he'd come or how much farther he had to go. It really didn't matter. He'd left everything that mattered to him in that campsite.

With an angry shrug, he shoved off the tree and started walking again, only to be frozen in place by the long, melodious sound of a wolf's howl carrying through the canyon. He gulped and spun on a heel, his heart thumping against his ribs. Was it Angie? Did she survive the transition? Was the merging a success?

He almost rushed back but caught himself before he took that first step. Loren would be able to help her far better than he could. There was no denying the truth. Loren was Jahehn, knew what she needed to learn about what she was and the person she would become. What did Mark have to offer? Not enough of what she needed. And nothing Angie wanted.

Dejected, he turned and trudged on, the small pack tapping his side with each step.

A hot shower and real cooked food did sound increasingly welcome. The thought of having either in the near future distracted him. Though it wasn't much consolation for what he'd left behind and lost. Honestly, the lost part sucked. He thought the last chance of being on the short end of the 'I got dumped' stick had happened in college when he'd lost his girl to another guy. Amazing how age didn't improve his chances.

He paused and glanced around, covering his eyes to gauge the time. He'd have to find a place to stop for the night soon. The sun was lowering a lot faster than he was making distance.

Dropping his hand, he searched through the trees, picking his next path with little real care. So long as he headed south, he'd eventually hit the gully washout crossed at the neck of the canyon. Once he found the truck, it was simply a matter of following the washout to the pass and then to the highway. Sure, easy, no problem. With one foot after another, he created more distance between himself and Angie.

TREES WHISKED PAST Angie, each long, loping stride a freedom she'd never tasted before. Colors ran like fluid paint in her vision. Sounds were crisp, and scents were distinct, each one separated and clarified instantly. Everything from the bark on trees to the pungent odor of other animals' markings. Each breath filled her lungs with sheer mechanical grace. Dirt and leaves beneath her toe pads barely shifted with her passing. The bunch of shoulder and hip muscles pulsed with every leaping stretch.

No wonder they revered and protected the knowledge of the bond. The sheer enormity of what she'd survived amazed her. This was what she'd suffered for. *This is amazing, really, truly amazing.* The words whispered through her thoughts, since she couldn't speak them.

A scent on the wind made her skid to a stop. She backtracked to test the ground. *Mark.* She was still on his trail. She closed her eyes and wished a heartfelt thank you to the animal's senses. Without them, she'd never have a prayer of finding him. Warmth flitted along her skin. A sense of awe stole her breath for a moment. She showed her appreciation, and the spirit brother acknowledged her. It was a humbling experience, so much to learn.

She spun and raced along the path Mark seemed to be sticking to. She had to find him. Remorse wasn't a feeling she'd felt in a long time, but considering how rotten she'd treated him... She let out a huff that would have been a sigh if she weren't panting.

Distance had no meaning. She only had one goal—reaching Mark before she lost him forever.

Shadows grew deeper, stretching farther. Every stride brought her closer. She knew it. He would likely stop to camp along the way, the same as they had entering the canyon. She wouldn't have that problem. Daylight was fading for the coming night, but she could see everything around her. The natural advantage of the animal in its environment allowed her to keep moving forward.

MARK RESTED ON his sleeping bag, flipping dry sticks into the miniscule campfire he'd built to drive away the darkest shadows. He'd had hours to think during the trek into town, to think about what and whom he'd left behind. Distance and time made little difference to him.

Crackles and pops pinged like tiny fireworks escaping the flames in front of his feet. It was really just to keep the night from looking so desolate. He had absolutely nothing to cook.

Even one of Loren's rabbits would have gone over like a feast for him at the moment.

Encircling a wrist under his fingers, he propped his crossed arms on raised legs. He wouldn't think about it. If he did, he'd only think about Angie.

*Sorry sack of shit,* he harangued himself. *What happened? Couldn't bring yourself to fight for her? Why not?*

So much for avoiding the question.

Mark was not a violent person. Ultimately he avoided uncontrollable violence. It was probably why he enjoyed defense classes. He could at least tell himself that they were to help the people who wanted to learn the basics. But put him in a bar-room brawl, and he'd rather pass for the exit.

It wasn't that he was against fighting for her. It wouldn't be easy, and he felt he could hold his own against Loren. It was his hate of physical violence. He knew that much. So what was stopping him?

She'd have to see him for Mark, the man who loved her, not her longtime friend.

*But wasn't Angie worth at least trying?*

He thought she was.

Staring into the darkness he'd traveled, he started to rise. He was willing to take the pain if it came from fighting for her, willing to take the chance. If Angie had survived, then he may still have that chance. If he could convince her that she was wrong.

*She laughed in your face, man. Want to go through that again?*

Mark shoved his hands into his pockets. "But that was before," he muttered to his conscience. He couldn't blame her for doubting him, not really. It was crazy, but he *knew* it was right. Wouldn't Loren have fought harder to deny it?

There was no doubt the free sound of the howl he'd heard was her. Absently he pulled his shirt off and hung it over a thin sapling branch. No sense in sleeping in what he'd be wearing the next day.

*If she'd loved you the way you thought she did, wouldn't she have listened?*

Maybe. He really didn't know. She'd always been stubborn and tenacious. Maybe Mark didn't know her as well as he'd thought or hoped.

He sighed, rolling his shoulders to ease the tension the internal battle was causing as he fought with his conscience. He couldn't recall the last time he was this torn up and miserable over a woman.

The toss of his thoughts distracted him from any sounds from woods or farther down the trail. He wasn't expecting company, which made the interruption that much more of a surprise.

"This is a lucky break," River said. Mark whirled and faced the councilman and his scheming grin. "I didn't think I'd find either of you this easily." A wicked-looking gun in his hand glinted against the flare of the small fire's flames.

River toted a sizeable pack strapped to his back, a rifle barrel visible behind him. Mark wasn't about to deny the obvious reasons behind River's appearance. He had followed them into the canyon. The sudden sickening truth hit Mark. He'd come personally to make sure Angie didn't return to town. The venom Mark had seen in the council house was right out front now that there was no one to hide it from.

Mark's hands slipped from his pockets as he relaxed, but his increased pulse belied the image.

"Why are you alone? Did she die?" River demanded, sounding a bit too hopeful.

The other man was practically bouncing with restrained anticipation. Mark was only too happy to deflate that happiness.

"No. She lived." He was willing to take the chance that he was right. He would do anything to keep her safe.

"Shit," River muttered, expelling a groan of irritation. He scowled. "That complicates things."

"Why? What difference does it make to you?"

River's gaze narrowed. He whipped the gun toward Mark, motioning for him to move. "Over there and kneel." He pointed to a tree a yard or two from Mark.

"What are you doing here?" His sudden appearance gave Mark a bad feeling. If River had come all this way...

"Quit with the questions, *notse*. Save your breath. I understand bleeding to death out here is a real bitch."

The tense snarl of River's voice raked against the calm of the night, not to mention Mark's already taut nerves. He didn't move.

A swift twitch of the gun in his direction told him River wasn't one to hesitate about using the weapon, and he was growing impatient.

Something inside Mark snapped. The clues fell together so easily. This man wanted Angie dead. It took him less than two seconds to make the connection that he was the same person who'd taken those shots at her in town. The rifle in his pack looked like a .45, the same caliber of the bullet Loren had shown him.

Whatever Angie was threatened River in some way. A big way if he was willing to murder.

Mark braced himself on the balls of his feet, flexing his hands. "Come and make me." He outweighed River. Unless he was some kind of trained fighter, Mark could easily take him and win. Mark was younger and far more agile without the weight of a backpack. River had to be close to sixty. Mark wouldn't hurt him, but he'd make the other man wish for it.

"I don't have to make you." He waved the gun and then steadied it to point right in the center of his chest. "A shot this close would kill you in less than five minutes." His grin reappeared, growing cold and cruel. "I don't want you to die that fast."

Mark lunged for the older man.

River fired.

# CHAPTER SEVENTEEN

THE GUNSHOT ECHOED down the canyon with a sharp crack. Angie jerked to a stop on the trail. *Mark!*

Trembles rolled over her body. She listened for more. Nothing followed. She leaped toward the fading sound, to race as fast as her tiring legs could take her. There was no way to know how far she'd traveled; all she knew was that she was getting closer. Sound and scent rushed her with every step, but there was only one goal—reaching him.

She soared over limbs and weaved past tree trunks like her body was made of butter. New scents grew distinct, filling her long nose. Fire. Blood. Her fear rose with each leap. Something had happened to Mark.

Focusing on his scent, on the acrid odor of the burning fire, she barreled into the campsite.

Shocked, she spotted River crouched over a prone Mark, holding something that could have been cloth in his hands. It looked like he was using it to stop the bleeding. Mark wasn't moving.

"Quick! He's bleeding," he shouted over a shoulder.

She did as River asked without thought. Somehow she found the strength to change into her natural form, feeling every twinge and grind as her body did as she asked. Whatever knowledge there was in it, she prayed she was doing what she could, and doing it right. This change seemed to take less time. Maybe there was less pain involved. It was more likely she was too numb with exhaustion and worry for Mark to feel the pain.

River held a shirt out between his fingers toward her. It was the shirt Mark had been wearing when he'd left camp.

"You're going to need this."

She gasped a thank you, feeling strangled and torn. What happened to Mark? Why wasn't he moving? How had he been hurt? How had he been shot?

Plunging her arms through the sleeves, she pushed buttons together with frozen, shaking fingers. River didn't face her as he hovered over Mark's body. He hadn't moved at all. Terror gripped her as the worst possible scenarios entered her mind.

"What happened?" She circled the fire, feeling her sight grow fuzzy at suddenly trying to walk on two legs after just running for miles on four. She inhaled and closed her eyes, finding her equilibrium. *Easy does it.* She was pushing herself into realms she'd never known existed. Exhaustion was bearing down fast now that she had a moment to be herself, in her own body.

River stood, spinning to face her, a gun in his hand. She caught a flash of something in his gaze that made her stumble on ungainly feet. Glacial hatred.

"I shot him. Turn around."

"Mark!" She screamed. She saw the cloth. It was stuffed into his mouth. His skin had an ugly gray pallor, sweat breaking out on his forehead. His eyes followed her, pain glazing them. Rope tied his hands together. Her gaze took in his entire body in an instant. The red stain just above his hip was impossible to miss.

She whimpered, reaching out for him. River blocked her rush to reach him, slamming a stiff hand into her chest. It knocked the wind out of her. Short of breath from running when she was struck, the blow made her see stars.

"I said turn around!" He backhanded her with the fist holding the heavy weight of the steel gun. She fell to her stomach, hard earth and grit filling her nose and mouth. Her stomach heaved with a rush of adrenaline-laced bile.

Sensations sparked through her as she fought to calm herself. She needed to breathe. Panic would do her no good. She sucked and gulped until her lungs began to work on their own. Her skin felt different. She shuddered, her mind racing to keep up with the influx of information.

Something was telling her to run. Something was making her skin tight. It didn't feel like the wolf. After spending hours in that skin, she hoped she'd recognize the feel of the wolf brother.

No, this was a sense of pure survival. A sense of something inside of her being pissed beyond recognition. It roiled and slid beneath her skin, making her itch to let it out. The sensation paced and crawled inside of her, demanding to be free, to strike out, to run. Confusion made it impossible to separate what had happened from what was happening to her in that moment. She forced herself from the feeling, working on one aspect at a time.

A grunt in front of her demanded she lift her watery gaze. Mark's face was blotchy and gray. The blood seeping from his hip terrified her.

He was staring right at her. Her heart slammed into her chest. She rose to her knees and felt her world crumble like the dirt beneath her hands. *I love you.* She prayed he could see the emotions tumbling inside her. It was too little too late, but she'd find a way to help him.

"Get up, or the next shot will be his last," River ordered. Wrapping a hand through her hair, he yanked viciously. She cried out in agony. Mark twitched, tied and unable to help her, lying in the dirt, slowly bleeding to death. Tears clogged her vision. River lifted the gun in his hand, aiming to point directly at him when she didn't move fast enough.

"Don't!" It was a choked sob. "I'll do what you say." She'd do anything to save him. As steadily as possible, she staggered to her feet.

He wrenched her head back. "I never doubted it," he whispered against her ear. "Walk." When she hesitated, fighting the strength in his grip, fighting to just make sense of what was happening, he told her, his breath hot on her neck, "You're going to die, but not here. You can't be found. No one else has to know you survived the merging. No one will challenge the council if you're dead."

Tears ran freely now between the sharp pain in her scalp and the rough and biting terrain beneath her feet. Her vision wouldn't clear enough to make it any easier. Constant yanks on her hair kept her moving. River was stronger than he looked, forcing her to march. The occasional jab of the gun into her side reminded her that she had few options.

MARK FOUGHT TO stay awake. It was dark now. Only the language of the nighttime world surrounded him, and it wasn't telling him much. There was a total void. A total absence of the creak of tree limbs, the scamper of quieting birds, or the whispered murmur of the wind through the leaves. It was eerily quiet.

He worked his jaw and tongue, pushing against the blockage between his teeth, ignoring the scratch of the fabric stuffed practically down his throat. It took what felt like hours, but the gag fell out. He managed to breathe easily for the first time since he was shot. The slightest movement made him hiss with pain, and twice his shift of weight was enough to streak stars across his vision.

He forced a calmness he didn't remotely feel. It was enough to sag against the tree with a shoulder, gasping, keeping as much weight as he could off his wounded hip. The last thing he wanted to do was bleed to death. River's threat was all too real at the moment.

He had no idea how far he'd come since he'd left the campsite, leaving Loren and Angie behind. Had no idea how close help was, if he even had a chance of getting it. The safest thing for him to do was to keep calm, stay still if at all possible, and do something to get his hands free. The bite of the rope was a constant reminder that he wasn't done yet.

A string of prayers for help and for someone to look over Angie were a constant litany in his mind.

ANGIE TRIPPED AND stumbled. The constant reining clutch on her hair kept her upright and moving. She didn't bother to ask where he was taking her. It didn't matter.

Her only thought was to get away. She had to get back to Mark. The sight of his blood, of the pain in his pinched expression was burned into her. It made each step harder and harder as distance increased between them.

Wherever they were, they were hours from where she'd left Loren earlier in the day. They were so far from town. She squelched the fresh flood of tears. Tears that were caused as much by what had happened to her as the biting pain she felt everywhere. There was very little that didn't hurt or ache with fatigue.

Shivers crawled across bare skin where Mark's shirt didn't cover her. Cool night air made the hair on her arms and legs stand up. Fear and anger battled like a maelstrom within her. Fear that she'd never see Mark again, never have the chance to apologize, to tell him what she felt. That fear made her angry. So long as she was angry, she was alive. So long as she was alive, she had a chance.

She needed a chance to escape. Just one.

Maybe knowing where they were going would help after all.

"Where are we going?"

"Shut up!" He tried to silence her again by twisting his fist brutally through her hair.

She yelped, stars bursting across her vision. Tears that hadn't stopped streaming down her cheeks with her best efforts sped up with the piercing pain.

"Why?" she choked out, fighting to stay on her feet. The urge to strike out was becoming harder to control.

Why was he doing this? Why did he want her dead? What did he think she knew?

The sensations she'd experienced before, feelings she hadn't been able to name at their first meeting—she knew them for what they were now.

The sensations were all too similar to Loren's, the 'understanding' between them. A sense that was created by a mutual blood bond between her and the guide—they traveled along her nerves with River right behind her, and they were not kind.

Angie's nerves screeched and rattled at the discordant warning. She kept one foot moving in front of the other, refusing to bow down to River's cruelty as she tried to make sense of it, but her tired mind and exhausted body weren't up to the challenge. He marched behind her, keeping her off balance with her head tilted and the gun a jabbing reminder that she shouldn't stop.

She remembered Loren's words, almost in cadence with the stilted, rushed pace River had set. If she could sense Loren, then why could she feel River now? How? They had to be related for the peculiar feelings to appear if what Loren had explained made linear sense. Then she had to be related to...

A sudden dizziness made her vision blank out for a second. Her world flipped, and suddenly earth was sky and sky was earth. She quaked and collapsed between steps, falling to her hands and knees. He stumbled, and the unrelenting hold on her hair loosened. Gulping air, she just managed to keep her stomach in place.

Her heart raced, pounding hard against her ribs until she thought it would jump out all by itself. Tremors shook her body with the sharpness of a resonating gong.

"Get up!" he demanded. Loose strands of hair were gripped again.

She sobbed, keeping her eyes closed when the world spun.

"How could you?" she breathed, although she nearly choked on the sourness of the words as they rose up her throat on the heated acid of her own shock. "How could you do this to me?"

There wasn't even a hint of remorse. "You weren't supposed to live! Stupid bitch. You know nothing. Why couldn't you have died? You *weren't supposed to live.*"

He yanked, and she screamed as he used her hair like a rope to control her.

He tipped her back, bending her like a reed until she was looking backward to him, arched and immobile.

For the first time in her entire life, she stared up at her father and knew who he was. The real one. The one who had impregnated her mother. The one who had given her the spirit of the Jahehn then left her to suffer. Who had chosen to let her die through that suffering!

"Not supposed to live?" Her breath erupted from her in harsh pants as she struggled to regain her equilibrium. Her world had never been more shaken.

River's face had turned crueler than she'd ever seen, cold and heartless.

"You weren't supposed to survive the merging!" he shouted into her face. "Get up. We're not far enough."

She trembled but forced her feet to obey. She *would* get away.

"Why?" She'd managed a few yards, but her legs threatened to buckle out from beneath her. She had to slow down and catch her breath, or she'd never have a chance of escaping. Her brain wasn't working fast enough to break everything down. She stumbled to a stop. "Why am I like this? Why my mother?"

He shoved a stiff hand into her back, propelling her forward. "You want me to tell you I loved her?" he sneered. "Do you want me to tell you I cared?" Cold and unfeeling, his eyes burned with a raw hate. "Because I didn't. She was nothing!" He inched lower, to where he stood a few inches over her. "She was a cheap college girl while I was in California with Croma, away all day handling tribal alliance business with his father. It was her fault for falling for me. She made it too easy when she lay on her back for me," he gloated with a twist of his hand in her hair.

"Don't ever talk about her like that," Angie ground out. "You left her pregnant! You left her with me." She straightened. "You. Left. Her."

He raised a hand to strike her. Instinctively she reacted. His grip wasn't fast enough to restrain her. The control he'd held over her by her hair slipped away as his anger escalated.

She swiveled on her hips and put all her weight into her fist, thrusting. A snarl rose in her mind, a wild, hissing roar that fed into her bloodstream. Her fist landed perfectly in his midsection. The impact was solid and jarring, causing air to gush out of his lungs. He wasn't prepared for the suddenness of the attack, not after pushing and controlling her, believing she was too tired to fight back. His underestimating gave her the opening she needed.

Her next hit was lower, driving upward with the heel of her hand. Skin crunched as the impact drove his scrotum into his bowels. He fell to his knees, his eyes glazing with shocked pain. The gun hung, then dropped from fingers that froze and clenched as his body curled in on itself.

Adrenaline pushed the exhaustion off her one more time, and she whirled. Hurrying as fast as her tired legs would carry her, she surged into a run to put distance between them.

She felt the merging happening and yanked the shirt over her head as her stride increased. The urgency was clear in the feeling. The wolf brother would help her escape. She breathed a welcomed thank you for the effort and gave in as renewed pain from the merging swept over her.

# CHAPTER EIGHTEEN

MARK BLINKED, seeing the world through a bleary haze. He'd dozed again. His shoulders ached and burned. He'd given up on freeing himself from the ropes. He didn't have the strength. He really needed to stay awake. Not that sleep didn't sound appealing. He was exhausted, but if he fell asleep, shock was likely. He didn't know how he'd managed to not go into shock as it was. Maybe he was and he just didn't recognize the delirium. The hole in his side burned and throbbed in intervals. It seemed to be what kept waking him up if he dozed.

He felt drained and so tired. Would it hurt if he rested for just a minute? Just for a minute...

Blood-encrusted denim pulled at his skin when he flexed. Cold. He was cold everywhere. It didn't feel right. Numb. He was growing numb in too many places. And tired. So tired...

His eyes drooped closed again. Two breaths later when his chin dropped to his chest, he passed out beyond sleep.


FATIGUE ATE AT Angie, but she couldn't slow down. Not for a second.

Wind rushed over her with each thrusting leap. Her lungs burned, but she didn't stop to rest.

The rattle of someone jogging toward her made her pause. Lowering into a crouch, she froze, waiting. She spotted Loren's lean shape as he came into view, and she leaped for him, too happy to stay still.

"Angie!" He knelt before her. She pressed into his hand, heaving for gulps of air. "The gunshot?"

She backed up and shook her head, unwilling to waste time with the transformation. If she changed her shape again, she'd fall over exhausted. She whipped around on her hindquarters. Hearing Loren follow, she prayed they were quick enough to help Mark.

LOREN HEARD HER low growl between hard pants. They had to be close. And something was wrong.

He knew she was exhausted. She'd stumbled several times but refused to slow or rest. He gave up pushing the issue. She stopped acknowledging him after the first two tries anyway. The only reason he could think was that whatever had happened when he'd heard that gunshot had happened to Mark.

Both he and the wolf before him stopped in their tracks when they burst into the mini campsite.

"Steven," Loren barked out on a harsh breath, finding the Sheriff dressed in civilian clothes, crouched over Mark lying on the ground, reaching to check his pulse.

The wolf that was Angie didn't even hesitate, leaping forward until she straddled Mark's bare chest, protecting what was hers.

"What the hell?" Steven snapped, falling on his ass as the click of teeth snapped loudly in the nighttime stillness right next to his face.

"She thinks you're going to hurt him more. She's exhausted."

"Crap! Angie?" Steven blinked, staring at the huffing wolf. Steven straightened, giving her room. He looked up at Loren. "She lived?"

"Ask another 'duh' question, Steven," he ground out, dropping his pack. "What are you doing here?" Suspicion didn't sit well, but this seemed too damned convenient to have him suddenly appear. He liked Steven's answer even less.

"Croma sent me to find you. Said things should have happened by now." Steven studied the golden wolf with a glare. He then gave Loren a gloating grin. "I guess it did. Hope you enjoy your banishment."

"Fuck off," Loren snarled at him. Angie added a growl of her own, still not moving. "She lived, and right now, Mark's barely living, so either help or get the hell out of here."

The wolf bared her teeth, and Steven backed up more. "Fine. What happened?"

She whined low as she looked over her shoulder. He knew what she was asking, and knew she had no reason whatsoever to trust the man on the other side of Mark.

"Go, Angie. We need to know what happened."

She slid a final look at Steven and lowered her head, growling her displeasure, but did as Loren asked. It didn't occur to him until she'd left that she should have beat him to Mark at least an hour ago, and she wouldn't have been coming back from the west wall of the canyon either.

"She survived," Steven muttered again a moment later, his gaze following her disappearing form.

"And she's royally pissed at everyone. Don't expect her to be thrilled to see you when she comes back."

Loren lowered beside Mark, carefully exposing the wound. He hissed. "Shit." He quickly reached for a wrist, knifing the ropes free that held him captive, and couldn't restrain the sigh of relief when he felt the strength of his pulse. His color was bad, but he wasn't down for the count. Fatigue and pain were playing with him as much as blood loss.

Steven hunkered down closer. "Damn. How'd that happen?"

"River shot him. He tried to kill him. And me," Angie informed them walking back on bare feet from the closet-like darkness of the trees, pulling a spare shirt out of Mark's pack to cover her nudity. She didn't bother to look in their direction, and dropping their gazes, they let her dress.

"River?" Both Steven and Loren chorused.

"You're wrong. River was in town tonight. I spoke with him myself before I lost radio contact."

She clenched her fists and stood over him. "Do not fucking call me a liar, asshole. He shot Mark. I don't care how he got anywhere, but he was here!"

Steven held up his hands. "Okay. Okay."

Loren slid Steven a telling look. He wasn't about to say anything to deny her the seething anger she felt. She had every right to it and more.

"Did you see River in town, Steven?" Loren asked quietly, already working over the puncture in Mark's side.

Silence. Loren bored into the other man's eyes. A man he'd once called brother, and friend. "Don't cover for him this time, Steven. This has nothing to do with Brelynn." His words were icy.

Steven glared in answer. "Why River? What does he have to do with either of you?" Steven shot back. Loren knew Steven was aware there had been a power play when it came to Angie. Steven might have been misled, but he wasn't an idiot. He wasn't ready to bend yet, but Loren knew it would only be a matter of time. River was hiding something, and Angie knew what it was.

The sharp words that fell from Angie proved him right, rending the pause between them apart with the explosion of a grenade.

"River is my father."

The sense of relief at the news was quickly demolished by a wave of shock.

Angie knelt next to Mark's shoulder. Her fingers brushed tenderly through his hair. Loren noted his pulse, his respirations, the color of his skin, relying on his training and his instincts. Time wasn't something Mark could spare. That worried him. He'd die before they could get him back to Inglewood. He checked his pulse again. Still strong, but he'd never survive the remaining trek into town.

"I heard the gunshot," she murmured. "I followed it here."

"I heard it too," Loren admitted.

Steven's lips thinned, but Angie ignored him when he didn't say one way or the other what he'd heard.

"He came to make sure I didn't survive the merging. I'm sure it's the same reason Croma sent you."

Steven avoided her heated, condemning looks. Loren caught this as he cleaned the wound, fighting to stanch the renewed well of blood. Mark's chances were quickly dwindling under the circumstances.

"I got here after Mark had been hurt. River had already tied him up, and I walked right into it. I couldn't see what had happened to Mark."

"Where is River now?" Steven demanded, suspicion making the question harsh.

She shrugged, a hand limply waving over her shoulder. "Out there somewhere, where he planned to leave me, the evidence of his tribal betrayal."

Loren watched her through his lashes. He realized she knew exactly what she was talking about and didn't doubt her in the least. The laws had been broken years before, and she was living proof. It was the living part that had ruined River's life.

He returned to Mark's wound, the seriousness of Mark's condition sinking in. The wound was deep. The problem of internal damage was possible. Fortunately the lack of blood loss seemed to point away from that. Regardless, there was also only one way he could save Mark from the injury he had.

Angie smirked, her gaze locked on Mark's face. "I know that's why he couldn't let me live. He *knew* the same as I did who I was when we met. I just didn't know he was my father. He had that knowledge on me. I've always been told I look like my mother."

Loren listened, noticing how she weaved with fatigue and exhaustion darkened the hollows of her face, but she didn't stop.

"It all makes sense now. He played you, Steven," she added. "He twisted Croma's responsibility to the tribe and warped his reasoning to you. He had a lot to hide. And then I lived, and his life became nothing."

"How do you know so much?" Steven's voice held the bite of authority and a wealth of untrusting suspicion.

"I have been Jahehn my whole life, even if I didn't live with the tribal acceptance. I didn't just live the legends; I breathed them in. I understood them, carried them. Mark was right." Her fingers trailed down his cheek, lifting to touch his lips.

There was no response to her touches. "But I was scared, and did what I've always done when I couldn't take any more. I fell back on what I knew. I wanted to find the talisman because it would mean I hadn't failed an entire people, an entire culture. If I failed, at least I failed...trying. The chance that it could heal me was just an excuse to keep myself looking, to ignore the pain, because I knew the seizures were going to kill me."

Loren looked up and for the first time noted understanding in Steven's eyes.

"You know I have no choice," he said, really only meant for the other man's ears. He wasn't sure Angie heard him anyway, as focused as she was on Mark. Her gaze was locked on every shallow rise of his chest. Heartbreak at the thought that she would lose him kept her attention pinned to him.

"The council will tear you apart."

The rare words of caution brought on by his understanding told Loren all he needed to know. For the first time in years, they agreed.

"I'll handle that when it happens. We need them both to live."

Steven grunted and stood, dusting off his jeans. Steven would know why there was no choice. Mark was Angie's. There would be no one else for her, and if what Loren suspected were true, the tribe really needed Angie. Not to mention with all of this going on, prosecuting his own uncle for attempted murder was going to be nothing less than a train wreck.

ANGIE FELT NUMB. Exhaustion, fear, anger, disappointment, worry... She could probably draw a random word from a fishbowl and find a way to acknowledge it in the knot of her emotions. She watched Loren remove stray strips and threads from around the wound with meticulous care, blotting away blood. The sight of all the blood didn't even stir her. She was on the other side of her endurance now. So long as he breathed, he had a chance. She waited for Loren to say it was time to do something to stop the bleeding after his examination, to prepare to take Mark to town, anything.

Instead he reached for his pack and pulled out items, placing them by his side. "Help me, Steven," Loren asked, adjusting Mark to a more relaxed position on the ground.

"Loren." He ran a hand through his hair, the tight warning in his voice noticeable.

Loren pinched his lips and shook his head. "There is no other way." After several seconds, Steven helped stretch Mark out, then moved away again. With little modesty in the action, Loren stripped Mark, baring him from his chest to below his knees.

Angie's eyes flared seeing the blood, the wound, and a very naked Mark. She looked up, searching for an explanation. "What? What are you doing? Why aren't you stopping the bleeding?"

Steven placed a hand on her shoulder. The sudden crackle of tension on the air made the hair on her skin rise up. She shook the weight off her shoulder. She lurched for something, anything that could cover Mark, but fingers shackled her wrist in a controlling grip.

"Don't, Angie." Steven's words were lowered, calm, although he gave Loren a disgruntled stare. "Just watch."

"Wha— What are you doing?" she demanded, but Loren didn't answer, focused. She shivered, unable to stop him, unable to move as Loren pulled out two pouches from the things he'd removed from his pack. "What are those?" Fear for Mark put a tremble into her words. Why weren't they helping him? Why weren't they covering him, packing the wound, doing something so they could move him back to town?

"Healing herbs," Loren replied absently, grinding the powder between his fingers to scatter over the wound. "They'll help."

"He needs a doctor!" Panic laced her voice.

"He'll never survive getting back," Steven explained from over her shoulder.

"He's right," Loren agreed. He palmed together the cold embers from Mark's fire and quickly rebuilt it. "This is the only chance he has to live through the night."

"But—"

Loren sought her across Mark's unmoving frame. "It's going to be okay, Angie. You were right all along. Except for this. I'm sorry for deceiving you. I had no choice."

*Had no choice?* What the hell was he talking about?

A rich sound formed, slipping from him on staggered rushes of breath. Slowly his hands rose, weaving, sweeping out to draw the wisps of wood smoke from the small fire toward him. It crackled in answer. The darkness surrounding them grew thicker as the light of the flames danced.

The chant he murmured grew in volume. Strength and power emanated in the words, on the very air surrounding them. Warmth embraced him, and she knew it had little to do with the fire that he'd restarted. The golden light of his eyes reflected the stars themselves, catching the night sky in the amber color.

She fell entranced into the melody of his words. Power snapped on the air like tiny fireworks, bright sparks that rose and shifted all around him.

Her hand dropped back to her side when Steven released her wrist. She sat, numb, shocked at what was happening in front of her.

Loren drew healing designs with his fingertips around the wound, blending together the blood and the ashen green color of the herbs he'd used. His voice never faltered as it rose and fell in cadence to the chanted words.

His hands hovered over the wound. His shoulders weaved and rolled, the depth of his chant deepening, reaching for her.

Instinctively, she placed her palm on Mark. She felt the steady rise and fall of his chest, thankful for the faint beat of his heart. Heat that had nothing to do with the nearby campfire rose on the air, encapsulating Loren.

That warmth undulated around his body, ebbing and flowing around him. It rolled over Mark's body in tangible waves. Loren layered his hands over the wound, a shot that had angled above his hip into his intestines. Her greatest fear was that he would die from it—from blood loss, pain, infection. It didn't matter. She couldn't lose him now. Not after all they'd been through.

Not after he'd believed in her, believed in the truth before she did.

The sparkling lights of power floating on the air around Loren began to sway with his words, began to swirl and dance as if orchestrated by his will alone. She stared in awe, watching the beauty of what he was doing.

"My God," she choked out as the fire behind him and the sparks in the air leaped without provocation. She *felt* the heat, felt the pure energy wrapped around him. Mark's chest rose and fell with deeper breaths, as though he had fallen under the trance Loren had poured into him.

With one hand holding Mark's side taut, Loren curled his other into a fist over the puckered wound of the bullet's entry, as though he were kneading the air above his hip. The words of his chant grew thick, and fine lines radiated across his features, proof of the amount of control and strength needed to wield the power in his hands.

With a final kneading pull, the squelched sound of the bullet exited. Without stopping, he dropped it to the side, focusing once more on the damage that had been done. Instead of the force reaching for Loren, it was spreading outward. The effect of it stole Angie's breath.

Pure and forgiving, it wrapped her up. She watched in wonder as that same blanket of power filled Mark, slowly suturing the wound closed. Little by little until the only sign of any injury was the slightest red gathering of pinched skin.

Loren continued his singsong chant. Tears blurred her vision as she realized what she'd just witnessed. Realized what he'd meant when he'd apologized for lying to her.

The talisman wasn't an artifact. It was a gift, a power, and Loren was the bearer.

The weight of her thoughts brought her chin down to her chest, tears falling freely now. She felt so out of her element. She was a scientist, a researcher, yet here in this canyon, her entire life's work had been put into a new light.

The lightest touch of fingers to her face snapped her up. "Angie?"

Loren looked ready to pass out. The toll of his choice was in the shadows under his eyes, the slackness of his shoulders. The brightness of his eyes had dimmed, like the fire inside had been doused until it was almost out.

"Rest, Falcon. I'll watch them in case River comes back." Steven spoke from behind her.

"Is he going to live?" She almost feared she was dreaming all of this. Her mind was beginning to reject everything. Had it only been that day when she'd found out about the merging, the reality behind her seizures? There was no real beginning to it, or an end. She was still living in that same day. And this was just another layer. She'd just witnessed the real strength and ability of the Anga talisman.

"He'll live." His smile was sincere, if tired. "Welcome to the family, sister." Black lashes fluttered, and his entire body went slack.

"Shit," Steven shouted, leaping to catch Loren's sagging body before he plummeted in the wrong direction. He laid him out to sleep. Steven gave her a drawn look over the sleeping body of the man who'd just saved Mark's life. "You might as well rest too. Tomorrow is going to be hell all over again." He grabbed the sleeping bag and, after unzipping it, draped it over Mark's bare body.

"What's going to happen?" She inched closer to Mark if for nothing else than to be able to touch him wherever and whenever she wanted, and know that he was going to live.

Steven stood and scowled at Loren. With a tired groan, he ran a hand over his nape. "Aside from breaking council law by saving your boyfriend, River shooting him to begin with, and you surviving— that will have to be explained whether he helped you or not. It's going to be a mess." He tried for a sympathetic look. He fell way short. "Just rest, Angie. There's nothing more to do. He's not going to move for at least twelve hours." He tossed a pointed look at Loren in disapproving emphasis.

"What about River? He's still out there." She searched the darkened shadows of the tree line, anticipating seeing the other man barging through the shadows. The absolute cold hatred that had been in his eyes was unforgettable. Her own father wanted her dead. It left her frozen inside.

Steven shrugged in answer. "I'm not going to let anything happen," he told her. Rising, he fingered through his own things and pulled out a second small blanket, handing it to her; then he gathered more firewood and took up a place to watch over the two men, unconscious on both counts and of utterly no help.

River wanted her dead because with Angie alive, it all but screamed his tribal betrayal. She didn't understand every nuance of the tribal laws but knew enough. She proved that he'd bred without claiming a wife or a mate. And if she wasn't the only one...

But that realization only brought more questions. Questions she didn't have the energy or the brainpower to decipher and answer. They swirled in her head, a morass of words that ran and bumped into the images and reactions of the day she'd already spent.

She gratefully pulled the thinner blanket up over her body, tucking herself in tight to Mark's side. She'd barely shut her eyes before exhaustion swept her under.

# CHAPTER NINETEEN

ANGIE FOLLOWED Loren into the house but he paused at the door. He looked tired. She knew how exhausted she felt after the days in the canyon and the return trip. She was sore and fatigued and in a foul temper that had taken massive restraint to keep in check the last three days. She'd barely acknowledged the helicopter ride, clinging to Mark, wearing borrowed clothes until the rest of their camping supplies could be recovered. He didn't regain consciousness the entire flight.

Somehow she'd just managed to sit through a three hour interrogation by the Inglewood council, and they weren't done. Just for tonight.

River was missing, leaving a large spectrum of unanswered problems and accusations, which weren't getting them anywhere.

"Look. Go get some rest. I'm going to go visit Andrew for a while."

She blinked, feeling groggy as she assimilated his words. Andrew. His brother. She'd met him briefly. She nodded, and he put a hand on her shoulder.

"It'll work out, Angie. You are innocent in all of this. They know that."

She almost sneered. It sure hadn't seemed that way to her. They'd all borne the same suspicion that the three had shown her during that initial meeting with Steven, Croma, and River. Innocent until proven guilty really wasn't a part of the council's mantra. If it weren't for the fact that Mark was still passed out in the borrowed bedroom, she'd have returned to Los Angeles without a backward glance to the town *and the people* who'd decreed her death. Let them think what they wanted about how she'd use her knowledge. She wasn't one of the tribe, as she'd been reminded over and over, and it was well past the point where she even wanted to be.

Without adding anything and a final glance of understanding, Loren turned and closed the door behind him, leaving her alone in the house with Mark. As she walked toward Mark's room to check on him before she fell into her own bed, the moments of the last few hours rattled around in her head.

The one bright spot in all of the accusations and demands from the council was Grace Lemon, the only woman on the council who'd looked her in the eye, and after two seconds, smiled and welcomed her without suspicion. She couldn't have missed Grace. Easily in her sixties, with purple hair—not just over dyed white, but real purple curls that hung to her shoulders. And it had sparkled. There had been glitter in her hair. She'd worn shoulder-length purple feather earrings and a matching necklace that hung halfway down her body. Once she got past the purple, there was no denying her smile or her laughter.

She'd taken Angie by surprise, but she immediately recognized an ally in the older woman. As a member of the council, her vote and voice were just as necessary as the next person's. And at that moment, Grace was about the only person on Angie's side against the overwhelming support of River.

Debate had been deep and constant as subject after subject had been shredded and ripped apart. River's absence had made half the arguments untenable.

The only thing they'd had no room to debate was that she'd survived. It was irrefutable that she was Jahehn and had been wronged by the entire council even if they'd not been party to the decisions. The tribal nuances had to be adhered to though, so every meeting with the council was a long, drawn-out affair, when all she wanted to do was curl up somewhere and sleep for a week. And go home.

She was out-and-out tired of Inglewood. She wasn't being held, but with Mark still recovering, she couldn't leave. She refused to leave him behind regardless of how he felt about her. He was still her friend, and she'd never leave a friend behind in a situation like this. Thinking beyond getting home was something she just didn't have the energy to do at the moment.

She paused outside his door and listened, but there was still no sound from within. A brief sigh slipped out. He'd been unconscious since they'd returned. He'd lost so much blood, but Loren had said with the power of the talisman coursing through him to heal the injury, he'd need nothing more than rest. There wasn't even a chance of infection. She'd put a lot of trust into him. Now she wasn't so sure. The thought of Mark not recovering rocked her deeply. She couldn't lose him and feared it was already too late.

She turned the knob and inched the door in, listening for his low, quiet breathing. The same sound she'd heard several times since he'd been put in the room to rest.

Silence filled the room. Worried, she pushed the door in wider and searched. He wasn't in his bed. The window was open, but that was the way it had been left. She hadn't heard him moving around somewhere else in the house when she'd come in. She wasn't expecting him up and out of bed at all. The sight of him lying in the bed for the last two days had made her want to curl up next to him and wait for him to wake up. She just hadn't had that liberty.

Suddenly the bathroom door popped open, flooding the room with light. He strode out wearing a low-slung towel on his hips and nothing else. And he looked so good.

"Mark! You're up!"

Joy stole away her exhaustion.

He spun with a startled look on his face. "Angie." He wavered on his feet, reaching out for something to hold on to, and she rushed to his side.

"You shouldn't be up yet," she admonished him, sliding up to help him steady himself. Heat and moisture clung to his skin. She wanted to wrap herself around that feeling but kept her touch light. Licking at the water droplets on his shoulders proved tempting. It almost killed her to touch him without knowing if she'd lost him completely or not.

"I'm fine if I'm not trying to dance out of my own skin," he grumbled.

It seemed to her that his touch lingered a moment longer than maybe he'd needed when he let her go, reaching to sit on the bed. She wasn't going to point it out. It gave her hope.

"You lived," he choked out. His eyes were bright, nearly glistening. "I knew you would."

"How are you feeling?" she asked.

His head sank to his hands propped on his legs. "Not skydiving wonderful, but I'm not dead."

She pursed her lips at his grousing tone. "Do you need anything?"

Mark shook his head. She wanted to run her hands over the breadth of those bare shoulders. She'd placed her things in the room next door but had spent most of her time sitting next to him or asleep in the chair Loren had put in the room so she could watch over Mark. He hadn't even argued over the request.

"Why am I not dead, Angie? I didn't imagine it, did I?"

Her gaze fell to the red pucker of skin just above his covered hip, the only sign of his injury. She was sure over time that would disappear as well, and not like in the life of a scar time, but because of the ancient magic of the talisman and its effects. He would've died, *should've* died under the circumstances, but he hadn't. She owed Loren everything for what he'd done to keep this man alive. It had been a risk for Loren to expose the truth, had been a risk for him to expend the energy. He hadn't fared much better than Mark or Angie after it all. He'd slept like the dead for almost a solid day.

She knelt at the bedside. Tentatively, she rested a hand on Mark's thigh and swallowed at the heat beneath her palm. She needed to get a grip on herself. Mark needed answers, not her slavering to lick every viewable inch of him.

"No. You didn't imagine it."

He shifted, reaching to touch the remains of the wound in his side. "I should have died. I thought I was dreaming. I was so tired." He cradled his head again. "I saw this white wolf."

He stopped talking with a jerk, staring in front of himself, at nothing with widened eyes. "That was you!" It rushed from him. "That was you. You survived." Each word was a little deeper, a little more raw.

She didn't deny it. What was the point? It was the only reason she was there in front of him. "I was looking for you. I had to find you. And then River shot you."

His arms were around her in a flash. He pulled her tight against his body, holding her as though she were a figment of his imagination. And then he kissed her.

Passionately. A kiss that shattered her thinking. Without letting her go, he maneuvered her to his lap. Her fingers drove through the fall of his damp hair. He tasted as good as he felt. She'd missed that about him.

"God, Ang," he groaned. "I thought I'd lost you." He paused, then dropped to suckle sweet kisses across her cheek and down her throat.

"You left me," she challenged him, although the real heat of her anger was absent beneath his kisses.

His arms tightened, but his kisses never stopped, his lips roaming freely along her neck and down her shoulder. "I had to. Half of Loren's battle was having me there. I couldn't see what was happening." He stopped kissing her to look into her eyes, holding her steady with a hand beneath her chin. "You wouldn't have listened to him had I stayed, either. We both know that. But I will never do that again. I don't care what the council or their laws say. They will have to pry me away from you. I died when you thought I'd betrayed you. I saw the pain in your eyes, and all I could think with each step was that you had to live. So you could forgive me."

"I—"

He shook his head and dropped his chin, losing her stare. She let him continue. He did with a heartbroken sigh preceding his words.

"If you've decided to be with Loren, I understand. He's Jahehn. He can help you with what you—"

"Be with Loren?" she asked, dumbfounded at the suggestion.

He lifted her away from him, putting space between them. "I knew he would be able to do something to help you more than I could."

"But I'm not interested in Loren," she sputtered.

"You're not?"

Every moment since he'd turned and walked away from her returned to play on her mind. She knew she loved him. Pretty much since the minute he'd followed her to Inglewood, since that first kiss in the hotel room when her world was so off kilter and he'd wanted to right it for her. She'd never had a hero love her.

"How could I be interested in him when I'm in love with you?" she asked him with a firm shove to his shoulder. He blinked. She'd struck him speechless. "I've been hoping you still care enough to give me another chance."

"Shit," he breathed. "You love me. Me. You love me?"

"Well, yes. That's what I said." Although she was grinning too much to make it sound as firm as she'd have liked. She moistened her lips, a flutter of worry sitting over her heart now. "What about you? Can you forgive me for being a bitch?"

He threw her down on the bed with a squeal she couldn't stop. "I could forgive you anything."

She giggled when he smacked a kiss to her lips again.

"There is something I want to say, Mark, and I want to make sure you hear it."

A worried bump appeared between his eyes when he frowned. She reached up and soothed it, completely unconcerned with the caging weight of his body over hers pressing her into the bed.

"I'm not very good at saying I'm sorry," she began, but he shook his head.

"You don't have to, Angie."

"But I do," she stressed. The honest openness in his eyes told her she had already been forgiven, but she needed to tell him, needed to physically say the words. "I need to know you hear it. I'm sorry for treating you the way I did. For not listening. For everything. I was scared."

His expression softened. She felt the way his body melted along hers. The tender whisper of his fingers stroked her face. "I know. And I love you in spite of your tenacity. I've worked with you all these years and loved you for almost as long. I think I know a thing or two about how your brain works."

This time she laughed deep enough to shake herself, him and the bed.

"I take it you're making it a personal mission to see I don't let it happen again?" She caught his chin, halting his wandering gaze, which was currently seeking down the vee of her shirt.

"One of many." He stopped what he was doing and asked, "You're not interested in Loren at all then?"

She shook her head. "He's going to help me with the laws and some training, but beyond that, no."

Relief raised a smile on his lips.

"Mark, Loren is my cousin."

He froze above her, milliseconds from her lips. "Your cousin?"

"I haven't had a chance to tell you. River is my real father, the man who made me like this."

He grunted, resuming his caresses and gentle motions. "That explains a few things, then. No wonder he didn't want either of us to return."

"That's just the beginning," she informed him with a sour pinch to her voice.

He gave her an understanding glance, already moving in for more of those warm-lipped kisses that she loved. "We'll look at it all tomorrow. Right now I have something very important I need to do." He brushed seductively to the inside of her arm, almost a feline caress as he ran a cheek up and down the smooth skin of her upper arm. The scratch of his unshaven skin gave her nerves a little shock. Her body tingled in answer.

"Oh?" she all but whispered, feeling breathless under his steamy glances and seductive kisses. "Are you feeling all right?"

He pressed his weight into her, and she purred at the hardness against her thigh where he pinned her. The towel hid nothing in that regard.

"I'm feeling perfect," he breathed against her neck. "I'm feeling you."

She closed her eyes as the sensual assault grew. Fires ignited and raced within. The slow draw of fingers trailed over her shoulders, then down her body until he found the hem of her shirt. She sucked in air when he scraped his fingertips across her stomach. The button on her jeans seemed to slip free all by itself. She kicked her shoes off and ran a foot up the length of his calf.

Burying her nose into his neck, she inhaled. Fresh, soap-scented, male musk filled her. She murmured her satisfaction, nipping anywhere she could reach to taste him on her tongue. It took less than two minutes to be completely naked on his bed. The man knew a thing or two about clothes.

Then the towel slipped away. She shivered as hot skin met solid muscle. The hard shapes of his arms and shoulders gave her hands plenty of play ground.

He took his time, studying every inch of her. He seemed to be taking quite a bit of time as he traveled across her body. She writhed beneath his seductive touch.

Hot breath and lips followed wherever his fingers led. Every spot received attention, every inch, from her shoulder to her hip to her knee. Deep sighs and pants of raging desire seared her lips. It made perfect sense that he was staking his final claim to her, and she wanted to be his. Every kiss was to ensure she was unharmed from her ordeal and trials, every breathed brush of his firm lips sealing her to him as irrevocably as any ceremony, as any vow.

She moaned when he brushed fingertips against her heat. The way he made her feel was taut and liquid at the same time.

Then she felt the strength of his tongue on her most sensitive spot, and she clutched at the bed in reaction. Quivers flowed over her, and she floated on the river of pleasure he created. Warm air blew against her folds, and she trembled. Rumbles of satisfaction speared through her, and she arched against him, pleading for the delicious torment to continue. He didn't disappoint, licking and suckling at her sex.

"Do it, Angie," he whispered up to her hoarsely. "Give yourself to me." She heard the words as they wound upward; then he renewed his intoxicating attack.

Sensations riffled through her. Nerves erupted in sensual falls of light on her eyelids as her orgasm built. Without warning he increased his tempo, increasing the pressure as he filled her center and she exploded, feeling herself spiral upward as he lapped at damp skin, wringing every breath from her body. She moaned deeply, soaring as sparks carried her heavenward, lost in the beauty of the fiery bliss pumping through her veins.

His weight moved above her, and he filled her slowly, excruciatingly. Hot and slick from his own desire, he slid along her until he lay perfectly against her body. His length pulsed inside her core, stretching her and touching parts of her that only he could reach, physically and emotionally.

"I'm never leaving you again," he swore, withdrawing only far enough to plunge into her in finality of his statement. "Never." He withdrew. She whimpered in denial. "Again." As he drove into her, she no longer cared about anything but his body and hers and the ecstasy between them.

She curled herself around him, enveloping him as he wrapped his arms around her in answer to hold her tight within his embrace. They moved as one, enraptured and carried by the rhythm of their loving.

Hungry kisses grazed her neck, and she arched into every sensation. She moaned, lost to his whim, when he rose and palmed a breast to suckle at the peak. Muscles clenched in answer, wanting more, hungry for everything. He swept them both higher, deeper and more beautifully than she'd ever known.

Captured together in the rise and fall of their passion, her release stole her last breath away. A throaty cry of desire, then heaven opened for her and welcomed them both.

At last, she'd found what she'd been missing. She felt healed in so many ways. She only prayed the meeting with the council the following day would be the end of it. She was ready to go home. She was ready to love her best friend, and let herself care again. She felt free, as though a weight had been lifted from her chest and she could breathe.

The only thing stopping her was River's disappearance. At least she hadn't been charged with murder. None of the trackers who'd gone into the canyon had found a trace of him. No one had come out and said anything in the meetings, but the level of animosity had been nearly palpable within the walls of the council house. Nearly all blamed her because he was missing. If she'd died like everyone had believed she would, then nothing would be at risk within their secretive community.

There were only a few exceptions on the council who approved of Angie's surviving her merging. The remainder liked the fact that River was missing even less. Add in Loren's help to keep Mark alive, and she wasn't sure how the next few days were going to end for them. They weren't being held, but they couldn't just pick up and leave either. She had a few questions of her own for River.

The tender heat of Mark's kisses brought her thoughts gladly to him.

"I love you," she whispered against the abrasive touch of his chin.

He nuzzled her in answer. "I love you too, Angie. Always have, I think." Slow kisses trailed from her hairline down her temple to her neck. "And I'm going to take as much time as you want to show you just how much I can love you."

She swallowed the pleased laugh at his reply. "Oh?" she tried to ask innocently.

He nodded, holding her closer, although he'd moved to keep his heavier weight from crushing her.

"I have years' worth of fantasies to enjoy."

She closed her eyes but could hear the devilish smile in his voice. She ran her hands up and down his spine in languid answer.

"We haven't even touched on them yet," he added.

She murmured a purr of appreciation. He rolled to his side, pulling her with him until she blanketed his body.

"Do that again," he whispered.

She opened her eyes and found him watching her.

Teddy bear brown and hot as summer fireworks, his eyes studied her in eager anticipation.

"What?"

"That sound."

She did, and he shivered, his eyes closing in pure delight. "That needs to be labeled as a dangerous weapon."

"Why?" She watched him quizzically but smiled. "It's something I've always been able to do."

"Not around me."

"Well, no. I've never really noticed when I make it. But you seem to easily bring it out of me."

He found her hand and formed her around his rigid length. He pulsed and thickened beneath her hand, already reviving from their first sensual romp. "*That* is why you can't do it. It seems I have a very strong reaction to it."

"Oh?" she asked again, arching a brow playfully. She lowered her lips to his neck. "So if I did it...here..." She purred, her lips just touching his still warm skin. His arms locked around her while a deep gusting groan rifled from his broad chest.

"Shit, Angie," he moaned. "Do it again, and I won't be held responsible for the results."

"Then try for some restraint," she challenged, meeting his gaze with a sultry stare of her own. With her hand still holding him prisoner, she lowered to his lips and kissed him.

He didn't complain at all the next time she purred for him.

# CHAPTER TWENTY

LOREN WAS WAITING for them the next morning in the kitchen. He held a cup of coffee in his hands, leaning against the counter, staring at nothing that she could see. He straightened when they entered. "Glad to see you're feeling better," he said in greeting to Mark.

"Incredibly better. If I move too fast, I still feel it, but I'll take that over being dead any day."

Loren grinned, then sipped at his coffee. Angie got cups for herself and Mark out of the cabinet. Loren had all but given them both the run of the house while Mark recuperated.

"I meant to tell you, your house is beautiful, Loren," she said, sitting down at the table. "I love the wards and the symmetry of the layout. You put a lot of thought into this house." She inhaled the fragrant steam and enjoyed the first quiet and calm morning she'd had in months.

He shrugged. "I did, but I worked on the plan in my head almost the entire time I was in the Marines. Took less than a year to build with my brothers' help."

"Has River returned?" she asked Loren.

He crossed his arms. "No. No one has seen him, which isn't like him. Or someone has and is lying." He glanced at Mark, then back to Angie.

She stifled the frown. The odds that someone was lying were plausible, considering what her reception had been from the council. Whatever information River had been feeding them, the undercurrent was strongly against Angie's recognition as a tribal member, regardless of the irrefutable proof that she was Jahehn. But if he hadn't returned on his own, where could he be? She'd only knocked his pride into the unknown. She'd never hurt anyone that much or with the intent to kill. The scouts that had been sent into the canyon to search for him and bring him back for questioning had found nothing. So where was he? She didn't trust him not to do something anyone else expected. His disappearance had been making her more wary with each passing day.

Loren tipped his chin toward Mark, breaking into her thoughts. "Unfortunately, with him up, the council is going to want to question him now."

Angie nodded. "We're ready," she said, about to swallow her coffee in a single gulp, but his reply stalled her.

He frowned and shook his head. "No. They want him alone. It has as much to do with you as what I did, and how he was shot."

"But we know you didn't do anything against the tribe. Either for me or for him."

"We do," he intoned, meaning the three of them. He set his cup down and crossed his arms again. "They don't."

"So you're still on trial?" she asked, feeling a growing bitterness at the unfairness of his treatment.

A single nod was the only answer.

"That isn't right," she said through a tight jaw. "They'd rather crucify a man for saving a life than bring the shooter to justice."

"It's the depth of the laws. I can't tell you how many we broke, the three of us." He scrubbed a hand down his sun-darkened face. "I've lost count, and the council has been digging them all up out of the histories."

"Because of Steven?" she guessed, angry and mortified at the same time. Would his bitterness toward Loren just keep going and going? She feared it would.

Loren let out a ragged breath. "Yeah, he's pushing it a lot, but he's not the only one. A few others are also."

"Others? They can't!" she nearly cried. She put her cup down a little forcefully, making a clinking sound against the wooden tabletop. "I'll argue every single one. You did nothing wrong."

"You survived. For Steven, that's all it took." He rubbed his eyes. "He's not going to win, but it's also a matter of face and trust. The council is there for a reason. Right now it's out of balance. Steven's anger, River's disappearance, and whoever else he tied into this game he started, has warped that balance." Loren looked at Angie. "Croma and the other elders—Grace, Margaret, Jacob—they all realize you may not be the only child from River's exploits. He's put the entire tribe in danger."

"Then he has to be found," Mark stated. "That much is a necessity."

"He will be, but until he is, they want to get this, you and Mark, out of the way, and my decision."

"What do you mean 'your decision'?" She studied him, not liking the flat tone he used or the guarded blankness on his face. That didn't sit well with Angie at all. She'd fight tooth and nail to keep Loren from being held responsible for anything that had happened in the canyon. He was the first family she'd ever had aside from her own mother and father. She'd be damned if the council found him guilty for saving Mark or for her survival.

Loren pinched his lips together and shook his head. "You'll see soon enough. The council requested"—though the word was said with some scorn—"your immediate participation as soon as you were up and mobile."

"They knew he'd be up soon?" Angie asked, aghast at their arrogance.

He shrugged. "They guessed."

She knew their behavior was rankling against Loren, their demands and omnipotent behavior. He hadn't stopped frowning since she'd sat down. Until he was off trial for his own transgressions, he wasn't part of the tribunal discussions or decisions about Mark or Angie.

"If they're going to interrogate him the way they've done with me, they can kiss my ass. I will not let them treat him that way. He was shot, damn it." She controlled the simmering anger and kept most of it out of her voice.

She stood and gripped Mark's forearms, falling into the brown of his eyes. Mark meant too much to her to let the council make ground meat out of him just after he'd regained his feet again.

"I won't let them go overboard on him, Angie," Loren said, trying to placate her.

Mark palmed her face. "Don't worry, sweetheart. What can they do? Really?"

She took a deep breath and let him enfold her into his embrace, just soaking up his body heat. She opened her eyes and pinned Loren with them. "If they do one thing to him, Loren..." she warned. "He's still healing."

"Never knew you had such a soft spot," Mark murmured to her.

"Apparently I do when it comes to you." She knew he was grinning. She heard it loud and clear. But he didn't push it, and she let it go. The feel of his fingers sliding up and down her spine and twisting absently through her hair, attentive to her abused scalp, helped her find a calmer center.

ANGIE WATCHED Loren's monster of a truck disappear toward the highway a little later after they'd finished their coffees, taking himself and Mark to Inglewood. Mark would be able to take the council's questioning, but she didn't like the idea of it, just the same.

She washed out their coffee cups just to give her hands something to do. Loren had been giving her information, training in spurts about what being Jahehn was, what it entailed, how they protected their secrets, and the tribe. She had accepted she had a long way to go to truly understand the animal soul she now shared a connection to. Considering last week she thought she was dying and this week she was alive and healed in a way she'd never anticipated, she was willing to listen to anything he had to say.

There was no doubt the council had concerns about her motivations—again—and whether it would be safe if they allowed her to leave with the knowledge, but she honestly couldn't put their worries first.

She had to find out why River had done what he'd done. If he'd had the opportunity to have more children like her. If he had done it intentionally in a fit of rebellion and had spurned the laws in youthful arrogance. The fear that there *could be* more on the loose in the world was real. Why would he ignore centuries of laws and protections? Was it just because he had been out and found the time to sow wild oats while Loren's dad was doing things elsewhere? She absolutely expected there to be more like her out there, but hoped not. The consequences would be devastating to anyone in her shoes with less information. Was her survival the only reason he didn't want her alive? What did it matter now, with the entire council aware she *had* survived? What was he protecting? Why did she threaten him?

She squeezed out the sponge for the last time with a ragged sigh of frustration, then placed it by the sink.

"Damn him," she muttered. "A little forewarning would have been appreciated."

Staring out the window, she watched a deer run across the front of Loren's property. She followed it with her eyes, staring in awe at the graceful animal as it disappeared like a bounding wraith into the woods again. There were some things that she never would see living in Los Angeles.

Loren and Mark hadn't been gone thirty minutes, and she was already too restless to sit still any longer waiting, worrying about what they were doing to Mark. Angie needed a distraction.

She marched out to her car and unloaded the boxes of Jahehn information and histories, bringing them into one of the larger living rooms to sift through and read. There had to be something in the files to give her a hint at River's motives.

Sitting cross-legged with sheets and photos surrounding her on the floor, she worked and wrote ceaselessly. One drawing after another, one line of their world at a time. What would it have been like to live centuries before with these people? Before the invasion of the white man, before they'd had to integrate with their tribal brothers to remain hidden? Before any recorded time?

Angie imagined what it would have been like, free to roam, to revel in the spirit brother's ways and learn the way of nature from the animals that lived in a symbiotic relationship with the world surrounding them. It was breathtaking.

She didn't know what her totem spirit was, not yet, though she was definitely curious. She was positive she'd felt it several times in the canyon but hadn't been strong enough to deal with it. Loren had cautioned her against searching too deeply for the animal's soul before she had a chance to grasp what was happening. She needed to know more about the laws and how to embrace the spirit totem the same way she had embraced the wolf brother. Loren had really only given her the tip of the iceberg so far.

She sat straight, looking about the room as her thoughts roamed. Did her spirit totem have anything to do with River? Did River have a spirit totem? Was there some secret to what she was? What if it was more than the spirit and the wolf brother?

She flipped through a couple of notebooks until she found the entries she wanted.

"*Upon the shaman's daughter fell the spirit of the winds,*" she read. She read further. *The gift of the mother's strength was blessed to the daughters, not the sons.* Whose strengths? What strengths? Her brows scrunched together as she tried to decipher the hidden meanings to the writing. *To each of the daughters, the good mother gave a spirit strength.* "Good Mother?" she spoke, flipping through her notes, on a mission. "Found it!" She brought it close to read the notes in Mark's handwriting.

*The earth, wind, rain (water) and fire, the four elements, were believed to have been gifted to the daughters of the tribe from the Good Mother. The gift of these believed strengths (powers) was part of the tribal hierarchy, passed from mother to daughter.*

"Okay, well, that leaves me out," she remarked. She didn't even remember reading this in any of the notes or their annotations before today, but then again, if she had, she would have immediately dismissed them under human ignorance because no one had this kind of power structure in their make-up.

Biting at her lip, she wasn't so sure now.

Did the current elders know this? Was it being protected, or had it been forgotten? She frowned. If the Jahehn of this century had any inkling to this kind of ability, to this kind of power... She slumped back, resting against the couch behind her.

This explained a lot toward why the council didn't want her just traipsing around with the knowledge. If any of the women were born with this and didn't know what was coming... It spelled catastrophe just like the merging had for her. Or if someone from outside found one of these women, found out exactly what those elemental gifts were, the repercussions to everyone would be devastating. When did the gifts appear? Did the gifts awaken like the wolf brother? Were they still in the spiritual makeup of the modern-day Jahehn? She was proof the tribal gifts, any of them, didn't lessen because of breeding, age, or ethnicity. No wonder they wanted to record rank and serial number as soon as a new member was born.

Okay. This was a possibility. But what did it have to do with River? And with her? She set that book aside and kept looking, searching for clues.

If it wasn't the gifts of the natural elements, then why? Why did he want her out of the picture? She wasn't interested in becoming one of the council. She still had a job to go back to—her vacation, as it were, was nearly spent. The Jahehn were her priority, but not in the sense she believed River saw it. Why did she threaten him? Other than the fact that he did try to kill her and Mark, what was driving him? Double attempted murder charges would be hard to get out of by itself.

Angie scoured through pages, skimming more of Mark's notes, more aware now than ever just how much time he'd spent helping her decipher the written language of the ancient tribe. The man's insight was amazing, the way he could decode entire passages and tell their stories in fluid sense. She shook her head, absorbed in the history as he saw it. Angie knew from her own memories that at the time, she'd been right there beside him, enthralled with the telling, lapping up the tribal dynamics like a thirsty lion. It was almost awe inspiring to see the places where he was exactly right—she was the living proof. Which meant...

She frowned, wondering where the idea came from. A cloud of a memory. *Something...* Where had she seen it? *Something...* She tapped her fingers on her knee, rushing to reach for the pile of notes across from her, shoving photos and stacks away.

Pages flipped like broad, pale leaves as she scoured through notebooks, one after another. File folders gave up little, but she knew she'd recognize it when she saw it. The whole enchilada. The reason for River's animosity, not to mention—now she was sure—his fear.

It hovered in the back of her mind. It kept circling, taunting her, teasing her memory. The history of the elementals, the spirit and the wolf brother, how they converged and became spiritually absorbed into the first tribal shaman and his wife and then his daughters. How the women earned the Good Mother's elements, when they were separate from the blood bond of the wolf pack. The sons were the first in the tribe to inherit the wolf spirit, and the blood ties only grew from there.

So what did that have to do with Angie? If she wasn't tribal born on her mother's side, she had no chance of receiving the elementals gift. She wasn't even sure how or why she had the totem spirit, especially since, as Loren had said, for women to carry the wolf was rare enough, but to carry that and a totem? She knew she had stumped him there.

Her brow scrunched. What was she missing? What was River's contribution to all of this? What did he know? What was he trying to protect?

A sickening thought hit her. Had he gotten her mother pregnant on *purpose*? Was it just Angie's mother, or several women? She held a hand to her stomach and swallowed the nausea at the possibility. Why would he dare challenge the sacred pact with the wolf brother like that? The consequences could devastate the entire tribe.

Ice coated her skin. Had that been his intent? Why? If that was his reason, why try to get rid of her when she came to town? Had she surprised him by showing up? Had he known about her from her first trip with the initial museum excavation dig? She searched her memory but she couldn't find River anywhere in the people she had met with during that first trip, and he didn't behave as though he had known her.

This was driving her insane! River hated her. River wanted her dead. Those facts were definite. Whatever he'd started almost thirty years ago, whatever the end results were now, he wanted her dead.

She hardly acknowledged the quiet sound of the front door, unconcerned expecting Mark and Loren to return, absorbed in her search. It was right *there*. The whole story. If she could only remember about when they'd discussed it, the finite details, Angie knew she'd recognize it. Given half a chance, she was positive she could recall nearly everything that was in those files, the information that had been deciphered and recorded over the years on the Jahehn's ancient society.

The popping sound caught her attention just as a sharp sting hit her shoulder. She whipped around and spotted the lengthy silver tube protruding from her upper arm, numbing her instantly. "What the hell?" She meant to shout it, but the gasped shout slurred, and her vision wavered.

A person walked forward, and she could barely make out the shape of the gun at eye level that had shot her; then her entire world went black.

# CHAPTER TWENTY-ONE

"DUDE," MARK GROUSED as they walked out of the council house some three hours later. "That was bullshit." A hard exhalation punctuated his frustration and anger.

Loren stalked next to him, no happier about the interrogation that had ensued. Mark had taken it all and dished it back, not falling once for the subtle traps they'd laid for him. What the council saw today and was finally forced to acknowledge, was what Loren had seen of the man in the canyon. He was just as knowledgeable in the histories as Angie, and just as honorable in keeping their silence. Even Steven had grudgingly acceded to the council majority. He hadn't liked having to do it, but Mark had proved himself several times over the past few hours. Steven had witnessed the healing and knew his input would be required for Loren's part of the council hearing. It was the one point that Steven couldn't get around. He wouldn't be able to lie from the background to implicate anyone.

Loren knew how much that had pained him. To have to give Loren his due for doing what he'd been trained for, what his gift demanded he do for any member of the tribe. Extenuating circumstances aside, Mark was Angie's male and part of the tribe through her. The rest of the arguments could just bite his ass for all he cared. They'd finally cleared Loren's participation from scrutiny for saving

Mark's life. Mark had vowed to take the secret of the talisman to his grave. His promise was the least of Loren's concerns.

River was still missing. And two of the other members hadn't been present for today's meeting. Loren wouldn't leave Mark to the council's examination to try to hunt for any of the missing three, but the fact that the others weren't there and River was still MIA bothered him and filled him with a growing sense of trepidation and disquiet.

"Why is River so intent on hiding his secrets?" Loren muttered, just tossing it out to be heard.

Mark shook his head, the angry tightness of his expression disappearing, obviously just as glad to finally be out of the council house and all the distrusting stares. "Damned if I know. At least Croma is done with his hypocrisy. They have no reason now—none—to deny Angie her fair place in the tribal records." He sliced a hand through the late morning sunshine in emphasis. His sense of fairness and justice on Angie's behalf proved more of Mark's devotion to her. That stalwart strength was essential in any outsider coming into the tribe. Their secrets had to be maintained.

Loren agreed with Mark's assessment. He was just as grateful his father had finally come around. "Thanks to Grace."

Mark paused almost to Loren's truck. "She knows something, doesn't she?"

Loren hesitated, then met the other man's stare. "She's the tribal seer. She knows everything if she has the opportunity to see it. She had warned Croma when I was just a baby about something happening within the tribe that would either tear it apart or help us regain a part of our bloodline that has been lost through time. His decisions would be the catalyst. She'd never mentioned my uncle or anyone else involved, but that might have been because she only told him the things he'd have a direct influence in. The only bloodline I know that I've never met is one my mother used to tell us about. The legends of the golden lion that would return. The mountain lion is almost as revered as the wolf brother. We haven't had a true puma-bred totem spirit in generations, in any of the factions that are scattered around the country. In her visions, the future that Croma would have a hand in, they were intertwined, this totem's return and the challenges it would cause."

The portent was alarmingly obvious, at least to Loren. Strength, cunning, survival. Angie showed those traits and more. And it made her that much more of a threat to those on the council if that was her totem. If others had already recognized it within her, it would place her above many because of the reverence held for that animal totem alone.

"Why would it scare them?" Mark's door popped open as he waited for Loren's answer.

"Because if it's Angie, she's not one of the tribe in the bred sense. She's an outsider to them. But if she's the key, then the elementals are returning if Grace's visions hold true. They were all tied together."

Loren frowned, and Mark caught on to his uneasiness, leaning in and lowering his voice. "Which means what?"

A brisk breeze caught at Loren's hair, tossing it off his shoulder as though in punctuation of his next words. "It's an omen. The elementals only occur as a warning for the tribe's future, a future that can go either way—in our favor or against," he explained. "The elementals, the tribal spirits, and the spirit brother converge. Together they have the power to save us or destroy us. As humans, when we face these challenges it is our folly or our success that determines our future generations. So far we've gone through the tests and succeeded, but River's actions are the first ones in Grace's and Croma's memories to challenge the laws like this. It's the only time as a whole we could lose the brother's pact. All the pieces come together, the natural, animalistic, and spiritual. It's a bad time to fuck up."

"Because someone broke the sacrament of the original promise?"

Loren nodded. "And it starts at the center and ripples outward, affecting each Jahehn family and genealogy. Everyone loses when one breaks the law of the pact. The sacred promise can never be broken. It's not forgivable. There is no second try."

"That explains the tight control your council keeps on things. Do you think it was just River fathering Angie?"

Loren hated to pin it all on his uncle, but it sure wasn't looking good for him. River had done the unthinkable and fathered a child without claiming the woman as his mate. Dangerously and just as likely, more than one child was walking out in the world, carrying the Jahehn spirit, and suffering. If they lived. "If it is Angie, and River destroys the chain he helped to create, the entire tribe will suffer. What has begun must be finished. It is the only way to ensure every promise is upheld, each test met and passed. We can't right a wrong by simply removing the mistake."

Mark's face paled at those words. "Shit! Angie..."

Immediately Loren understood. River had already tried to get rid of Angie twice. He would try again. They jumped into his truck to get to Loren's house.

ANGIE GROANED. Her head ached, and she had an awful taste in her mouth. She tried to move and trembled when her body resisted. Inch by inch, her body awakened. Tingles poked like burning needles into her skin and nerves. Slowly other things became clear as she tried to focus. She was lying in a huddled position in a dark space. There was the smell of rubber, gas, and oil. She bounced as she became aware of motion, hearing the sound of pavement beneath her ear. She was in a trunk. The awful taste was from breathing in fumes and whatever was stored in the trunk.

Flexing her fingers, she winced when she moved her arm. The arm she'd been shot in. She groaned again, unable to hold it in. She was stiff from being stuffed into the trunk. She inhaled then coughed and tried to get her bearings. Moving in slow increments, she found she wasn't bound, so that was one in her favor. Just cramped space.

There wasn't any way to judge distance or time. She had no choice but to wait until they stopped.

The near-smoothness of the road began to get rougher as they left the pavement. Not long after that, the trunk popped open. She blinked, adjusting to the sudden, blinding sunlight. The first thing she spotted was a gun pointed at her.

"Get up!"

She startled. "Jacob?" What did he have to do with this? She knew the woman from the council but had forgotten her name. Probably not the thing to point out at that moment. River stood to her side.

"Okay, okay," she complied in a conciliatory tone, easing herself out of the trunk, grimacing when cramped muscles complained. Clambering out, she took a deep breath to cleanse the stench out of her nose and lungs. It had been early morning when she'd been attacked. By the depth of the sun, it was now late afternoon. She'd been out at least eight hours. She kept the shiver of fear from slipping free, keeping her face a mask of calm indifference. She was royally screwed. "Now what?"

"I say we just shoot her and get it over with," the woman remarked, ignoring her.

*Uh, yeah, I have something to say about that,* she retorted silently but refrained from stating it.

"No. We have to make amends," River snapped.

"Don't you mean *you* have to make amends?" The other woman rebuked River.

His lip lifted with a snarl of anger.

She faced him. "I did my part. I'll have to explain to the vet when we inventory why a high-dosage tranquilizer vial is missing."

"Fine!" River snapped. "Wait in the car, then."

That would be fine with Angie. It evened the odds. The woman glowered, then turned and stomped off. The slam of the car door made it evident that she'd done exactly what she'd been told to do.

Angie crossed her arms and leaned against the bumper, ignoring the gun. "So why am I here? Care to enlighten me?" She wasn't scared of River, or Jacob, who had to be older than the hills, or at least older than River. No wonder they had the woman. She doubted these two could've moved her by themselves with her totally conked to the world.

"No," he stated, then waved the gun. "You won't be so relaxed in a few minutes."

"Oh?" Angie searched their immediate area. "You have more than him to help you with your oxygen and your medication?" she quipped, flipping between the two men with a caustic glance. "Did you miss one too many senior citizen field trips?"

Jacob's mouth slackened. He looked at River, then back to her, then started laughing uproariously. She arched an eyebrow but waited for the inevitable explanation.

"She is definitely your daughter," he spewed, gasping through his laughter.

River lurched his arm as though to strike Jacob with the hand holding the gun. She jumped, gripping his wrist. His dark gaze latched on to hers, filled with hate.

She refused to let it bother her. He was not the father she loved.

With his thin wrist clutched in relentless fingers, she shoved him.

"This is between you and me," she warned him icily. Whatever his part in her abduction, Jacob's sins against her were far less than River's, and he didn't deserve River's wrath. She'd be willing to bet he hadn't been the one who had shot her with the tranq gun either.

Staring into his seething gaze, Angie knew this was the type of man who would—could—kill.

"Fine!" River snarled between her and Jacob. Making his decision, he waved the gun in the direction of a leaf-covered animal track that disappeared into the woods. "After you."

"River," Jacob said, his expression torn, watching.

"Wait in the car with Margaret. I'll be back before sundown."

She almost snorted but stopped herself. He was such a big man when he held a gun to her back. "Gonna take me out and kill me in cold blood? Take notes, Jacob. You've just become an accomplice to murder." She gave him an evil grin. Psychological warfare was completely legal at this point.

Jacob's face slackened.

"Hadn't thought of that, had you?" she taunted, giving him a chilling stare from beneath her eyelashes, giving him the full impact with a dose of reality. "Right now it's assault with a deadly weapon and aggravated kidnapping. Why add more to that?" Jacob looked ready to crack.

"Shut up!" River struck. Blinding pain erupted against her side. She collapsed to a knee. With her palm pressed to her side, she gasped for a deep breath. Warmth oozed over her palm. Shock collided with anger, and she swallowed a snarl. He'd stabbed her.

He clutched a short-bladed utility knife in his fist. The tip was coated in blood. At least it wasn't a killing wound. She gritted her teeth. Just painful as hell.

Angie purposely showed Jacob the blood on her palm. Jacob held his hands up. His face had completely blanched stark white, his dark eyes wide and blank with fear. "River." Jacob choked out the man's name.

The following seconds happened in a blur. All she could do was rely on instinct and basic reactions. The only way she could describe it later was actually feeling the impact when River snapped. Like a branch breaking under pressure, the fibers and bark bending until it just gave with a loud crack that only she heard or felt.

River's hand swept up again, pointing the gun toward Jacob. Angie lunged from her crouch, smacking into River's waist with a full tackle. The gun fired. A scream erupted from inside the car. She heard the engine roar to life with her next heartbeat pounding in her ears. The car dug into the ground and lurched forward, leaving the three of them in a spray of dirt, leaves, and dust. It vanished down a dirt path that disappeared between the trees.

She grappled with River, rolling with him on the ground, fighting for the gun. From beneath her, he crammed a palm under her chin, forcing her head up at a painful angle. The pain in her side evaporated as she fought him for the weapon. It shouldn't have been hard to disarm the older man but his strength surprised her. Madness gave him a strength she hadn't expected. He sliced toward her again, and she dodged, rolling with him to avoid the sharp tip of the knife fisted in his grip as he aimed for her face and arms.

Grunts and curses came from the both of them as she wrestled with him, trying to avoid the knife. Just trying to get the upper hand. She blocked a wild swing, and his palm jerked open, sending the blade flying across his body to land in the ground debris several feet away. He growled a low snarl of rage.

"Why couldn't you just die?" he roared, wrapping one hand around her throat, forcing her up to breathe. Dark hatred flared in his eyes. The only way she could escape his hold would be to release his arm. "You don't deserve to live. You are not one of us!"

She ignored his taunts. They meant nothing to her. He refused to release the gun when she pinned him, smacking his hand into the ground, ignoring the pinching grip on her throat. His single hand on her windpipe gripped like claws, making her throat burn, but she knew how to break the hold. It would have just been easier if she could have used both hands. One was needed to keep his other arm pinned to the ground, the hand holding the gun.

Rolling all her weight forward, she slammed the inside of his elbow with the bone of her forearm, spinning away when he bellowed in pain, his arm falling slack from around her throat as the known stinging pain raced from his elbow to his shoulder. The only problem was it still left him armed. Winded and still determined, he pointed the gun in her direction. He fired a shot as he gained his feet. She spun out of the way, keeping him moving. Off balance, he couldn't find her to shoot at her.

She raced into the trees, diving deeper into the shadows as he tried to regain his balance and find her at the same time. Youth did have its advantages with this fight.

He fired once, hitting a tree a few feet behind her. She ducked as she ran with bark splintering in all directions. She bit her lip to hide the sudden cry of fear. Her skin itched, trembled now that she wasn't focused on fighting him. She felt the urge to change but was still too close. Any sudden sounds, and River would hear her. The need for silence kept her listening intently, gentling even her breathing as she heard River's attempts to find her where she hid, pressed to the trunk of a large tree.

She'd felt this once before, in the canyon when she'd needed to escape before, but had been too exhausted to listen. This time she embraced the sensation. Time seemed to crawl as she put distance between herself and River a foot at a time.

"Come back here." The rage in his voice was so deep it shook with every word. "You're going to die. You can't live."

She resisted the urge to shiver at his adamancy. The man was definitely insane. She took two more gliding steps in the opposite direction.

"You are only one! You are not worthy to carry my spirit totem," he shouted, his footsteps crunching through the leaves and twigs with each step. He was off her right and moving further away. She barely blinked even as he continued his tirade. No other sound came from the end of the track where Margaret had left her and Jacob to face River's scheming. There was little hope that Jacob lived if he'd been shot just as she'd feared. She focused on River's ranting to keep space growing between them, slowly removing clothing. She could hear him quite well in the silence surrounding them. Every few seconds, he seemed to be a few more feet away. She kept her own pace deliberate and delicate to not make a sound.

"You are not pure," he continued, his snarled voice snaking between the trees. "You are no child of mine. You don't deserve to live!"

She wholeheartedly agreed that she wasn't his child. The venom in his voice was unmistakable. Leaning against a tree, she slid off her sneakers, listening as he continued.

"You'll never be as powerful as I am," he challenged her. "No daughter ever could be!"

She refrained from telling him how wrong he was. She just had a different kind of power and had openly embraced it. Thanks to Loren's history and her own, she knew just how wrong he was. River had either intentionally, or not, forgotten much of the tribal history. Or chosen to ignore the depth of that power to make himself bigger in his own mind. A man with a power that no one else in the tribe held or knew. A power to contend with on the council. A man to fear.

She didn't fear him. She pitied him.

"You must know that," River said in a taunting chant. "The daughters never received the gifts the sons did. The brother made sure of it. You are all abominations."

She arched an eyebrow as she silently slid from her jeans and crouched on the ground near the base of a large tree, hidden in the deeper shadows as the sunset darkened the ground. That explained a little bit more. *How very wrong you are.* He was an egomaniac. The 'I am more than you' line of thinking. Male over female. As though it were his will that dictated what spirit gifts fell to whom within the tribe. She noticed he hadn't once used her name either, as though he didn't want to label the person he was determined to destroy. The daughter of his own blood.

Hiding in the shadows was the dangerous part. Taking a slow breath, she listened for him for several long seconds, waiting, pacing his steps and the distance between them. He didn't even try to hide his tromping through the woods, snaps and crashes as he marched between trees and branches, looking for her. She'd never called on her totem spirit, and until the merging was done, she was vulnerable. She was pretty sure the absolute surprise of facing the very thing he denied within her would be his downfall. His own ego wouldn't accept that she had a totem protector. It was obvious in his voice alone how much it galled him that she had been called by the brother, and worse, survived the merging. He didn't know her at all.

She also knew she could outrun him easier on four feet than two. All she wanted was to get away from him. Provided her faith in her totem spirit wasn't misplaced. It would suck to be a field mouse.

Inside she cleared her mind, finding the heartbeat that thudded against her ears like a hollow drum, seeking the soul that she knew was her kindred spirit, her totem, her protector. The rest of his complaints were heard with half a mind as she concentrated on embracing the change that enveloped her just like the wolf brother's spirit had only a few days before. She swallowed the first whimper of pain. It was sharp against her nerves, making her arch reflexively where she crouched on bare feet. Agony erupted with explosive force, drowning out everything but her own heartbeat. White light flashed like lightning across her vision, pulsing red with the pain in her jaw, sharp and undeniable. She forced herself to relax, felt the grinding and popping of her muscles and bones as they took on the new shape. She welcomed the change, and the pain began to recede.

Dropping forward, she felt the thickness in her hands and the arch of her legs as she shrank and bent into a new form. They were sensations she now recognized, but she immediately knew the shape was vastly different from that of the wolf brother. The clench of muscles twitched and flexed as she crouched, absorbing the new her. Sinew, strength, senses—they all felt different as she drew deeper breaths, becoming accustomed to the animal she'd been blessed with.

She rolled her tongue and found the sharp points of long canines and felt the weight of a tail zag once behind her.

She lifted a paw and stared in amazement, then thrilled at the wonder as claws appeared with a flex of her fingers. A mountain lion. She thought of all the statues, crystal pieces, and paintings that she had at her apartment, even on her desk at the museum, and immediately felt comforted in the knowledge. Some part of her had known all along. Some part of her conscience had felt the kindred spirit.

Bowing her head, she gave her thanks to the spirit protector who called to her, who embraced her as one of the daughters of the blood, even if her own begetting father couldn't give her that respect. The truth of her spirit totem raised more questions for her, questions she hoped Loren and Grace could answer, but before she had that chance, she had to get away from River without being hurt more. Her side still burned, the puncture burning in her haunch above her hip where the human wound had been.

The crash of steps alerted her. River was moving in her direction again. Too late to bury her clothes to hide her intent, she slunk low on the forest floor, winding between trees close to the ground. His scent was acrid, pungent compared to the tang of the trees and natural life surrounding her. She barely blinked as she circled back around, stalking him rather than being the hunted.

Loren had pounded the laws into her since the moment she'd first awakened, when they had been brought back from the canyon and every day since.

No blood drawn in any of the gifted shapes, either the wolf brother or her totem spirit. No killing. No hunting. No harm. The price was beyond comprehension. It was one rule she didn't want to tread even close to breaking.

But that didn't mean she couldn't scare the shit out of him.

# CHAPTER TWENTY-TWO

SHADOWS LENGTHENED as each cautious step brought her closer behind River, his angry taunts falling on deaf ears, ears that at that moment were pinned, flat against a feline skull. Her vision was perfect in the rapidly disappearing light.

A breath. A pause, then a slow, cautious step. She repeated it, stalking him easily through the growing darkness. He was the one who was combing farther into the shadows. She merely followed. All the while her mind tumbled.

She didn't want to kill him. She needed him alive to explain his fear. His absolute hatred. His anger was fueled by something she didn't understand but could almost touch. She'd been close. It was there, just out of reach of her memory. Had he intended to challenge the wolf brother somehow? She couldn't see it. The spirit was a pact, centuries, maybe even millennia old. He'd destroy the entire tribe.

"I know you're out here," he crowed, waving his gun around as if it were a magic wand to make her appear. In her given form she couldn't snicker, but it was her choice reaction. He was a walking superiority complex.

Thank God she took after her mother in more than just looks.

She paused several yards behind him, hidden in shadow and frozen like a statue. Her gaze followed his every step, his every move.

Pictures flitted through her mind. The files she'd been reading before they'd drugged her and dragged her out into the wilderness. Studying him and listening to his ranting, the truth clicked for her rather suddenly. It shocked her so badly, she didn't have time to be sick over it, because she never would have anticipated it.

She doubted anyone on the council even had a clue.

He wasn't trying to destroy the tribe. He was trying to reclaim the shaman powers for himself. All of them. To rule the people.

And she proved he had failed. He had tried first by getting her mother pregnant, in his mind forcing the pregnancy, leaving her when he'd accomplished his goal, then believing he could control the wolf brother's call to her. Believing that if she died, he'd have his answers, that it had been River's powers that had killed her, denied her the ability to merge. She heard it all as he ranted. Which all but guaranteed she wasn't the only one. To control the wolf brother's abilities, meant a child first had to be born with the ability that he sought. She shivered beneath the puma's skin. She prayed like she'd never prayed before, for all his folly, that she was the only one the wolf brother called to.

He was from the original shaman bloodline. Anything less was impure. And he'd wanted that power, the decision over life and death. But the spirit didn't work that way. River's depth of knowledge was lacking or he was arrogantly dismissing the rest. She hadn't even had the training, and she knew no one person commanded the wolf brother's call to merge. The age of the pact was ancient, the price immeasurable. River's deliberate egotism was a crime against them all. She almost wished someone else were there so she could tell them what she'd discovered.

Waiting in the shadows, it was only her. And River. She continued to follow him, invisible in the darkness.

CROMA STOOD OVER Jacob's body. Loren rose after checking his pulse. His expression said more than any words could convey. His pulse had stopped long before they'd arrived.

"This has gone far enough," Croma decreed.

Loren glared at his dad, boiling anger making his voice sharp. "His death was greater than Angie's?" Out of respect to the tribe's feelings, Mark had stayed near Loren's truck, waiting for the judgment to be made. Loren was thankful Mark couldn't hear his father and himself. Mark's nerves and patience were shot through, and Loren couldn't blame him. He also doubted he'd be able to restrain him much longer. The last few hours—finding Angie gone again, then following Margaret's directions—had put him on his last nerve.

Croma's shoulders sagged. "No. There are many things I've done wrong. Let's pray I can stop them here." He leaned on his ceremonial staff, the exhaustion of the last few days showing their toll on his once robust frame. Time and age had finally caught up with him, and they weren't being kind. Margaret sat silently, red-eyed in the back of Steven's cruiser, watching them all.

People milled around the site, collecting information and photos. Soon Jacob's body would be covered and carried away.

Margaret had called Steven in a hysterical fit to say Angie had shot Jacob, but quickly fell apart and admitted that she, Jacob, and River had drugged Angie and taken her deep into the wilderness. River had planned some elaborate sacrifice to the wolf brother, and Angie was to be the sacrificial lamb.

She'd hated Angie on sight for surviving, mocking her son's death when he failed his merging. She'd never believed River would take it so far as to shoot one of them. When she'd heard the gun and saw Jacob crumple to the ground, she knew she had to get away. Her bitterness had cost her a friend and her freedom.

"Where are they now?" Loren searched the woods, where there was nothing but shadows. A glint on the ground several feet from Jacob's body caught his attention. Standing, he held the bloody box knife covered in a sealed baggie in his hand. With only a single look at his father, he handed it to one of the deputies. He feared he knew whose blood would be on the blade.

"Falcon," a voice called several feet into the tree line. Ignoring his father, he strode toward the call. The deputy was taking pictures of the bullet hole in the trunk of the tree when he arrived. "How old do you think that is?"

He touched the still leaking sap. "Not long, maybe an hour." He looked around his shoulder, surveying the woods. "I'd say they're still in the area."

Loren nodded and began to search for other signs. It was only a few minutes later when he lowered once more to the ground, but not for a blade this time. With a sigh he gathered the clothes and reversed himself to the waiting vehicles.

Loren didn't even bother looking at his dad. He set his find on the tailgate of his truck. Mark was at his shoulder as soon as he realized what Loren had found.

Lifting the shirt, Loren found the blood and the all too obvious hole. A neat slice, about the size of a cutting blade.

Mark's entire body went rigid with fury. His hand shook when he ripped the shirt from Loren's fingers without apology. His fingers held it so tightly, his knuckles turned white under the pressure.

"She's tough, Mark," Loren said, knowing what was going through his head already.

"What is it with you assholes?" He snarled quietly. Pain, anger, and fear were in his voice. "How many times does he have to hurt her before you will do something?"

"It will end here," Loren told him.

"It fucking better," was his adamant ultimatum. Every man had a wall, an absolute limit to what he could take, and when it came to Angie, Mark had hit his.

A sudden caterwauling wail erupted through the trees, a crying, carrying yowl that made the hair on the back of his neck stand straight up. He'd never heard anything like it before in his life. So demonic, utterly shrill and nerve chilling, he wanted to run himself. Before it had even faded, a male scream of terror rocketed to them. Gunshots reverberated through the night, and Mark tensed, ready to charge through the trees.

Loren gripped his arm, halting his movements. "Wait. She's driving him back to us." The howl repeated, longer, deeper, and Loren swallowed, unable to not feel the threat in that roar of anger.

"That doesn't sound like a wolf," Mark pointed out, his gaze whipping back and forth, the same as every person standing in the little group, all of them trying to pinpoint the direction the roars were coming from.

Motion within the cruiser showed Margaret murmuring, swaying, and shaking. Praying.

"Because it isn't."

Mark blinked, blanching a sickly shade of gray, then drew a breath, steadying himself with a hand on the frame of the truck. "You were right," he managed, choking the words out by the sound of them.

"I almost wish I weren't." Then he turned to face the direction of those God-awful feline screams.

MARK FELT HIS legs shake, locking them so he wouldn't fall to the ground. Shock was encasing him, almost a welcome kind of numb. That scream had crawled down his spine with the chilling finesse of ice. Loren was right. As a third roar carried to them, it was decidedly louder, more punctuated. With that powerful, screeching howl, she was driving River back to them.

Steven drew his weapon and urged Croma behind the cruiser, opening a door to block his own body. His deputy did the same, flanking the cramped space on the other side of the small track they'd driven to, searching for Jacob. Loren's four-by-four hung at the back.

Crashing footsteps reached them. Someone running and uncaring as to what lay in front of him. As soon as his body was visible, Steven hit his headlights, and River tossed up his arm to block the blinding light splitting the darkness.

"Drop the gun, River." Steven's hand was steady, braced on his doorframe.

The arrest was anticlimactic for Mark after days of trials and mistrust, after the threats and attacks on himself and Angie. Mark watched River fall to his knees, exhausted, surrendering without a fight. Stark terror gave his face a dead, gray pallor. The gun in his hand fell to the ground. Steven approached him, grasping a wrist to snap the handcuffs on him. River didn't even seem aware when he was pulled to his feet and escorted to the car to sit with Margaret.

Mark felt relief, but after everything, it just didn't feel deep enough.

Something nudged him above his knee, and he looked down, spying a mountain lion rubbing at his leg.

He collapsed at the sight, his legs finally giving out on him. He'd never fainted. Never believed men could, but this... *This* was pushing his limits. She didn't hesitate, just crawled onto him and sprawled in his lap, panting, like a giant housecat. A cat that could take a chunk out of him if it had been anyone but the woman he loved.

Mark bent over her, pressing himself into her thick fur to hide his tears.

"HOW DO YOU get used to something like this?" he wondered evenly, his hand stroking her side. They were due in the tribunal house for the tribe's final acceptance of Angie into the Jahehn of Inglewood, and he was stealing the last few minutes without even a twinge of guilt.

A few stitches had taken care of the cut on her side, and Angie had bounced back from the whole affair. It felt like it had taken longer for her to explain River's plans and what she'd overheard from him than it had for her to get over being the revered puma spirit. Unfortunately, it also meant they would have to be diligent in finding others, if River had more children than her with other women. River's mental capacity had slipped further on an almost daily basis.

Her fingers trailed his naked chest, stopping at the snap of his jeans to return in languid patterns. She was already dressed. She wore a ceremonial doeskin dress borrowed from Grace, beaded with lovely bright colors and soft as butter beneath his fingers, and likely just as giving against her skin. Her hair was braided, ending in a knot with a single bead at the end. She was beautiful to him no matter how she dressed.

"I imagine the same way you take on any other new challenge in your life. One day at a time."

He stared up at the ceiling from their snuggled position on the bed, his arms wrapped around her. Was it really that easy? "How do you feel? Are you okay?"

Her hands didn't hesitate in their meandering. "I feel fine. Overwhelmed at times, if you want the truth."

He tipped downward and kissed the top of her head. "Always." Looking at his watch, he groaned. "Time to go."

She rose and pressed a single warm kiss to his lips, sharing her devotion and love with him before they faced the council for the last time since her ordeal began.

A few days had passed since the final showdown with River, and Mark was almost feeling normal again, or at least as normal as he'd ever likely be. Letting Angie slip free, he sat on the edge of the bed, sliding his arms into his shirt as Angie studied herself in the mirror to ensure she'd done no damage while sharing the brief minute of 'them' time.

Dressed, he stood behind her. He placed his hands on her shoulders and met her gaze in the reflection. "I know we don't know how things are going to stack up from here on out."

"Hopefully today will be the end of it. I'll go home, make a short presentation to divert interest from the talisman and the Jahehn, but give them enough to chew on to believe we really found more of their tribal work, which we did in the writings in the caves. And that will be the end of that."

He nodded. "Then that only leaves one thing." He turned her beneath his palms.

"What?"

Her skin was soft when he cupped her chin, stroking her cheek with a thumb. He felt the pull of her deep green eyes and took the plunge before he lost his nerve. Or the moment.

"Loren had asked me if I'd be able to live with what you would become when you still had to meet the wolf brother. I told him without a doubt, I couldn't live without you. I want you to know, even with the status you're going to have within this community, the years you're going to have ahead of you to learn what it all means, and the responsibility you're going to bear, I wouldn't want to be anywhere else." He took a deep breath and lowered to a knee. "I don't have a ring to offer you, but I'm asking you to marry me. Be my wife, and I'll cherish you and all that you are until the day we die."

Tears filled her eyes to spill over like raindrops from her lashes. Her voice was thick with happiness as a whispered yes fell from her lips. "Yes, I'll marry you."

He stood, sweeping her into his embrace, loving every inch of her body so close to his. Setting her down was a bittersweet feeling. There was no choice, but this was only the beginning.

NEARLY AN HOUR LATER, Croma stamped his ceremonial staff on the hard-packed ground, the gray striped feathers at the top bouncing with the motion.

"Then let it be. Angela Merrick will be Woman of Two Spirits." He smiled, graciously bowing his head to her. "Let us welcome the newest member of our community to our circle."

Angie stood from her kneeling position by the fire pit, the ceremony complete as someone removed the naming shawl from her shoulders. The council had discussed for nearly thirty minutes the extent of her inclusion to begin her journey with the tribe and their knowledge.

She expressed some willingness but had held her ground on not wanting to join the council as River's next of kin. Time might change her decision, but for the moment, many animosities would have to be healed and forgiven before she'd even consider it, if they should ask her in the future.

The one thing she did want to do was learn from Grace. The feeling that Angie could be the next tribal historian intrigued and appealed to her. It would keep her deep-seated love for the Jahehn close to her, but also allow her to continue her work at her own pace for the museum projects.

With Mark at her side, members of the council approached her to welcome her; however, it was apparent in their gazes a few were still unwelcoming to her as a person. She was fine with that. She wasn't there to win anyone over. She was there to complete her registration with the council and then go home.

Steven had already expressed a low level of apology, but she felt it was only made under duress. Steven really had no like for Mark and left as soon as he'd greeted her.

Loren waited for his dad near the side door to the council house. She watched the elder approach with Grace at his side. His dark gaze was still troubled but softened and became welcoming when he caught hers. The future would be a rocky one now that the wheels had been put in motion. The only thing she could give them was her vow to do what was right to uphold the promise of the pact and to revere the spirits.

She studied the elder and realized that the entire situation with River had been draining on him. She noted while he still looked tall and regal in his appearance he also appeared more haggard and worn than he had at their first meeting. He'd lost ground within the council and within the community for placing sole faith in one person's words. And she'd almost paid the price for it. Her anger at the council was still there, but with Croma's acceptance of her place and change of heart toward her, she didn't hold it against him any longer. It would take time to assuage the pains of the last few days for the remainder of the council who had seen fit to side with River, against the very laws that should have protected her.

"I must share my deepest apologies, Angie. We were all mislead and lied to. My son and your words and actions have proven that we were grossly wrong, that we wronged you. Anything that you need to know about the laws and the tribal knowledge will be at your disposal to learn. It will require returning, though."

"Thank you, Croma. I will...consider it." The warmth of Mark's supportive arm around her waist felt perfect. "I have a lot to learn and would like to know what is ahead for me." There was complete honesty in her reply.

"Don't forget your children," he offered with a kind smile.

She blinked, surprised at the suggestion. "I can't. I'm barren."

He hesitated, tilting his head to the side to study her. "Had you tried before your transition?"

"For years."

"You are *taka-ja-meh*," he said simply, then shook his head, a severe frown slicing between his eyebrows. "River has much to answer for."

He lifted a hand and touched steady fingers to her forehead between her eyes, where the mythological third eye would have rested. The knowing gentleness she'd seen the last few days filled his expression. "Welcome home. I look forward to answering your questions. Strength does indeed run in our family, as it will run in yours."

Croma left, leaning a little heavier on his adorned walking staff than he had days before. He must have spent a long night in meditation, searching for the right answers to today's meetings. Loren held the door and walked out with his dad.

"What is that supposed to mean? All this proper talk makes my teeth itch. Can't they just say what they mean and get it over with?"

She shook her head as he led her to the door. She waited until it drifted closed behind Croma and Loren. "You know better than that. It's all in the way it's handled, the manner of the voice, not just the words." She, however, was wondering deeply at his final rejoinder. She put a hand over her stomach, only to let it drop as first the idea exploded for her, then vanished as so much wishful thinking. She knew she couldn't conceive. Her life was already jam-packed. Not being able to get pregnant was almost a relief in the whole bag of issues she was now facing.

Angie had a new heritage to learn the nuances of, to follow in Grace's footsteps. She had a wedding to plan and work still waiting for her in LA. Looking up at the man at her side as he held the door for her to the outside world, she couldn't believe how far she had come in the last two weeks, from believing she was dying to realizing she was a lost soul of the Jahehn.

"You know," she started, walking next to Mark, "we're going to have to find a way to come here, and often."

He nodded, his arm linked warmly around her. "I had assumed as much." He glanced down and grinned lovingly. "I see that thought behind your eyes. You've already figured out a way to do it, haven't you?"

She smiled, rubbing against him where he held her snugly. "I have an idea or two." His light chuckle warmed her until his lips and his hands could warm her completely.

## About the Author

With more than half a dozen eBooks currently to her credit and her first print book released in 2008 to rave reviews, Diana Castilleja has kept busy since she started writing professionally in late 2004. Diana currently resides in central Texas with her husband and son. When not focusing her energy on her family and her writing, she loves to travel and haunt bookstores. She's lived in several states across the south and Midwest, as well as traveling to Mexico. With moving every year or changing schools since the fourth grade to her sophomore year, she learned reading was a fast escape. The freedom to read about anything and everything has fueled her adult imagination. She is most likely currently sitting at her desk, having it out with her keyboard writing her next book.

Visit her site for more information about the upcoming Aiza Shifter books and others.
http://www.dianacastilleja.com

She can be reached at:
Diana.Castilleja@gmail.com

Diana Castilleja also writes under the pen name Diana DeRicci. Feel free to learn about these stories at her website.
http://www.dianadericci.com

PURPLE SWORD PUBLICATIONS
Romantic Speculative Fiction
www.purplesword.com